SCORING CHANCE

A COMEBACKS NOVEL

A.J. TRUMAN

TRUMAN BOOKS

Model Cover Photography: Ren Saliba

Model Cover design: Breathless Lit

Illustrated cover: Bailey McGinn

Header images: DeviArts

Editing: Bookworm Yogi

Thank you to my "Zucchini Lover" Patrons: Mari, ReAnna P., Kara G., Amber N., Allison B., Jeremiah N., Naomi E., and Rebecca F. Y'all are the best!

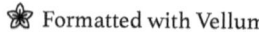 Formatted with Vellum

1

DES

When I have sex with someone, I always put my phone on *Do Not Disturb*. It's a polite thing to do. I may be an animal in the sack, but I'm also a gentleman. However, there's one person in my life whose texts and calls I allow to come through.

I pick up my phone, and my eyes bulge at the text from Tanner:

Tanner: Crap, I just got fired.

"Oh shit."

Maya, the woman currently on all fours on my California king bed getting rammed by yours truly, looks back over her shoulder.

"Oh my God, are you coming?" she asks.

"No, no. My friend just got fired," I inform her while continuing to thrust inside her.

"That's awful. I'm sorry. Fuck!" She drops her head and moans into my comforter.

My phone buzzes again from Tanner.

Tanner: I thought I was going into a weekly check-in with my manager. I was ambushed.

Des: Those fuckers. Screw them.

"He thought he was going into a regular meeting with his boss, and they canned him right then and there," I tell Maya as I fist her hair.

"Yes!" she gasps out. "I mean, that's horrible. Why are you answering your phone right now? I thought it was on *Do Not Disturb*."

"It is, but Tanner's my best friend and emergency contact."

Tanner sends through another message: five crying emojis.

I know that Tanner isn't actually crying. It can take a lot to make him turn on the waterworks. Tanner was born with an even keel. He isn't prone to emotional outbursts unless absolutely warranted. I remember holding him at his wife's funeral, feeling his sobs vibrate through his body. Seeing your friend cry unlocks a new level of friendship.

"He'd just gotten promoted six months ago."

"That made him more expensive to keep," Maya says over the sound of our most sensitive areas slapping against each other.

"Damn it. You're right." I stare out the floor-to-ceiling windows. Not even the gorgeous view from my condo can mask the anger I feel on his behalf.

While one hand rests on Maya's back as I pound into her, I text him back.

Des: Hey buddy, that fucking sucks. You're allowed to say "fuck" in this instance.

As it hit send, the phone flips out of my hand and hits her in the back.

"Ow!" she yells.

"Shit, I'm sorry. I'm being really fucking rude. I should stop."

"No, don't stop," she yells louder. "We're working professionals."

In the corner of the bed sits Maya's phone; her two dogs gawk at me from her lockscreen. Who says business and pleasure can't mix?

She thrusts back against my dick. "Stop texting but don't stop fucking me!"

God, she's so hot. Tight brown curls on creamy mocha skin. I don't want to stop. I can multitask. I am a highly paid professional. I have very strong executive function.

I pick up the phone from where it fell and read Tanner's reply.

Tanner: They're doing layoffs. I couldn't even go back to my desk. They said they'll box up and ship all personal items to me.

I grumble, pounding into Maya with my seething frustration. Corporate America will fuck you as hard as I'm fucking her.

"What's wrong, baby?" She looks back over her shoulder again. "Are we still dealing with your friend?"

"This is cruel. That's what it is. Tanner worked so hard for that company. I told him that he should have been looking for a job once that merger was announced because he's in HR, and they don't need duplicate HR teams. But Tanner and his fucking optimism. 'No, it'll all work out. They really like me there. It'll be fine.'"

"Can we switch positions? I'm starting to get a crick in my neck."

"Yeah. Sure thing." I pull out and flip her onto her back. I throw her legs over my shoulder and slide back into her. She unleashes a loud moan that echoes through my very large apartment.

"Fuck me, Des. Just like that."

Maya is getting close. And I'm...checking my phone again for updates. It's going to be an uphill battle for Tanner to find another HR job. Guys in their forties have to deal with ageism. Luckily, I've avoided it by working my ass off for my company, but I also don't have a family pulling away my attention.

"Hey, do you need to stop?" Maya raises her eyebrows, losing some of the flush on her face. "Do you need to call him?"

I look at my phone. "Fuck, I am such an asshole, Maya. If it was anyone else...but we're always there for each other, no matter what."

"God, are you two sleeping together?" she asks.

"Me and Tanner?" I laugh. I push her knees to her chest and thrust deeper inside her. She squeals with delight.

"I know you're bi. You'll stick it in anyone." She shrugs her shoulders. "Your words, not mine."

I'm an equal opportunity hole destroyer. But there are some people that are off limits; Tanner being number one on that list. "Tanner's been my best friend since forever. Please. The man has a million kids. I wouldn't want anything to do with that. I'll call him when we're done."

"He sounds cute. Is he single?" she asks.

I shoot her a look.

"What? It's not like you and I are exclusive." Maya cocks an eyebrow.

I don't do exclusivity at all. My bedroom is like summer camp. We're here to have fun and enjoy ourselves.

"Can you go a little to the left?" Maya asks. A benefit of a fuck-buddy is honesty in the bedroom. We're two professionals on a time crunch in the middle of a busy day. "Fuck yes!" She throws her head back as I shift my position.

"He's single. He never dates. He's still getting over his wife."

"Did she leave?"

"No, she died. It's a sad story I don't want to get into. That's the real boner killer."

"Poor guy. Well, you can call him in a minute," she says.

"A minute?" I scoff. I toss my phone on the floor. "You're wildly underestimating me."

———

AFTER WE BOTH get our cookies in the end, Maya puts on her clothes, and I chill in my boxers. I met with a client this morning, and I'm working from home for the rest of the day. Maya, however, has to get back to the office. She checks herself in the full-length mirror, smoothing out her skirt and cream-colored blazer.

The only doors in my apartment are for the bathrooms. The kitchen, living room, and dining room are all one big space, currently glowing with sunlight from the floor-to-ceiling windows. A sliding door separates the open space from my bedroom. I stare out on the gorgeous mountains and rivers that make up the Hudson Valley. The first leaves are beginning to turn for fall, and soon, I'll basically be living in the middle of a postcard.

I waltz into the living room and make myself a post-coital, afternoon martini. "Do you want one?" I yell back into the bedroom.

"No. I have a meeting at four." She joins me in the living area, sinking into a plush black leather couch. "We're brainstorming on a pitch for our client. They're coming out with a new wart remover. Sexy."

She snorts a laugh. The thing about working in advertising is that not every account you work on is an iPhone or Coca Cola. Even the boring things we use every day need to be marketed and sold. I spent last weekend perfecting taglines for mustard.

"Silq Cosmetics is looking for a new ad agency," she says while putting on her pearl necklace.

"Oh?" My ears immediately perk up, which makes her smile. People love the power that comes with knowing something others don't.

"I might've whispered your name in their ear." She slides bracelets down her hands onto her wrists. We learned from trial and error not to fuck while wearing jewelry. They have sharp edges where you least expect them.

"You're not going after this?"

"We work with a competitor, so we can't."

Maya and I met at an advertising conference where our companies each had a booth. Over the course of networking mixers and cocktails, we discovered that we both had a love of modernist art and no-strings-attached sex. When our schedules align, we treat ourselves to a midday fuck.

"You look stunned," she says.

"Silq is one of the fastest growing companies in the country."

"And they could be yours." She shoots me a wink, aware that the only thing that gets me turned on besides sex is work.

"Sex and business opportunities. What an afternoon." I pour her a glass of sparkling water. I sit on the couch arm and flash her a winning smile. She openly checks me out. Will there be a round two?

"Don't you need to check on your friend?" she asks.

"I've already interrupted our time together once. I'll call him in a few. Thanks for understanding."

"Hey, I'm impressed that you managed to stay hard while texting."

Maya hands me her business card. "I think my company might be hiring. Your friend is welcome to get in touch with me."

I lean down and kiss her lips.

"We had a great time this afternoon. I love when you work from home, Des," she tells me, nibbling my ear. "We should do it again soon."

She puts her hand into my boxers, gives my cock a stroke. Her hand sinks lower and pauses. I can feel the slight tensing in her touch, the signals she's sending to her brain about why this guy's sack feels off.

I pull her hand back gently.

"Sorry," she says. "I still forget sometimes. You fuck better than guys with two balls."

I take a pretend bow from my sitting position.

"Does it feel any different for you?" she asks.

"Nope." I don't like to talk about having one testicle. It's a memory that doesn't need to be resurfaced. "It's better to be down one nut than to have cancer all over my body."

"That's true." Maya gazes into my eyes for a beat longer than we usually do. "Maybe next time, we'll have a meal together and then have sex."

I wag my finger. "That would be a date, Maya. And we know what dating leads to..."

"Oh yes, it'd be horrible. Love. Wedding. Marriage. Sounds brutal." She's being sarcastic, but I nod my head in agreement.

We walk through my beautifully appointed apartment as I escort her to the door. I paid an interior decorator a fortune to help me design this place. It's beautiful—upholstered couches, vibrant art on the walls, a sculpture in the corner. One of the benefits of being a wealthy bachelor is having a very nice bachelor pad.

I tip her chin up. "Thanks for understanding about..." I hold up my phone. "Next time, I'm locking my phone away in my safe."

Maya nods, not falling for my bullshit. "Yeah. Well, tell your friend to call me if he's still single."

"Will do," I say.

I give her a peck on the cheek, and she leaves.

I stroll back to my martini waiting patiently on the coffee table. I grab my phone from my bed, put it on speaker, and pace in front of the gorgeous view.

"Dude. What happened?" I ask when he answers.

"It wasn't my favorite day," Tanner says in his sweet voice. He doesn't sound sad, just tired. Or more tired than usual. "Last week, my manager and I were talking about back-to-school shopping, and today, he could barely look at me. He read off a script."

"God, I hate this," I say. "Don't they know you have, like, a zillion kids," I say.

"I have four children."

"It feels like a zillion. I mean, how are you gonna afford diapers?"

"None of my kids are in diapers anymore." He chuckles.

"I was talking about you."

That gets a full-fledged snort. I believe that if someone is able to laugh, then all hope isn't lost. During the darkest days of my chemo-therapy, if I could crack a joke, it meant I still had hope.

"What does the severance package look like?"

"Two weeks."

"Two weeks? That's it? That's nothing. Fuck those fucking pricks." Since he won't curse, I'm spewing f-bombs to cover the both of us.

"They said they loved me at my last quarterly review. I guess they didn't love me enough."

"Let me guess. They used to call the office a 'family,' right? 'We're one big family at Fuck Off Corp.' I've been telling you, man. When companies merge, HR is hit. Accounting is hit. All these services where they don't need duplicates. But it's okay. We're gonna find you a new job."

I wish I could give him a hug over the phone. I'd pull him tight.

"Des, I'm scared," he says.

"Don't be," I tell him. "It'll be okay. I got you covered. I know a lot of people at a lot of different companies. We'll find you something really soon. Think of this as a two-week vacation. And you know, if you ever need a loan or anything..."

"Hopefully it won't come to that," he says.

Our financial situations are very different. I don't know how Tanner affords four kids, but he makes it work. There are no priceless works of art in his house, just lots of crayon on the walls.

"Look, we've been through worse." A loaded silence hangs between us. "But no matter what, we got each other's backs. This sucks, but you're gonna get through it. It's gonna be okay. We're gonna help you through it. Do you still want to come to hockey tonight?" I ask.

"I should be with the kids."

"Have you told them yet?"

"No. Crap. How am I going to tell them?"

"We can tell them together, if you want. Come to practice. The guys will cheer you up, and you can let out your frustration on the ice."

He heaves out a sigh. "Okay."

"Good. I'll see you there tonight. And buddy, look up. It's gonna be okay."

2

DES

Once upon a time, way before losing wives and testicles, Tanner and I were hockey all-stars. We claimed back-to-back championships as part of the winning hockey team at South Rock High School a million years ago. Or more like the late '90s.

Last year, our old captain Bill had a crazy idea: we should come back together and join an adult recreational hockey league in town. Even though we're all in our mid-forties and not moving like we used to, I couldn't resist the pull of getting back on the ice with my best friends. We call ourselves The Comebacks. I guess The Old Fucks was taken.

And hey, we still got it. We won the championship last season against a much younger and faster team led by Jack, a former NHL player who is now dating my teammate Griffin. With the fall session starting up, maybe we can clinch a back-to-back victory.

But whatever happens, there's always a post-game beer. Or a post-game martini in my case.

I get to practice a few minutes late. I had to catch up on emails I'd missed during my midday rendezvous with Maya.

I skate onto the rink and immediately glide up to center ice, where the guys crowd around Tanner. I push past them and throw an arm around my friend's shoulder, giving him a supporting squeeze. With his dirty-blond hair and beaming dark blue eyes surrounded by the beginning creases of rugged wrinkles, Tanner is aging like a fine wine. He's a daddy, but he's also totally a capital-D Daddy.

"I fucking hate layoffs. We had a round of them last year, and I fought like hell to keep my team safe. But I still had to let a few go. I felt terrible." Bill narrows his no-nonsense eyes that match his no-nonsense beard. You know how hockey players can look scary in their official roster photo? Well, that's how Bill looks all the time. If I worked for him, I'd be shaking in my boots. Although, his old assistant fell in love with him, and they're still together. So I guess he does have a soft side at times—but definitely not on the ice.

Bill gives Tanner a fist bump. "If I hear of any openings at my company that need to be filled, I'll let you know."

"You mean, besides your former assistant?" I can't help myself. Bill's face turns bright crimson.

"Des, I'm two seconds away from ripping off your one functioning ball."

I blow him a kiss. It's still just as easy to rile Bill up now as it was back in high school.

"Thanks," Tanner says to Bill, getting between us before any blood gets spilled.

"Don't worry. You're going to land on your feet," says Mitch, who plays defense. He has a thick beard like Bill, but kind eyes. He was out last season with a bad back for the daredevil behavior of sneezing too hard. The perils of turning forty!

"Oh, don't give him that bullshit line," I chime in. "Don't say 'land on his feet,' or 'you'll find something better,' blah blah blah. I mean, all those things are true, but let's not make his day worse with clichés."

I return my arm around Tanner, where it fits so naturally, and pull him close. I catch a faint whiff of his citrus shampoo in his thick hair dotted with gray. He turns to me with bright eyes and the sweetest smile you will ever see in your entire life. It truly is astounding that someone with this good of a heart can play a sport this nasty and violent. Tanner's strength, though, doesn't lie in pushing around guys and getting into fights. He's all about speed and agility. So am I. That's how we make a great offensive line.

"I will help you find something," I say.

"If you ever want to be a fireman, you know you can start training," says Derek, another defenseman who also rocks a thick beard, big chest, and big gut.

Hank, our goalie, with his sloppy smile and red cheeks, skates around us. "And hey, you know, you can always be my apprentice with plumbing. You make good money. I mean, it'll take a few years..."

"But he doesn't have a few years, Hank," I say.

Unfortunately, Derek and Hank's line of work won't work for him.

"I can see if they're hiring at the airport," Griffin says, his eyebrow lifting over his eye patch. He lost his left eye in a brutal hockey game our senior year. So we're both missing a ball.

"Tanner has a fear of flying. His last flight was a decade ago," I say. I convinced him to take a quick getaway to Miami years ago. The guy dug his nails into my arm and drew blood during takeoff. I got him situated with those little bottles of alcohol, and he was fine the rest of the flight. My arm hurt like a bitch all weekend, though.

"They have front office positions. Sometimes, there are openings." Griffin scratches at his beard as he thinks. Derek and Bill do the same.

Tanner and I are the only ones bold enough to use a razor, it seems. Hank has scruff, but I can't tell if that's because he's trying to grow a beard or he's just lazy. With him, it's fifty-fifty.

Tanner's been rocking stubble as of late, and I have to say, it really adds to his sex appeal. Objectively speaking. "Thanks, guys," Tanner says. "I'm still in shock a little. But it'll be okay."

"We got your back," Bill says, with the others chiming in their hardy agreement.

"We've all survived a lot of hard times on this team." I pound my hockey stick against the ice. "I survived cancer." I then point to each of the guys. "Griffin survived getting an eye gouged out. Hank survived being married to Cruella de Vil."

"Hell yeah!" Hank raises a fist.

"Derek survived losing his wife. Mitch almost lost his bar, but he survived. And Bill, somehow, survives having a stick permanently lodged up his ass everyday. So we all struggle."

Bill smacks me in the stomach. He cracks the tiniest glint of a smile. I get one of those a year.

"I don't want to talk about it anymore. I just want to play hockey." Tanner skates past us, making big glides on the ice.

"Let's get to it," Bill says.

In high school, Tanner and I were a brilliant offensive duo. Our passing was innate and crisp. It was like we could read each other's minds. We knew when to pass, when to skate around...and despite not playing hockey for a good twenty years, it's like we picked up where we left off.

We play a scrimmage and skate around our teammates with ease. Griffin and Derek on defense definitely give us a fight, but I nail a pass to Tanner, and he slips it into goal.

It's like we're dancing.

Tanner and I have just always understood each other. You know, I love all my teammates, but he and I have a special bond, forged through tough times and inside jokes and all the little stuff in between that builds a friendship.

"Damn, you guys still got it," Hank says.

After a good hour-long practice, we get showered and dressed.

"All right, who's up for a beer?" Griffin says. He points to me. "Or a martini."

"Excuse me for wanting something a little bit nicer," I say.

Tanner takes his time getting dressed. I glimpse his chest and some of the golden hairs on there. I don't mean to—it happens so fast. I'm proudly bisexual. I think women and men are both beautiful in their own ways, and finding your friend beautiful is something that's bound to happen. I dismiss the thought, though, and avert my gaze. He's the safe harbor away from the stormy seas of my sex life.

"I'm gonna pass on drinks tonight," Tanner says. "I gotta get home to the kids and break the news to them."

I grab his arm before he goes. "Hey, if you need help with anything, we're here. We got you."

I peer into his eyes, letting him know that I mean that more than anyone here.

"We're not gonna let you starve."

He gives me a nod, and I watch him go, absentmindedly checking out his ass in the process.

3

TANNER

Spending time with my kids is usually the highlight of my day, but tonight I'm dreading it. I'm dreading having to tell them that their dad is out of a job, unemployed, on the verge of being a deadbeat.

As a dad, I need to be the strong one. I've always needed to be the strong one, especially after their mother passed away. I want to be the example that you can get through hard things.

And luckily, this is nothing like losing Katie. But still, it sucks. I don't want them to see me fail. They just started a new school year. They're adjusting to so much; I don't want to add this.

I pull into the garage. In the rearview mirror, I force one of my regular dad smiles onto my face. I'll crazy glue it on there if I have to.

Inside the house, my five-year-old, Lulu, runs over to me, easily one of the top moments of any day. She hugs my legs first. I pull her up into my arms.

"Hey, baby, what's up?"

"Daddy," she says in that gleeful way that goes straight to my heart. "I painted a picture of a bunny rabbit today in school."

"Really?" I say. "That's incredible. Oh, I want to see it."

The art that gets sent home from class is a bit excessive. There's only so much you can put on the refrigerator. Especially when the kids were younger. They'd scribble on paper and the teacher would send it home with them where it'd have to go on the fridge for a few days. However, this bunny rabbit picture actually resembles a bunny rabbit. She's chosen pink for the body and green for the ears.

My seven-year-old Dean strolls up to me with chubby cheeks that I have to resist the urge to pinch. He wears a red sparkly bow tie from a magician set he got last Christmas.

"Dad, would you like a piece of chewing gum?" He holds out a pack of gum with one piece—only one piece—sticking out.

I play along. "Oh yes, I really could go for some gum. I'm so glad you have some, Dean."

I reach in. As soon as I grab the piece, it sends a shock through my body. It stings every time. But the laugh on Dean's face is worth it. He's a total jokester, something he does not get from me. Didn't really get from his mom, either. It's something all his own.

I walk with my two youngest into the living room where my two oldest are watching TV. Lena is doing some homework while the TV is on.

"Dad! Watch this!" Davy, my ten-year-old, plays with his plastic hockey stick and puck in front of the TV, practicing his moves. He shoots the puck into a wastebasket leaning on its side on the carpet. He's begun parting his blond hair the same as me.

"He shoots; he scores!" I yell. I give him a high-five.

"Hey, Dad." Lena looks up and gives me a smile. She's fourteen, so it's not the beaming grin of her younger siblings. There's a little bit of a wariness to it, a little something that she's always holding back, as is her teenage way.

She started high school this year, and I hate that I have unemployment stress hanging over my head—that I can't fully be there for her. But luckily, she has a good head on her shoulders.

"Dean and Davy have permission slips that need to be signed. Also, Lulu refused to have any meatballs with her spaghetti tonight. She says she no longer eats them," Lena informs me.

"You're not eating meatballs anymore?" I ask her as she runs up to the couch.

"I'm a chickatarian!" Lulu proclaims.

"It means she only eats chicken," Lena tells me, a tired smile on her face.

"Thanks for watching the kids tonight." I kiss my oldest on the top of her head. There's only so much affection she'll let me show her nowadays.

I'm grateful that Lena is old enough to look after the kids for the one night a week that I have practice. Luckily, my friends chip in to help with watching the kids when they can. Lots of play dates.

"Are you wearing a new perfume, Lena?" I ask her.

"Oh, just trying something from one of my friends at school." My little girl is growing up so fast. I can't keep up. "Is it okay if I go to a friend's house on Friday night? Michelle is having a few of us over to watch a movie."

"Sure. That's fine," I say.

"Dad, check this out," says Davy, moving the puck.

He snaps a shot, and it nicks the edge of the wastebasket before sputtering onto the bookcase.

"Dang." Davy sighs.

"Next time," I tell him.

Dean tries to grab his stick. "Hey, can I try?"

"No, Dean, you hate sports." Davy holds tight to his hockey toy. Even though it's a toy plastic stick, he regards it with sanctity. Davy loves the sport as much as I do, and he's kicking butt in his junior hockey league.

"I bet I can make this hockey stick disappear. One, two, three!" Dean swipes it from his brother and throws it behind the couch.

"Hey! Stop—" Davy swipes the prank gum from Dean's front pocket.

"Dad!" Dean yells.

"Dean, your brother cares a lot about his hockey gear, just as much as you care about your magic tricks. So don't touch each other's stuff." As a dad, 80 percent of my job is conflict resolution.

I plop on the couch. It's exhausting having four children and being a single dad. It just is. Doing it solo wasn't the plan. Katie and I made a great team, and since she passed two years ago, I've been trying to keep everything together, keep the plates spinning. It's like trying to play hockey by yourself. No way can you beat your opponent that way.

Oddly enough, once I admitted to myself that things were hard, then everything got better. I was no longer deluding myself into trying to be this superdad. Just make it through the day. That's my mantra.

Des is my only friend who is proudly child-free. He thinks I'm suffering in silence. I've learned I can't really talk to him about the nitty-gritty parts of parenting, because he thinks it sounds like the worst thing ever. Anecdotes about dirty diapers or stomach bugs that go round and round in our household are funny in retrospect, but to Des, it sounds like a horror show.

The stressful parts of parenting are always temporary, and then you're left with the good stuff. I'll have an incredibly stressful moment with my kids where I want to scream followed by watching them do the sweetest thing which makes my heart swell until it's about to pop out of my chest. And that can all happen within the span of fifteen minutes.

This right here is a good and bad moment. All my kids are gathered around me. They're healthy and happy. And now I have to break the news to them. My heart dips.

"So everyone, we need to have a talk—a family talk."

Their happy smiles immediately go away. Except for Lulu. She's too young to remember her mother. But the other ones—they know. They know what happens when I shift into serious mode. It's never good news.

I hated having to be the one that told them that their mother passed away.

Lulu puts a hand to my heart.

"Daddy, your heart is having palpitations," she says.

I love the way the *P*s pop in her mouth. It's a bright moment before I dive into the ugliness.

"So I got some news today. It wasn't great." I take a breath. Parents have had to tell their kids bad news forever. If I can tell them about their mother passing away and have us survive, we can get through this. "My company has decided that there are too many people in the company, and so they had to let a few of us go. And they're letting us look for new jobs."

"You got fired?" Lena asks.

"In a way, I did. But it happens. And it's just a job. I can find another job. But I just wanted to let you know. And it's gonna be okay. The important thing is, nothing in your life is changing. Everything will be fine.

"Davy, you still have your hockey practice and you're still going out for your traveling team. Dean, I still want all the jokes and magic from you. Lena, you're still in high school. You're being a great student. Everything's going great.

"And Lulu...you just keep being Lulu. You got it?"

She gives me a thumbs up. Her big eyes and cuteness melt my stress away.

"Are we gonna run out of money?" Lena asks, her forehead creased with concern.

"No, we will not. We have savings. We are fine."

The mental calculator starts going like crazy in my head. Things add up fast. How long will my savings last? That's something to freak out about in private.

"I have a joke! I can cheer you up," says Dean. "What do you call a fake noodle? An impasta!"

It's so dumb I have to laugh.

Lena groans. Davy punches him on the shoulder.

"Davy, you're gonna hurt his cardiovascular system!" Lulu says.

She started watching some kid science show on YouTube, which is her new personality. Hopefully, this means she'll be a doctor. Should I be letting her watch YouTube? About fifty times a day, I question whether or not I'm a bad dad.

I hear a knock at the door. Des strolls in with cupcakes—gourmet cupcakes—from the fancy bakery in town, and a six-pack of beer hidden in a paper bag. His tall, broad-chested frame glides through the front door. With his fancy suits and hair neatly combed to the side, sometimes Des can feel like an anachronism, someone who stepped out of the 1950s.

"It's my favorite little humans!" Des gives them high-fives.

Dean runs up to him, about to give him a hug. Des stops him. "Dean, you gotta wipe your hands off. I see they're covered in some kind of sauce...or you just committed a murder. I'm hoping it's the first one, right?"

Dean runs back to the bathroom to wash his hands. God forbid anything happens to one of Des's fancy outfits. I once borrowed a T-shirt from him. I looked it up online.

It was three hundred dollars. For a T-shirt!

"Are those cupcakes for us?" Lulu asks.

"Nope. This is my dinner. Sorry. None for you guys." Des hugs the box close to him only for a second before putting it on the coffee table. The kids immediately start grabbing cupcakes. "Let's wait until your dad and I get plates and napkins. Lots of napkins."

Des may say that he hates kids, but he loves being Uncle Des. He can be the fun uncle and then leave when things get too loud or annoying. My soul lifts having him here.

"Hey," he says to me, his voice low. His deep chestnut eyes study mine. "Everything good?"

"Yeah. I was just telling the kids that I'm going on a new job adventure."

"Adventure!" Lulu echoes.

"Your dad is amazing." Des peers around my cluttered living room as he sits next to me on the couch. "He's so smart. He's gonna find something new, and those...c-words are gonna get what's coming to them."

"What's a c-word?" Dean asks.

Des is usually really good about swearing, but he is not perfect. He gets to swear all day in his life. He doesn't have to worry about watching his mouth. He doesn't have to worry about the words he's saying influencing a young child.

"C as in...curmudgeons. They're curmudgeons," he says.

"What's a curmudgeon?" Lulu asks.

"It's a big, grumpy person. Those grumpsters at your dad's job, they are dumb for doing this."

"Wow, these cupcakes are so good," Davy says.

Lena licks the frosting off with her finger. Dean and Lulu dive in, stains be damned.

"Dean, use a napkin. You're making a mess," I say.

Dean reaches across the coffee table to get a napkin and knocks a glass of Lulu's milk off onto Des's leg.

"Fiddlesticks," Des says, really emphasizing the *F*. I give him a thumbs up.

"Oh, sorry, Uncle Des," he says before grabbing his preferred cupcake.

I race to the kitchen for a washcloth. Patting his leg dry, I take notice of how strong his thigh muscle is. I hand him the rag before I think anymore of it.

"It's okay. It's okay. Tell me everything that's going on. Dean, how's hockey?" Des asks.

"Davy plays hockey," Dean says, annoyed. "I'm a magician. Say, do you want a piece of gum?"

He takes out his trick gum.

"Is it sugar free?" Des asks.

"Uh...no? I don't know. Try it and find out."

"I'll pass. I prefer Altoids."

Dean puts away his trick and takes a big bite of his cupcake. Des remains oblivious.

"There's a traveling team that I want to try out for, and I really think I have a shot. Like, I play with some of the guys who are trying out, and I can totally beat them," Davy says.

"Sweet. Just keep practicing." Des gives him a thumbs up. "Lena, you seem quiet. How's high school?"

"It's fine," she says. A typical teenager's vague response that I will have to get used to. She used to babble as much as Lulu, but those days are very much over.

"Who do you have?" Des stares at Lena. He has that power to make you feel like the only person in a room.

"I have Bright for history. He's nice, seems a little odd. And Mr. Bradford for French, who's obsessed with this old show from the '90s. He's dating the Spanish teacher Mr. Shablanski. It's so cute."

Des and I share a look. We don't recognize any of these teachers. South Rock High has totally changed. The last time I went there, I felt a pang when I noticed all their pay phones were gone. Yes, I know it's ridiculous that they'd still be there, but please let me have my nostalgia.

"Is Mrs. Barnes still there?" Des asks.

"Yes. She's so old. I'm glad I don't have her. I heard she's kinda scary," Lena says with a giddy laugh.

"God, I remember she busted me when she caught me smoking under the bleachers." Des chuckles.

"You smoked cigarettes?" Davy asks, shocked.

"Oh, they weren't cigarettes—"

I smack Des in the stomach before he can explain further.

4

TANNER

Des cleans up while I put the kids to bed. When I come back downstairs, he's wiping frosting off the coffee table.

"I tried. There's only so much I can do to clean up around here," he says.

"It'll never be immaculate like yours." I shrug. There's a general layer of dust and grime on the house. Shelves are crammed with toys and books and Legos and random junk. Clutter fills the house. I could never be one of those parents who are strict with their kids about cleaning up. I don't have the stamina. "My motto is clean enough."

"I brought an adult treat for us." He nods to the paper bag on the recliner.

A few minutes later, we're sitting on my roof drinking beers. This has always been a great place to think. Each time, I worry it's going to collapse, but it keeps surprising me with its strength. I suppose we have that in common.

From up here, I get a nice view of my neighborhood, the mountains way off in the distance. It's nothing like Des's view from his condo that is just breathtaking—worth every penny.

I'd love to go over there, but Des would have a heart attack if the kids were in his apartment. It's like an upscale hotel and my brood is definitely not Eloise.

"How'd the kids take it?" he asks.

"Fine. I really tried to sugarcoat it as much as possible."

"Okay, between us, how's it *really* going? Because, Tanner, I know when you're stressed. You may put on a good game, but I can tell, man."

I rub my hair. The accountant in my head is screaming and pulling the panic alarm. The realities of my situation are quickly catching up with me.

"Do you need money?" he asks.

"It's not the money. It's...it's the insurance. My severance only covers two weeks, and then I'm kicked off the company's insurance plan by the end of the month. And, you know, luckily, there're no major medical things. But the kids—they still see a therapist. Davy is always having sports injuries he has to go see a doctor for. And if something really should go wrong, we won't be covered. I'm trying to sift through options. There's COBRA, but it's so expensive."

I had a coworker who had to go on COBRA when he was in between jobs. He'd been laid off, and COBRA allowed him to stay on his company's health care plan with a HUGE markup. I know why they call it COBRA. Because it's a snake that will suck the life out of you.

"Lulu just started kindergarten and Lena just started high school, and now I have to deal with this," I say.

Des rubs my leg. I try not to seem so worried, but man, is it tough.

"You've handled worse surprises," he says with a loaded pause. It all happened so suddenly. For our anniversary, Katie and I went to Vermont for a weekend, just the two of us. We were biking in the woods, when Katie hit a tree root and got thrown off her bike, hitting her head on the ground.

She said she was fine and didn't need to go to the hospital. Katie complained of dizziness the rest of the day, and when she lay down to take a nap, she didn't wake up. It happened so fast, and left me with a mixture of grief and whiplash, like the universe was playing a con on me that I didn't figure out until it was too late.

I was a complete mess for weeks. If it weren't for my friends stepping up, helping with the funeral and spending time with the kids, I don't know if we would've made it.

"No matter what, we've been there for each other," I say.

"You were there for me when I was going through chemo. That's what friends do." A wistful smile takes over his face, creasing his freshly-shaved cheeks. "Do you remember high school?"

"Yes and no," I say. Some things feel like just yesterday, some things feel like a million years ago. I didn't know I felt that old. I didn't know time could pass so quietly, so cruelly, escaping like an Irish goodbye. "I went to South Rock for Lena's freshman orientation, and it was just—I was speechless. I can't believe that we used to go here. It's so different. But then you spot these little corners in the school that are still the same. A stretch of hallway that hasn't changed. The same creaky chairs in the auditorium."

There was a time in my life when all I had to worry about was homework and hockey. Wild.

"You know, I remember when we were in high school, we probably all thought, 'We'll get married, we'll have kids,' and now, like, here I am—and my oldest is *in* high school." I laugh and gaze up at the night sky.

"I never thought that," Des says proudly. "Didn't want it then, didn't want it now."

"I never got why you were so against it."

"I'm not against it. It's not for me. There's fun in playing the field. I enjoy playing the field, and I don't really see a need to stop, you know? Keep things fresh and interesting. And no offense, man, I see you and your kids—and your kids are so wonderful, and you're so wonderful with them. But that is not for me. That just seems exhausting. And a slog. And tiring. And dirty. I like just being able to come and go. I like having my freedom. But I can see how freedom is overrated."

Des's full lips crack a smile. Even with me, he knows how to charm.

"Some things haven't changed," I laugh. "You were a ladies' man in high school. I remember you were dating these two girls at once, and you sent me to break up with one of them."

"Oh God, that was rough. I can't believe you said yes. Didn't one of them slap you?"

"It's what we do for our friends," I say.

He just looks out, sips his beer. "And you had one girlfriend all through high school. You love your monogamy. We were on top of the social food chain back then. You could've been with anyone. You could've played the field, Tan."

"I save my playing for the ice." My high school girlfriend and I broke up after graduation. She was going to college very far away, so we both knew it wouldn't last. It was amicable. Unlike Des, I've never gotten slapped over a breakup.

At a post-graduation party, she tried flirting with Des, but he firmly said no, even though I said it was fine. I always appreciated that about him.

"You're still on top of the social food chain." I sip my beer. "You managed to peak in high school and as an adult. I mean, you're super successful, with an awesome bachelor pad, and a very active social life." There's a part of me that would like to have that life for a day, to see what I'd be missing.

"It's pretty sweet," he says.

While it does seem pretty sweet, I don't know...I feel like it would get boring after a while. Different strokes, I guess.

"It's kind of a miracle that we became friends." I was the good, dutiful kid. Des was the bad boy—hooking up with everyone. People couldn't believe that we were friends. We seemed so different. Des is loud and boastful and extroverted as heck. And I've always been more thoughtful, more cautious. But I don't know—it worked. Maybe we both see something in each other.

"I think we balance each other out," Des says. "No matter all the parties I went to, all the people I hooked up with. They couldn't come close to just hanging out with you, chatting about life and shit. And plus, you were there for me when I needed it most—my shitty parents and then shitty cancer."

Luckily, it was caught early and they were able to remove the testicle that was impacted. I can't believe it's been four years already. There's been no recurrence, and for all intents and purposes, he's in the clear. But I still get nervous when he goes in for his annual cancer screen. I've seen firsthand how quickly things can change. One fall, one nap, one doctor's appointment...your whole life can get turned on its head.

"We've gotten through a lot together," I say. I clink my beer can against his.

"We have." His lips pout. Des is a very attractive man. I've always thought so. People love his dark eyes, his cut jaw. But for me, his lips are his best feature. They're full and pouty. Welcoming. Anyone who gets to kiss them is very lucky. They amplify any expression he has. A smile with those lips is a beam of sunshine. A frown is a dark cloud.

Right now, they are adding to the mysterious, pensive look on his face.

"I have a crazy idea," he says.

"What?"

"What if we got married?"

I burst out with a laugh. It's the best laugh I've had all day. I knew my friend would always be there to cheer me up.

"Des, this is why you should not be drinking beer. It's doing stuff to your head. But that was a good one."

"I'm serious. I think I'm serious."

He arches his eyebrows. The wheels turn in his head. I can tell when Des is really thinking about something—and this is one of those moments. The lips are in full pout.

I sit up. "Wait, you're actually thinking about this?"

"Well, if we were to get married, you can go on my insurance plan. And then you and the kids would be covered. My company has great insurance. When I had cancer, I had very little medical bills. Most of it was covered. So that would extend to you, right? I mean, if we were married. And really, marriage is one of those events where you can have someone join your plan right away. You don't have to wait till the end of the year."

"That's true," I tell him. Being in human resources, I know this like the back of my hand. "It's a qualifying event."

"So we can get married, you and your kids can immediately get insurance, and then once you find a new job, you can get off and go onto that, and everything will be fine."

In theory, this sounds very logical and very helpful. But still—it would mean that we would get married.

"You're asking me to marry you? For insurance?" Des would be *my husband*. "Is this fraud?"

"I don't know. Let me check." He asks the question into his cellphone. Google pops up with a response.

"Nope. Not fraud. It's not illegal. Frowned upon, but not illegal. If someone comes to us and asks if we're married, we know each other so well, we could easily say that we are. We can easily pass that test. And most marriages are sexless, so we're right on track with that."

My mind is spinning with this proposal. That's what this is. I'm being freaking proposed to. By my best friend. I told myself I would never get married again after losing my wife. Does this count?

Des gulps his beer and heaves out a sigh. "Tanner, I guess...will you marry me?" He caps it with a belch, not a ring.

Still, I say yes.

5

DES

For the record, I never want to get married, but if I had to, I'm glad I'm marrying my best friend for insurance fraud. Legal, insurance fraud.

"Wow, I can't believe my friends are getting married," Hank says, a wobble emanating from his throat.

"Are you okay, buddy?"

"Yeah, I'm fine." He sniffles as he paces behind me. "It's just weddings. They bring it out of me. Don't let my hyper-masculine demeanor confuse you: I'm an emotional guy with a lot of feelings."

Hank's very pale, and that means the slightest bit of emotion can color his face like a tomato. I was never one to cry at weddings, and I'm certainly not going to cry at my own fake one.

"It's not a wedding, Hank," I tell him, straightening my tie in the mirror. "We're simply having a legal ceremony performed so that Tanner and his kids don't wind up like Fantine from *Les Misérables*."

"Oh God, that musical was so sad. Now I'm gonna get more tears all over again," Hank says.

I dip my head to my fingers, pinch the bridge of my nose.

I love my friends, but also, they can be a little strange, especially Hank. One time junior year, he sat upside down at lunch for a week to test the fact that humans can still swallow in that position. Maybe he got one too many pucks to the head as goalie.

He proudly marches to the beat of his own drum, and you can't hate a guy like that.

"This isn't romantic, Hank," I tell him. "We're in a men's room in a county courthouse."

In fact, right behind us, two guys are using the urinals, and there's a guy in the toilet stall who seems to be having some issues pushing one out.

"Yes, I know, I know," Hank says. "But still...you're getting married. We never thought you would get married. This is an exciting day."

"It really isn't."

Hank brushes aside my objections. "My friend's getting married today," he tells one of the urinal users, a young lawyer in a suit who comes to wash his hands. "Oh, and you should use more soap."

The lawyer gives him an odd look that must be commonplace for Hank at this point before leaving.

I grab my friend's shoulders. "This is not a real marriage. I am helping a friend out. Remember the time when your car broke down and I let you borrow my backup Lexus? This is just like that. My company's insurance plan is a backup Lexus for Tanner."

"You're right." He brushes aside whatever emotion he's daring to feel. He looks at me in the mirror and fixes my tie. I smack his hand away.

"Hank, I can always find another witness."

"This may be a fake wedding, but I want you to look nice," he says. This coming from a man who tucks in his shirt 10 percent of the time and doesn't own a pair of non-sneakers. Although to be fair, today Hank tried dressing up. His dress shirt is ironed, and his shaggy, dirty-blond hair is combed into submission.

"Now, I brought some things. Don't get upset." He holds up his hands, steeling himself for my reaction. But with Hank, it's always something, so I just roll with it.

"What is it?"

He claps his hands together, does this little jig with his feet. He grabs an old Jansport backpack from the floor. I shudder to think that's the same one from high school. He reaches inside, and I hold my breath. With Hank, he could literally pull out anything.

"Even though it's a fake wedding, nothing says that we can't have some real traditions."

He hands me his old high school student ID. The South Rock letters are mostly worn off. I can make out an *S* and an *R*. Hank is twenty-five years older than this picture, but he still has the same goofy smile, same shaggy hair, same ruddy complexion.

"Your high school ID."

"That's something old."

"Oh good Lord," I scream out.

Next, he hands me one of his credit cards.

"Your Visa card?"

"That's a brand *new* card I just got. You can see the expiration date. Something new. Get it?"

"Nothing says romance like a credit card."

"That's what my ex-wife used to say—well, before she wrecked our credit rating," Hank says. Back into the bag his hand goes. "Then, here's this. It's kind of a two-for-one."

He pulls out a CD case with a blue blob artwork on the front. Third Eye Blind's album *Blue*. I've instantly been transported to the year 2000.

I flash back to memories of putting CDs into my car stereo and flipping through my big book of CDs while driving—something that was probably ten times more dangerous than texting and driving.

"That's my Third Eye Blind CD," says Hank.

"Why do you still have this?"

"I believe in keeping physical media." He takes the CD, then makes a big gesture of handing it back to me. "I'm letting you *borrow* it. And, could you tell me the name of the album?"

"*Blue*," I say flatly.

"Yes! Something borrowed *and* blue! Take that, wedding traditions!" His voice echoes off the bathroom walls. "Maybe there's a song in there that we can play...for your first dance with Tanner." Hank chokes up, and I shoot him all the daggers in the world.

"There's no first dance, no last dance, no dancing at all," I remind him, "because this is not a real wedding."

I want to give back these things, but Hank's eyes are so wide and so hopeful. And what's the big deal if I hold onto this crap for the few minutes of legal proceedings?

"Yes! I knew you were a quasi-romantic," Hank proclaims. The CD case barely manages to fit into the front of my jacket pocket.

I wave his credit card. "I guess lunch is on you."

I turn and give Hank a final check. I lick my thumb and smooth out his eyebrows. He's a good-looking guy, one man-size puppy dog. I straighten the collar on his shirt.

"Hank..." I notice him looking up, trying to hold tears.

"I know, I know. Just let me have this moment, since you're not gonna let me make a best man speech."

"You're not my best man. Hank, you're a witness."

"But if you were having a wedding, I would be your best man."

"If I were getting married, Tanner would be my best man."

"Well, you can't have your groom be your best man."

I decide not to go down this rabbit hole. I let Hank have the victory. "Yes, Hank. You would be my best man."

He pulls an empty, plastic champagne flute from his backpack and fills it with sink water. He clears his throat to ensure none of the other bathroom users interrupt him.

"Des, I've known you for more than half your life. None of us ever thought that you'd get married. You were so scared, you thought it was like a venereal disease. But Tanner has always been the one to get through to you. He's been able to open you up and make you this warmer, gentler person. I don't know the twists and turns of the universe that brings two people together, but I'm so glad you two found each other. I think you make a really wonderful couple. You're gonna make an excellent father."

I shudder at him calling me a father.

"You know, just take care of Tanner. He's been through a lot, and he's a good guy."

Despite everything, Hank's speech actually wedges into my heart. It makes me think of Tanner and how wonderful he is. And damn, now I'm looking up at the ceiling, holding back tears.

Maybe Hank isn't so bad at speeches.

"Thanks, pal." I wrap an arm around him, kiss him on his head and realize his hair is in place thanks to a gallon of hair gel. "Okay, let's get freaking married."

———

WE WALK into the judge's chambers. A big window looks out on a huge oak tree, sun shining through the leaves. Hank immediately starts humming "Here Comes the Bride." The judge sits behind his oak desk, surrounded by shelves of law journals. Tanner and Griffin, our other witness, are sitting in two chairs on the right side. Two chairs on the left side are empty for Hank and me.

Technically, I am walking down *an* aisle, not *the* aisle.

"That's enough," I mutter to Hank to end his singing.

Tanner stands up from his chair and turns to face me. Fuck. I am not a romantic, and this is not a real wedding, but the wind kind of gets knocked out of me for a second. His fiery blue eyes and sweet, hopeful gaze pull me like a tractor beam down the aisle—I mean, *an* aisle. We're actually getting married. Like we're going to sign a legal document and be husbands. It's hard to tell what's a scam and what isn't.

"You look very nice, Des," he says.

"Well, I always look nice. It pays to have a tailor on speed dial." I adjust my cuffs in a James Bond style.

The judge welcomes us into her chambers. She's an older woman with a mane of gray hair and big, black-framed glasses. She looks like she could've been a lesbian bookstore owner in a past life.

"Good morning. We're here today to witness the union of Max Desmond and Tanner Chance in marriage," the judge says. I stand next to Tanner. His sandalwood scent blurs the lines even more today.

"It's so weird hearing someone call you Max," Griffin says. He gives me a supportive nod and stands behind us observing. He's really taking being a witness to heart.

"You can just call me Des," I tell the judge. "Max was my father's name."

The judge motions Tanner and me to take step forward. She comes around to our side of her desk. "Today marks the beginning of your shared journey, built on a foundation of honesty, respect, deep friendship, and of course love. Marriage is not just a celebration—it is a profound and enduring commitment."

I gulp a nervous lump back in my throat. I didn't expect the judge to go so hard.

"Ahead lies a future rich with joy, new experiences, and the challenges that life brings. With unwavering support for one another, you will face each moment united, growing stronger with every step."

I look at Tanner, and I get that lump in my throat again. This can't help but feel real as much as I try to remind myself it isn't. Tanner doesn't break eye contact with me, making this even more intimate.

The judge turns to me and asks me a question I never thought I would ever be asked. I take a deep breath, my heart thumping in my ears. I'm about to say two words I never thought I would say. But there's no one I'd rather say them to for the purposes of insurance coverage.

"I do."

Tanner bites his lip slowly. It's a small tell he has—that something is really affecting him. I guess he feels the weight of it too. This isn't just a little story between friends. We're involving the United States court system.

"And do you, Tanner, take Des to be your lawfully wedded husband?"

Tanner opens his mouth. Nothing comes out at first. He looks at the judge, then looks back at Griffin, looks at me. His eyes are big and nervous.

Then I get nervous. Fuck. Am I gonna be left at the altar at my fake wedding?

"I do," he says. His voice is shaky, and I wonder if he's going to cry. I squeeze his hand.

"Do you have the rings?" the judge asks.

Griffin steps forward and removes them from his pocket. He hands one to me. I stare at it for a second.

"You're supposed to take it," he tells me, as if I just landed on earth.

I was the one who picked out the pair of white gold rings. If we're going to have a sham marriage, we might as well do it right. I picked the first pair that looked decent and weren't cheap metal, then went to work. But now the rings are in front of me, and they're...rings. Actual rings.

I open my palm and Griffin drops a ring in. I can barely think straight as I watch myself slide the ring onto Tanner's finger.

My body vibrates with nerves and terror and joy as Tanner slips a ring onto my finger. This finger was supposed to stay naked for eternity. I check out my hand. I was never a jewelry person, but it looks good with a ring on.

"Des and Tanner, by the state of New York, I now pronounce you married. You may kiss," she says.

"We don't have to do that," I say.

She cocks her head. "Why wouldn't you want to kiss your new husband?"

Shit. I guess we can't lie about that.

"Sorry, I had a...garlic omelet for breakfast." I wonder if such a thing does exist.

But before I can second guess, Tanner steps forward and plants a kiss on my lips. I've kissed a lot of people, but no kiss has ever taken my breath away like Tanner is doing at this moment. His hot lips press against mine for a flash before pulling away, quite possibly leaving me changed forever.

This kiss is magic. I'm not a romantic, and I don't believe in magic, but...my wand is starting to stand up.

"Okay, well, where do we sign?" I ask.

She hands over the documents, and I get back to something I know: signing contracts. That is my specialty. Marriage and love? That is not.

"Stop crying," I tell Hank as he signs the witness part. A few minutes later, I exit the courthouse with...my husband? We stand on the majestic courthouse steps, staring out on the green.

"Well, husband, what should we do?" he asks.

"I actually have a call I have to get to at work. I told them I had a doctor's appointment."

"Yeah, fair enough. And I have to get home, with job hunting, and then do some grocery shopping and laundry. There's always laundry to be done," Tanner says, laughing.

It really is a beautiful laugh—deep and warm like the perfect cup of coffee on a chilly winter morning. It breaks the tension building in my chest.

"Well, I guess I'll see you at practice." I shrug my shoulders up to my ears.

He laughs. "Yeah, I'm not sure what to do either. I mean, we're married."

"We *are* married."

"I know what I'm gonna do," I say. "I'm going to change my insurance status with my company." I hold up the marriage license. "Qualifying event, bitches! I'll get you and the kids on the plan in no time. So no worries."

"Great."

"Okay." We walk to the parking lot. A wind rustles the leaves. "I'm parked down this way."

"And I'm one aisle over," he says. The word aisle causes a twist in my stomach.

"Cool." We stand there, a bit unsure, a bit dazed. We decide on a hug goodbye.

"Goodbye, husband," Tanner says.

"Goodbye, husband."

6

TANNER

arried life with Des is a lot like regular life with Des—only now we text like we're starring in a sitcom with a laugh track.

Des: Your husband demands tacos tonight. This is nonnegotiable.

Tanner: Already thawing the beef, my love. Shall I pick up limes too?

After our wedding, there was no reception, no honeymoon. Des and I went back to our normal lives. I had chores and school pickups and grocery shopping to do on top of searching for a job. Every so often, I'd remember that Des was now my husband, and I'd chuckle to myself. I texted Des reminding him of this fact, and our text chain quickly morphed into us cosplaying domestic bliss.

Des: God, yes. Who did I marry, and how did I get so lucky?

It's stupid. It's completely ridiculous. But I catch myself smiling every time my phone buzzes. I've been smiling more lately, which is... strange. Nice, but strange.

Tanner: How was your day, honey? Do you need me to fix you a post-work cocktail?

Des: Make it a double.

Being a widower is like having a giant invisible sign around your neck that says *Caution: Fragile.* You get used to walking around cracked. You learn how to smile at PTA meetings, laugh at your kids' jokes, even flirt a little with strangers who smile a second too long—but underneath it, you're always split open somewhere. And then Des—rakish, confident, infuriating Des—puts a wedding ring on your finger and calls you "husband" in a text, and it doesn't feel like a punchline.

It feels like someone reaching out and sliding the sign off your neck. As soon as I got home from the courthouse, I took off the ring. But every now and then throughout the day, I put it back on and feel myself inching toward being complete again.

I'm not saying it's real. It's not. He did it for my kids. For the insurance. Des doesn't even *like* commitment. But still, when he sends me:

Des: Did my darling husband remember to pick up peanut butter?

And I text back:

Tanner: Creamy, as you like it. I live to serve.

I feel it. That little jolt in my chest like I'm back in something warm.

———

A WEEK after we exchanged fake "I do's," I'm parked outside the kids' elementary school with the windows down and radio off. Lulu's class lets out first, a stream of tiny humans galloping toward parents like they've just been released from captivity. She spots me and yells, "DADDY!" with all the subtlety of a fire alarm.

She launches herself into my arms.

"Hey, baby girl," I say, catching her with one arm, her backpack with the other.

"Miss Melling gave us gummy bears," she reports, breathless, "but I dropped mine on the rug and then Tommy stepped on them so they got rug on them and I didn't eat them but I *wanted* to."

"I am so sorry for your loss," I say gravely.

She nods. "It was very hard for me."

Davy walks out flanked by his friends, reenacting a play from his last hockey game. Dean comes out five minutes later, walking slower, head ducked. He lives life on full volume. A muted Dean is never a good sign.

"Hey, bud," I say, ruffling his hair.

"Hey."

His teacher Mrs. Yoon follows behind him. With her curated vintage skirt and top, she's way too stylish to be serving looks in a suburban elementary school.

"Dean was being a little *too* funny in class today," she tells me. She kneels down to his eye level. "We love joking around with our friends, but not during reading time."

He shrugs. "It was *boring.*"

"Still gotta pay attention," I say, wanting to show his teacher that I have this under control. "Being funny is great, but not if it gets in the way of your learning."

I guide my brood into the car, which I imagine is as challenging as herding wild animals. I'm getting Lulu in her booster seat when I hear my name.

"Tanner?"

I turn. It's Russ, tall and trim, patterned dress shirt neatly tucked into his jeans. His boys, Quentin and Josh, are in Davy's class, and he's one of the few dads I actually talk to at school events. His husband Cal is the brother of my teammate Derek. All of us go way back. Also, widowers tend to find each other in a crowd. Like stray cats.

"Hey, man," I say. "How's it going?"

"Can't complain. Josh made it through his math test without crying, so we're calling it a win." He grins. "You?"

I gesture at the kids. "Trying to keep the circus in order."

"Hey guys!" Russ waves to them, then turns his gaze back to me. "I see you haven't signed up yet to bring in a snack option for back to school night." His words are polite, and his smile is big, but he's also blocking my path to the driver's seat. "It's in a week."

"Oh. It must've slipped my mind." Typically, I'm good at keeping a mental to-do list running, but PTA requests tend to fall off.

"When you get home, could you fill it out? It'll only take a minute. There are still a few options for what to bring. Cookies or brownies are always welcome, even if they are, y'know"—he steels himself for a moment—"store bought."

"Right." Derek told me Russ makes pizza from scratch—crust, sauce, and shredding his own cheese. Russ would shudder if he saw some of the store-bought meals I threw together for my kids. None of my kids are going to bed hungry, which is the most important thing. "I've just had a lot going on. I lost my job so I've been focused on that."

His face immediately shifts. Russ may be uptight, but he's not callous. "Tanner, I am so sorry. Don't worry about back to school night. I have it covered. I can whip up a batch of brownies. If I hear of any openings at my company, I'll keep my ear to the ground."

"Thanks. I appreciate it."

"And if you need help with anything else, let me or Cal know."

"Of course. Thanks." I wonder if I keep thanking him, will I eventually get to go into my car?

Russ puts a hand on my shoulder, gives me a solemn head nod. "How are things going besides that? If you ever need to talk about... it's only been two years. It's still fresh."

I gently move his hand off me. Talking about the sadness around missing my late wife isn't appropriate pickup line conversation. "Thanks, Russ," I say definitively.

His gaze drifts to my hand. I realize, too late, that I'm still wearing the wedding ring. I forgot to take it off before I left the house.

Crap.

"Wait. What is this?" Russ catches my hand. "Did you...get married?"

"Married?" Lulu gasps from the car.

I shut the car door.

"What? No, this is...nothing."

"Doesn't look like nothing." Russ takes my hand and gets up close and personal with my new accessory. "That's white gold."

Not to stereotype gay guys, but how the hell was Russ able to clock that so fast?

"I felt like wearing it. For old times' sake." I know I'm a jerk for invoking my late wife in a lie, but desperate times. My marriage to Des cannot become local news. Gossip spreads faster in Sourwood than crabs in a college dorm.

"That's not your old wedding ring. It was black silicone. It was better for all the rugged hiking and biking you and Katie used to do." Russ, who apparently has a photographic memory when it comes to my life, arches an eyebrow at me. "That's what you told me after she passed."

Bless Russ for being a great listener and an attentive friend. But also...crap.

I laugh too loudly. "Oh, it's, uh, it's a long story. Just a kind of legal thing."

"Is that why you went to the courthouse with Uncle Des?" Davy asks from an open car window.

"Why did you open your window?" I try to sound stern but it comes out panicked.

"Because Dean farted."

"Davy farted first!" Dean yells from his seat.

"You went to the courthouse with Des? For, like, a marriage license?" Russ raises his eyebrows.

"Technically?" For someone who's involved in a fake marriage and fraud, my lying ability needs work.

"You and Des are married?"

"It's—I'll explain it later. I need to get the kids home. Thanks for baking the brownies."

I pivot and twist away from Russ, not unlike maneuvering away from an aggressive defenseman on the ice. I let out a long, slow breath as I slide into my car and shut the door. My head is clouded with spiraling thoughts and the stench of my sons' flatulence.

I peel out of the pickup lane at ten miles per hour—twice the speed limit.

Another A-plus parenting moment.

Nailed it. Kind of.

————

BACK HOME, I make grilled cheese and tomato soup. That's as close to pizza from scratch as I can muster. Dean helps by doing impersonations of the Swedish Chef, and Lulu helps by trying to eat all the cheese.

Lena is studying at a friend's house, and Davy gets picked up for hockey practice. I can fill them in later. They're old enough to hopefully have a better understanding of what's going on with Uncle Des. My two youngest need more handholding.

"Okay, guys," I say as we sit down. "We need to talk about something."

"Can I get a rabbit?" Dean asks.

"A rabbit?" I hand them napkins to put on their laps.

"Not as a pet. To pull out of my hat."

I notice then that Dean is wearing his magician's hat.

"Can I get a pet rabbit?" Lulu asks.

"You don't like rabbits," he shoots back.

"Yes I do! Daddy, can we get a pet rabbit?"

"This rabbit would be part of my act. He's not a pet." Dean dips half his grilled cheese into his soup, then his mouth. "How do magicians get rabbits to stay still under their hat?"

"Dean, you are so delusional," Lulu says with a slight lisp. It's her new favorite word that she picked up from her older sister. I doubt she actually knows what it means.

"No rabbits. We need to talk about Uncle Des."

Dean narrows his eyes. "Is he okay?"

"Yeah, he's fine. He's great." I tap my fingers against my leg, nerves pinballing around my stomach. "The thing is...remember when I told you Uncle Des and I had to go to the courthouse for something last week? Well, we technically got married."

They both stare at me, their little brains trying to compute.

"To each other?" Dean asks.

I nod yes.

Lulu gasps again, delighted. "You're *princesses!*"

"Close," I say. "It's a...special kind of marriage. It's not the same kind of marriage as your mom and I had." I get a little sting at the back of my throat, as if my body's betraying my explanation. "Some people get married because they're in love and want to live happily ever after. And some people get married to help out their friends."

Crap, am I falling into a backdoor explanation of green-card marriages? Why did I have to wear that stupid ring outside the house?

"Uncle Des and I got married so that Uncle Des could help us out with something really important. But it's not forever." I let out a quick sigh of relief because I didn't blatantly lie to my kids. I merely distorted the truth. And yes, there is a difference.

"We don't need to tell people about this favor Uncle Des is doing. It's not nice to brag about good deeds because it makes them less special." I feel like that guy who walked on a tightrope between the World Trade Center. Careful. Caaaaareful.

Dean and Lulu's face squiggle with turning wheels as they digest this news.

"Does that mean he's our...stepdad?" Dean asks.

"No," I say quickly. "Still just Uncle Des. Same as always."

"Did you guys kiss at a wedding?" Lulu makes smooching sounds.

"What?! Who told you that?" A flash of heat hits me when I think back to our kiss and how absolutely nothing about it felt fake.

Dean shrugs. "You have to kiss. That's what people do at weddings."

"We're getting off track." I sigh and take a bite of grilled cheese. "Look. The point is...we don't need to tell all of our friends that your dad married Uncle Des. Because nothing is changing in your life. Uncle

Des is still Uncle Des. He's just helping us out. A temporary favor." I snap my fingers, a brilliant idea coming to me. "This is like a big magic trick. And a magician never reveals how he pulls it off, right?"

Dean nods. "I don't get it." He leans back in his chair, thinking hard. "So...you're married, but not?"

I blink. "Dean, I think I'm changing my tune on that pet rabbit."

His and Lulu's faces instantly light up, the confusing dimensions of my relationship with Des left in the dust.

"A rabbit for both of you to share," I say.

Once we get into eating, I let them turn on cartoons while I clean up the kitchen. I check my phone. There's a text from Des.

Des: Everyone is asking us where we're going on our honeymoon. We have to do Hawaii. What do you think, honey?

Tanner: Hawaii sounds great, dear.

I close my eyes while my hands are deep in the depths of dirty dishes, and I dream. I dream of walking along the beach with Des, of honeymoon suites with heart-shaped beds.

Of laying in that heart-shaped bed with Des as he pulls me close and drags my boxers off, then runs his hands between my thighs until he grabs my—

"Daddy!" Lulu yells from the living room. "Can we get a white rabbit?"

"Sure," I call back, eternally grateful that my daughter interrupted that daydream.

7

DES

I text Tanner to let him know that the insurance documents are in. Once we're cleared, we should be good to go, and his kiddoes will be covered.

Des: I've submitted the paperwork, darling. You don't need to nag me anymore.

Tanner: Good. I'll have a meatloaf waiting for you at home tonight.

I stroll into my office with a dopey smile on my face. It's not a corner office, but it's one of the biggest on the floor. During one late night trying to brainstorm a pitch, I measured the other offices. Not my proudest moment, but sleep deprivation and stress will do that to a guy.

I read through my emails and look over some new taglines that my team came up with for Brenner's Mustard and their new spicy mustard.

"Hey," Kyle says, doing his annoying knock on my door. It's up there with the sound of drilling into a tooth, which is appropriate since dealing with him is as joyful as a trip to the dentist.

Kyle exudes golden-boy energy that's totally unearned. He only got this job because his dad was one of the agency's founders. Even though his dad retired years ago, Kyle's still here—still thinking he owns the place, still acting like the little kid who used to ride his tricycle around the office and bother everyone with his ideas. We're both associate creative directors. I got my position through tirelessly climbing the ladder over fifteen years; Kyle got his because of the right DNA.

"Kyle. What's up?" I ask with the minimal acceptable amount of pleasantness.

"How are things going with Brenner's? I heard a rumor that your team had to redo everything. They weren't happy with anything you presented." He curves his lips down into an exaggerated frown.

"It happens from time to time. Well, for you, it's a regular occur-rence from the rumors I hear." I flash the same exaggerated frown at him. "I appreciate your concern. You can run along now, nepo baby."

"Ouch. I haven't heard that one before." His chuckle sounds like a dog throwing up, but less pleasant.

I look up, and his dumb face is still in my doorway.

"What?" I keep my eyes glued to my computer in the hopes he'll run along soon.

"You want to hear another rumor going around?" Kyle asks.

"If it's the one about you catching gonorrhea on a Disney Cruise, I've already heard it."

"It was a staph infection, and it was pretty serious." He drops his ugly smile.

My junior copywriter Craig comes in—at six foot five, he should be in the NBA in my opinion— and lets me know Stan, the agency's creative director, is calling a meeting for everyone.

"Everyone?" I ask.

"Everyone," he confirms.

"I wonder what it could be..." Kyle flits away from the door, his knowing grin only adding to my anxiety.

Stan doesn't do a lot of meetings. He's generally busy with older clients and long-standing accounts. So why talk to the whole office?

"Do we know what this is about?" I say to Craig under my breath.

I have to stand on my tiptoes so he can hear; I almost trip over a wastebasket.

"I heard a rumor." He flings his pretty boy hair out of his eyes.

"What's the rumor?" I ask. Being out of the loop is new for me.

"Stan's retiring," Craig whispers back just as we reach the traffic jam to enter the conference room.

Holy shit. A huge pit plops in my stomach.

I signal for Craig to zip it so others don't hear us talking, especially Kyle in front of me. He doesn't hold the door open for either of us. Typical.

The room's walls are filled with framed pictures of past ad campaigns, for cereal and travel agencies and fax machines. Petty/Marsh has managed to remain relevant for over forty years. I could've tried to get in with a bigger agency in Manhattan, but working my way up at a boutique outfit has let me get more experience.

Managers and above sit around the conference table, with assistants and junior employees taking the seats around the perimeter. At the head of the table is Stan Beecham, in his navy blue suit, wearing his trademark bow tie. He liked impressing people at parties by showing them how to tie one because most have no idea how. His black skin pops against his light blue dress shirt, and the white of his tight curls gives him a regal quality.

"Yes, happy Friday to you all," Stan says. "In advertising, brevity is key. We only have six seconds to grab the consumer's attention. So I'm going to cut to the chase. I've worked here for twenty-five years, been creative director for nine of those, trying to fill the hole left by the great Drake Petty." Stan nods at Kyle, who makes a heart with his hands.

Barf.

"It's been a great ride, but I've decided to pack up my spurs and go. I promised my wife I would retire, and I have to keep that promise."

Nobody gasps out loud, but you can feel a collective shift in the room at the news. It's the end of an era. I have Craig sit on the opposite wall as me so we can slyly communicate during these meetings. He and I both have the same stunned look. This is real shit.

"Now, you're probably wondering who will be my successor," Stan continues. "Well, I'm not leaving until the end of the year, so I'll be using these next few months to look at candidates in-house, and also some external candidates, and see who would be the best fit. Because being creative director—it's tough. You're running a whole agency. You're interfacing with clients and their needs. But I know one of you can handle it. There are already a few at the top of my list."

His eyes find me in a split-second glance. After bouncing around in my twenties, not knowing what I wanted to do with my life, and getting no guidance from my parents, Petty/Marsh, and Stan in particular, became a home to me. They were the place where I learned to be a functioning adult. I love it here. I want to stay here. I *know* I can lead here. This is what I've been working for.

Some people say it's bad to only care about your job, to be job-obsessed. I disagree. The satisfaction that comes from work is unparalleled. I rub my finger absentmindedly, surprised to find myself looking for a ring to swirl. I left that wedding ring on all weekend by accident. Big mistake.

"Since we're all here, let's take a few minutes to go around and give a quick update on your different clients—who you're working with. Des, you go first. How's Brenner's?" Stan spends some of his time teaching marketing and advertising at a local college, and he's become fond of calling on us as if we're his students. You always have to be prepared in a meeting with Stan Beecham.

"We're presenting new creative to them today. In it, we're playing up the excitement that spicy mustard can bring to a regular sandwich. We're transforming the way people think about lunch." Sometimes, I hear myself talk and have to laugh. Am I selling mustard or helping to elect the president of the United States?

Stan tepees his fingers together and nods with utmost seriousness. "Send me what you have after this meeting. I want to look it over. I wonder if we should be thinking less about transformation and more about a fun moment in the day? Transformation sounds very serious. Adding a little twist to your sandwich won't change your life, but it's..."

"Something different to look forward to."

"Exactly."

"I'll work with my team to tweak some of the messaging." Stan may be getting up there in years, but he's still a fountain of wisdom. He has this innate ability to understand what people want. I'm grateful for the opportunity to have worked under him all these years, and I feel confident I can take the mantle.

"Well, my team and I have a lot cooking," Kyle interjects, never one to let a moment exist without him. He used to see me as an annoyance, until he realized I was the real deal. "Ardmore Expedition Stores has been so enamored with our work that they're considering..." Kyle pauses for effect. Damn it, even I lean forward in my seat, intrigued. "Advertising in the Super Bowl. And they'd want us to make the commercial."

Stan's mouth falls open, while the rest of his face beams. The conference room lights up with excitement. "We've never done a commercial for the Super Bowl. One hundred million people seeing our work."

"More than that. The right commercial can go viral. We might be looking at billions. Quite a spotlight for Petty/Marsh," Kyle says.

I grumble while keeping a polite smile on my face, something I've mastered through years of listening to scathing client feedback.

"Great work, Kyle," Stan says.

"Ardmore has been so impressed with our work that they want to expand their advertising, and what better way than the Super Bowl?" Kyle flips a pen in his hand. The joy radiating off him turns up the panic in my chest.

"That's awesome," I say, and before I can think it through, the words keep coming out. "I also have some exciting news. I'm going to make Silq Cosmetics a Petty/Marsh client."

That quiets everyone and pulls focus back to me.

"No you're not," Kyle shoots back.

"They're unhappy with their current creative. They're about to put their agency into review." I silently thank Maya. For the great sex and possibly saving my career.

That elicits actual gasps around the room. Stan, a man with a great poker face, can't help but raise his eyebrows. Even Kyle has a flash of shock.

"Really?" Stan asks. "They just hit the Fortune 500 list. Some people think they could eclipse Revlon soon."

"If they have the right creative," I say, keeping cool. "We should be getting their RFP next week."

After Maya's tip, I found out that Silq's head of marketing is connected to Bill on LinkedIn; they met at some corporate function and stayed friendly. I sweettalked Bill (a challenge) to get me an introduction, then I sweettalked the head of marketing to get us an invitation to compete.

"We're going to land them. I have the best team working with me. I don't have any doubts." I manage to be cooler and calmer than George Clooney sipping his branded tequila. Inside, though, I'm freaking the fuck out.

This would be a wonderful sendoff gift for Stan. Landing Petty/Marsh's biggest client ever, a true sign of how he's been able to build up our agency during his tenure. There's no way he could deny choosing me for creative director after that. Now I have to do the damn thing.

"If we get the Silq business, does that mean we'd get free products?" asks Ainsley, a mid-level graphic designer. "Asking for a friend, of course."

"We'll see," I say.

"You think we can get Silq?" Stan asks.

"Absolutely. We've never gone after a client of this size. But we have it in us." My stomach tumbles around like the most aggressive dryer cycle.

"Well, if you need help, Des, I'm happy to assist," Kyle chimes in. "You know, since I have a fresher, younger perspective."

Kyle is only thirty-five, nearly a decade younger than me. He had less of a ladder he needed to climb thanks to daddy.

"I think I've got it from here, Kyle. Thank you."

"Competition—I love it!" Stan rubs his hands together. "I'll be making my decision on my successor by December. Let's see what you boys got."

Just then, Stan's secretary Myrna enters. She's a lifer, knows the birthdays of every single person in this office from memory. She whispers something to him, which elicits a look from Stan I'm not used to: giddiness.

"Des," Stan says, "do you have any big news you want to share?"

"Does it get bigger than Silq?"

"Anything else you want to tell us about?"

"We've finally convinced Vernon Auto Parts to start a TikTok."

"Not work-related. Is there *anything* else going on in your life?"

I rack my brain. Is this a trick question?

"I might be getting a new car?" I offer.

Stan rolls his eyes. "Des, you love to keep us on our toes. Apparently, you filed to change your insurance plan today...because you got married."

Suddenly, all eyes are on me. Not the kind of focus I prefer. I take a breath, tight and shallow.

"I did," I say slowly. Very slowly.

"This is news to us!" Stan says, slapping his knee. "We never thought you would get married."

"That came out of nowhere," Kyle adds. "Did you get drunk and marry someone in Vegas?"

"No, Kyle," I mutter.

I want to remind him that his dad allegedly did just that on a wild work trip years ago, but I don't want to burst his bubble.

"Oh, you know...it was just time," I say.

Myrna looks at the form. "Tanner. That's your friend, isn't it? He came to the holiday party with you a few years ago."

She never forgets a face. Ever.

"We've been friends for a while." I think about Tanner and our dopey text chain. The times on his roof. That adorable sweetness that radiates off him. "We've known each other since high school. We played on the hockey team together. We've just...been through it. Through highs, through loss. And over the past few months, we realized this friendship was something more. Something deeper."

Despite myself, a smile crosses my face. I remember that I'm in advertising, and my job is to sell people on new realities, and I'm damn good at my job.

"He's funny. He's sweet. Sometimes I don't know how he stands me, but...he does." My colleagues hang on my every word. They may be more emotional about this than about Stan retiring. "We realized we wanted to make it something more permanent."

"Dude, you just up and got married? You said you were taking it easy this weekend," Craig says.

"When you've been with someone this long, and know them this well, you don't need a whole ceremony. That can come later. With school starting, and the kids going back—Lulu's starting kindergarten, Lena's starting high school—there's just a lot of transition. We didn't want to add to that. So we kept it low-key."

"He has kids?" Stan asks.

"Four. I'm crazy about each and every one of them."

"That is so sweet," Myrna says.

"So you've been together exclusively this whole time?" Kyle asks.

"It's been a few months since we decided to be exclusive. You know, when you get to our age, you know what you want. What you don't want. You don't need all the pomp and circumstance. We went to the courthouse."

Some coworkers let out an *aww* at that. I flash back to those crowded chambers, holding Tanner's hand as I slid the ring on, feeling a slight nervous tremble in his fingers.

"You are so in love. It's so cute. I never thought this day would come," says Rishi, an account manager sitting across from me.

"I'm sorry I didn't mention anything." I turn to Stan. "But don't worry—I'm still laser-focused on my work."

"I hope so," he says. "Because you have four new dependents. And kids are a handful. Wonderful, but a handful."

Myrna nods and laughs. I wonder if this is some kind of HIPAA violation, reading my life out loud in front of everyone.

"I love being a father," I say, grateful I didn't choke on that absurd statement. "But as I said, Stan—I'm ready to help lead this agency. We're gonna get Silq. So don't worry about any distractions."

"Oh, I'm not," he says, waving away my concern. "Des, you've been a bachelor for so long. That can be fun. But having a marriage and a family...it gives you stakes. Now there's a real reason for you to come into work. You've got mouths to feed. People to support. Something real."

He smiles. I feel a little dinged at his opinion, though. As if I wasn't serious about my job when I was single.

"And maybe that's old-fashioned of me. I support whatever life-style people choose, but a family keeps you grounded. I'm excited to meet them."

I do a double take. "Meet them?"

"Of course! We want to meet your new family."

"Oh. Well...if there's a work event, maybe you'll meet Tanner or something."

"No, I mean really get to know them. I've met spouses and kids over the years at holiday parties and company picnics." Stan loves playing wise old grandpa to everyone's kids. He dresses as Santa at Christmas parties.

"Well, I'm sure you'll meet them sometime."

"Myrna, can you work with Des to schedule dinner? I'd love to come over one night—if that's okay with you."

Before I can answer, Kyle says, "I'm sure Des would *love* to have you over."

"Wonderful idea," I say through gritted teeth.

"It's settled," Stan says. "I'm excited to meet them. And Des— welcome to marriage and fatherhood."

Everyone claps and cheers.

I act gracious; inside, I feel like I'm melting at the speed of light.

8

DES

T he martinis are over-chilled, the glass rims frosted perfectly, the twist of lemon curled with surgical precision.

I've done everything right—except relax.

Jeremy watches me with mild amusement as I adjust the cocktail napkins *again* and glance at my phone *again*. It's been over an hour since I called Tanner, and still...nothing.

Not a single text. Not even a "lol."

"You always this fidgety before a drink?" Jeremy asks, propping a sockless ankle on his knee. He's somewhere in his late twenties. He does something with computers. And he's some version of preppy cute.

We'd been messaging on Milkman, allegedly a gay dating app that's really a gay hookup app. Things had petered out a few weeks ago, but the stress of today compelled me to reopen the app. He messaged *wut up?* and that was enough for me.

Sex is nature's mood stabilizer.

Jeremy should be exactly my type. Tall, symmetrical face, good shoes, ready to get it on. He slipped out of his clothes within fifteen minutes of arriving, claiming that he thinks better in just his underwear. My cock should be raging to get inside him, but right now, he might as well be a lamp.

"I'm not fidgety," I lie, scrolling my messages for the fifth time in the last two minutes.

Jeremy leans back on my sofa, the one that cost more than my first car. "You're checking your phone like you're waiting for lab results." He sits back up. "Wait, are you waiting for lab results? When was the last time you got tested?"

"Recently, and I'm all good on that front."

"Me, too," he says, not wanting to be left out.

I hand him one of the martinis. My hand brushes the screen of my phone, and I catch sight of the last message I sent.

Des: Stan wants to come over and have dinner with us and the kids.

I swallow a sip of lemon-infused vodka and try not to feel nauseous.

"Are you in some kind of trouble?" Jeremy asks, watching me with that slightly predatory look people get when they sense drama.

"No." Another lie.

"Well, you're acting like someone whose ex just posted a tell-all on TikTok."

I press the martini glass to my temple. "It's nothing."

This wasn't supposed to happen. We were supposed to have a secret wedding, and then his kids would have medical coverage until he got a new job in a few weeks. But now my *entire company* knows we're married, and my boss is dead set on meeting my new "family." If Stan finds out any of this is a lie, I can not only kiss creative director goodbye, I can kiss my job at Petty/Marsh or any future job in the ad industry goodbye.

I'd become an anecdote laughed about over happy hours for generations to come. *Did you hear about that ad guy who lied about having a family so he could get a promotion?*

All it would take is one of Tanner's kids accidentally saying something they shouldn't, or Tanner and I messing up our timeline. Fifteen years of building a career would vanish overnight.

"You seem so stressed." Jeremy holds out my martini to my lips. "Drink your juice, Shelby."

"I'm fine."

"Are you sure?"

I refresh my messages, hoping for a reply. "I'm waiting to hear from my husband."

Jeremy chokes on his drink. "I'm sorry. Your *what*?"

Fuck.

"My friend," I stammer out.

"No. You said husband. As in husband."

I take Jeremy's hand, trying to get back to my suave self. "It's nothing."

"I'm not a homewrecker. Oh God." He looks around my apartment. "Is this like your secret residence where you take all your side pieces so your family doesn't find out? Do you and your coworkers own this apartment together and take turns bringing your mistresses here for illicit sex?"

I don't know what kind of expression I'm making, but it sends him leaning forward, curious.

"It's...complicated," I mutter, staring down at the lemon twist floating like a smug little snake in my drink.

"So you're not married then?"

"No!" I bite my lip. "Well, technically, I am."

"Technically?" His mouth opens so wide I regret that I'm not going to get a blowjob from him now.

"We're not really husbands."

"This is so messed up." Jeremy picks up my phone before I can stop him. "Oh my God, *Tanner*? You mean *this* husband?"

"Hey—" I reach for the phone, but he's already reading.

He scrolls through our messages, disgust wiping across his beautiful cheekbones. "Des: Your husband demands tacos tonight. This is nonnegotiable. Tanner: Already thawing the beef, my love. Shall I pick up limes too?" Jeremy throws the phone back at me. "Nope. Doesn't sound like a husband at all."

I feel my face getting redder as this hole I'm unintentionally digging gets deeper. "That's a joke between us."

"What kind of idiot do you take me for?" Jeremy throws a martini full of very expensive vodka in my face. "I'm not wasting my 8 percent body fat and deep throating abilities where it's not appreciated."

Jeremy grabs his shoes and clothes and launches himself to the door, a tornado of admittedly justified anger.

"Jeremy, stop. Please! I'm sorry. This is all a big misunderstanding."

"You can find someone else to explain it to." He yanks open the door and marches down the hall. He jams his hand against the elevator down button. "Asshole!"

And of course, like the devil summoned by my panic, the elevator doors open and out steps Kyle.

Kyle's eyes go from the pantless, fuming twink to me standing behind him. He's holding a bottle of wine and a smug expression. "Well, well, well."

I freeze. Jeremy pushes past me and Kyle, and disappears into the elevator.

Kyle watches him go, then turns to me, one eyebrow lifted like he was *hoping* for a scandal and just got served one on a silver platter.

"You live here, Des?"

"What are you doing here?" I ask, willing the normal color to return to my face.

"My friend Hiram lives here. We rowed crew together in college. Anyway, he's throwing a little thing tonight. Small world."

"Too small," I mutter.

"Who was that half-naked man leaving your apartment?"

"That was a friend of mine. He was helping me with something... and he thinks best when he's in his underwear."

"Don't we all." Kyle's Grinch-like grin stretches up to his beady eyes.

I turn and walk back to my apartment. I can feel Kyle's dull spirit behind me.

"Are you following me?"

"Hiram lives here." Kyle points to the apartment two doors down from mine. I vaguely remember Hiram from when he moved into the building. He seems nice. Don't understand why he'd willingly have Kyle as a friend. "Is this your apartment?"

Kyle steps around me and peers into my place. "I heard you had an amazing bachelor pad. Where are the little ones?"

"They're at home," I grumble.

"This isn't their home, too? Typically, when you get married, you move in with your spouse and his kids. And typically, you don't have naked guys running out of your apartment." Kyle crosses his arms and has a grin the size of Times Square on his face. "That is, unless you're not actually married."

My spine stiffens. "Actually, I was about to go home."

"Mmhmm." Kyle smiles like he smells blood.

"I'm in the process of selling this place."

"Right." Kyle nods, taking it all in. "Well, enjoy your night. Hope you and the husband can sync calendars soon."

He disappears into Hiram's apartment, and I race into mine.

I close the door, lean against it, and sigh so hard it feels like my lungs deflate.

I stare around my spotless condo—the ambient lighting, the curated art prints, the cold, hard edges of everything—and realize that not a single thing in here feels like home right now.

A few hours later, I'm on Tanner's front steps with two roller suitcases and a duffel bag.

The lights are on. I can hear music coming from inside, something poppy and chaotic from a kids show. I take a deep breath.

This is it.

This is what the plan demands.

If Stan wants a married man with a family, then I have to *be* that man. I can't just phone it in from my luxury condo like some sleazy consultant. I have to show up. Be present. Be believable.

And, somehow, not ruin Tanner's life in the process.

I knock.

A few seconds later, Tanner opens the door.

He's wearing an old hoodie and jeans, and there's a splotch of spaghetti sauce on his shoulder. I may be stepping into the middle of chaos, but for once, it feels like a chaos that might actually keep me grounded.

"Des?"

"Honey." I sigh. "I'm home."

9

TANNER

Telling your kids you're fake-married to your best friend isn't something they cover in parenting books.

There's no section that says, "If your buddy from high school ends up in a sham marriage with you to get around America's broken health care system and keep your four kids insured, and now he's moving in with you to keep up the ruse, here's how to break the news to your children without sounding like a lunatic." So I improvise.

We're all gathered in the living room, the air heavy with anticipation. With Russ and now Des's entire company aware of our marital status, we had to get serious about keeping up appearances.

The kids sit like a half-interested audience—Lulu in my lap, Davy cross-legged on the rug, Dean balancing a pencil behind his ear like he's taking notes for a future roast, and Lena perched on the armrest, arms folded, chin raised in skeptical judgment.

Des stands in front of the TV like he's about to give a corporate keynote.

"So," he begins, clapping once. "I have an announcement, team."

I give him a look. "Don't start with 'announcement.' You sound like you're launching a new product. And we're not a team. We're a family."

He frowns slightly, recalibrates. "Right. Okay. So...you guys remember when we said your dad and I got married?"

"It was like a magic trick," I remind Dean and Lulu. While Davy and Lena are old enough to get the gist of what's happening, I'm terrified of how my two youngest will process this. Rule number one of parenting: don't teach your kids to lie. Though, all kids learn how to anyway, so maybe I'm fine.

Some lies are good lies, right?

All four kids nod—Dean with a mischievous smirk, Davy with a confused blink, Lena with one raised eyebrow that says, *This better be good,* and Lulu with a happy little gasp like she just remembered cake exists.

Des continues, brave man. "Well, technically, we told the truth. Just...not the whole truth."

Dean leans forward. "So you're *not* married?"

Lulu gasps. "*Lies?*"

"We're sort of...pretend married," I explain. "Just for a little bit. It's so Des can keep his job and you guys can see a doctor in case you get hurt."

"Why does Des need a job so we can see a doctor?" Lena asks.

There aren't enough civics classes to explain that one. If we lived in Finland, this wouldn't be an issue.

"That's just how it is," I say, using my firm dad voice to put an end to her questions. "And now his boss wants to meet his...family. So Des is going to live here for a little while."

I hold my breath.

There's a moment of silence, which is rare in this house. Then Davy squints.

"So it's like...a spy mission?"

Des perks up. "Yes. Exactly."

Dean beams. "Awesome. Do I get a code name?"

"You can have five," Des says.

"Can I be Agent Thunder?"

"Sure."

Lulu pats my face. "Are you still my real daddy?"

I pull her close. "Always, bug."

"And Des is like...my pretend daddy?"

Des squats down in front of her. "If that's okay with you."

She beams and wraps her arms around his neck, a moment of sweetness amid this chaos that squeezes at my heart.

I blink, a little stunned by how easily that just happened.

"Are we gonna have pretend holidays?" Dean asks, bouncing now. "Because I've got some ideas. I think we should have a pretend Christmas once a month."

"Keep dreaming," Lena says.

"It's hard to dream when your perfume is choking us," Davy shoots back.

Lena squirms on the couch arm. I didn't want to say anything. She's been wearing a lot lately. She's fourteen. New to high school. Trying new things. Makeup, perfume, new hairstyles. It's all new terrain for me that makes me wish her mom were still here. Katie was effortlessly gorgeous, and she'd know the right shade and style and scent for our daughter. I feel so out of my depth with Lena, and this fake marriage will only magnify that.

"What do you think?" I ask her. "Honestly."

"I think it's kinda weird, Dad. Uncle Des is now my dad. He's going to be living here? How long is this going to be for?"

"Only a few weeks—"

"At least through the end of the year." Des cuts me off. His eyes meet me, letting me know there's a reason here. I don't question it.

"Do I have to tell all my teachers that I have a new stepdad?" Lena asks.

"No." I truly hope this lie does not spread that far. "Only if anyone asks, which they shouldn't. And Uncle Des won't be here for long. A few months." I rub her shoulder. Lena is wise beyond her years. I'm grateful that my first born turned out so mature. She's been through so much, and she's handled it all with grace.

"You're asking us to lie." A gotcha smirk comes on her lips.

"It's for a good cause?" I offer a weak smile. It's the best I got. "One day, when you get older, you'll value having good health insurance."

"I'll try to keep the others in line," she says, always looking out for her siblings.

Des points at her, something he'd do on the ice when I scored a goal. "Thank you. I'm buying you a car when you get your license."

"Des!" I turn back to Lena. "No, he's not."

He mouths *yes I am* to Lena. She nods once, not exactly approving but not storming out either. Which, from a fourteen-year-old, is high praise.

"You're all cool with this?" I ask, checking in with each of them. "Really?"

Davy gives two thumbs up. "Des can help me prepare for the hockey traveling team tryouts. I'll have two coaches at home."

"You're so delusional," Lulu says with an eyeroll. I assume that's a yes.

"Dean?" I glance at my son.

"It's Agent Thunder," he says with a wink.

I glance at Des, who looks as dazed as I feel.

"Outstanding!" Des plops onto the kitchen chair brought into the living room. He lets out a rip-roaring fart.

Dean kicks his legs as he howls with laughter.

"That was not me," Des says, leaping out of his seat. He pulls out a whoopee cushion from under him.

My kids crack up. Dean doubles over with laughter. "I thought you were going to look before you sat, but you didn't, and you—" He blows a massive raspberry.

Des stares at us blankly. I imagine he's questioning every decision he's made over the past week.

"Dean's into pranks. Whoopee cushions are a new fave," I explain.

"Noted," he says, shaking it off. "Well, if we're gonna make this look real, we need evidence."

I raise an eyebrow. "Evidence?"

"I need a family photo for my desk." Des rummages through his work bag. He pulls out his phone and a sleek little stand like he's about to do a cooking demonstration on Instagram live. (Not like I watch those in bed religiously...)

"Because nothing says 'we're a totally normal family' like a last-minute picture taken under duress." A bemused laugh rumbles on my lips.

"Exactly."

"Should we pose in front of the bookshelf of chaos or the laundry mountain?" I ask, deadpan. Des's apartment is sleek and could qualify for Architectural Digest. My house is a mess of clutter a few steps removed from a *Hoarders* episode.

Des glances around, trying to find a photogenic background in the living room. Slim pickings there. "Let's keep it simple and all gather on the couch. Should be quick."

We'll see about that. Parent makes a plan. Children laugh.

He sets up the phone on the fireplace mantle, accidentally knocking over a few picture frames in domino fashion. He herds us like unruly cats onto the couch. Lulu climbs directly into his lap. Lena stays put on the couch arm. Davy and Dean jockey to sit next to Des. As a perpetual peacemaker, I sit on the other couch arm, so both boys can flank their new fake stepdad.

"Where are you going?" Lulu asks helplessly when Des stands up. It's been a long day; she's still adjusting to school.

"I need to set the camera timer. I'll be right back." Des gets his phone ready and double-checks the positioning. "This is going to look perfect. Alright, we go in ten."

"Minutes?" Davy asks.

"Seconds." Des pulls Lulu back onto his lap.

"Starting from when?" Dean asks. "Are we in the ten second countdown from when you pressed the button on your phone or from when you sat back down? How many seconds are left?"

"I don't know. Just look at the camera," Des pleads with desperation.

"Dad, can I switch sides with you?" Lena asks me.

Des shushes her.

"Dad, I'm hungry," Davy says. Kid appetites are like natural disasters: they happen anytime, anyplace, without warning.

"We'll eat after this," Des grits through his teeth.

Dean begins poking his cheek for reasons only known to him.

"Dean, stop that," Des hisses.

Click.

Des puts Lulu down to check out the picture. She begins crying. I stroke a hand through her hair to calm her down.

"Lulu, what's wrong?" I ask.

"Uncle Des doesn't want to sit with me."

"He does. He'll be right back," I tell her. Little kids are detonated bombs in the evening. If you don't get them to bed on time, they will explode, as my daughter is demonstrating.

"I'll be right there, Lu." Des checks out the picture. "Lena, you were blinking. Davy, you were looking way off camera. Dean...I still don't know what you were doing. We have to do this again," Des says. "Okay, the ten second countdown starts...now."

Des races to the couch and swoops Lulu into his arms, which only partially quells her crying. Lena and I race to switch sides.

"Dean, you're making a stupid face." Davy leans over Des to mock his brother, who's winking and pointing at the camera.

"Your face is stupid all the time," Dean shoots back. He throws a pillow at Davy just as the flash goes off.

"Dammit," Des mutters. He plops Lulu off his lap and races back to the mantle, immediately sending her into a sobbing fit. I take Des's spot on the couch and hug her tight.

"We can sit together," I coo.

"I want to sit with Uncle Des!" Tears stream down her face. The bright side of a tantrum is that Lulu will probably go to sleep very easily. But first, we must get through this picture.

"Des, can't we use one of the previous ones?" I ask.

"They weren't right. We can get a great shot."

"Take three!" Des zooms back to the couch. He puts Lulu on his lap. I move to the couch arm. All quick, barely coordinated chaos. "Eight seconds! Lulu, it's okay. I'm here."

But the Lulu bomb has already gone off. Best any of us can do is take cover. Des rocks her on his lap, but she continues to cry. Davy throws the pillow back at Dean.

"Hey! Stop!" Des says, trying out his stern dad voice. It makes me sit up straight. Pretty good for a newbie. Six out of ten.

Unfortunately, he couldn't see Dean giving him rabbit ears behind his head as he reprimanded Davy. I try to swat Dean's hand away, but I'm too late. The flash goes off.

Des looks down at a crying Lulu, and a quieted, shamed Davy. He sighs, totally defeated. "Let's call it a night."

I grin. "Welcome to parenthood."

———

FIFTEEN MINUTES LATER, Lulu is calm, the boys' détente is back up, and I'm putting the finishing touches on reheating leftovers. The kids haphazardly set the table for dinner.

Des emerges from my room in an old *South Rock Hockey* tee and jeans that are about an inch too short on him. He's barefoot, and his hair is sticking up in a very un-Des-like way.

He catches me staring, his full lips curving into a lazy grin. "What?"

"You look normal."

"I think I got Lulu snot on my slacks. It's probably smart not to wear designer labels around kids."

I nod, heartily agreeing. I like Des in a T-shirt and jeans over a fancy suit any day of the week. He immediately looks more relaxed, more like the Des I know.

Lena scrolls through the photos and snorts. "You guys need a couple pic, too. It's gonna look weird if there're no photos of just the two of you."

Des looks at me. "I guess she's right."

I nod, heart skipping for no good reason. "Alright."

"Let's get our rings back on, just in case they're in frame." To my surprise, Des pulls his from his pocket. Does he carry it around everywhere with him? Or is he just prepared in case we need to put on a show?

Mine is also in my pocket, though not for preparedness. I slide it onto my finger, sending another wave of conflicting feelings through me.

We stand in front of the fireplace shoulder-to-shoulder as Lena holds the phone. "Closer," she says.

"How close?" I ask.

"Married close." She puts a hand on her hip.

Des wraps his arm around my waist. His hand rests on my side, firm and casual and way too familiar. I can smell his cologne—clean, woodsy, expensive.

I look up at him.

He's already looking at me.

And not in that smirky, smug way he usually does. It's soft. Studying. Like he's trying to see something that isn't quite visible yet.

It hits me like a sucker punch: we've been pretending so hard, I forgot what it feels like to be really looked at.

I swallow.

Dean's voice cuts through the tension. "You guys gonna kiss or what?"

Des huffs a laugh, not taking his eyes off me. "Sorry, Agent Thunder. This one's PG."

The shutter clicks.

We step apart. The room suddenly feels too warm.

Des heads to the kitchen like nothing happened. He claps his hands twice. "Dinnertime! Let's eat!"

He stands with the kids hovering over the leftovers and begins spooning food onto their plates. I watch for a second longer, rubbing my arms against the goosebumps.

And wondering how many more pictures like that I can take before this whole fake marriage starts to feel a little too real.

10

DES

I can't remember the last time I had a home cooked meal. My dinners usually consist of take-out, hip restaurants, or office snacks on extra late nights. The kitchen in my apartment is pristine simply because it's rarely been used. There are no food smells in my domicile.

But here I am. In a suburban dining room that smells faintly of pasta and Crayola markers.

The kids swarm around their plates like little velociraptors. I don't know all their table dynamics yet, but I can already tell that sitting down for a calm family meal here is as likely as getting a workable family picture.

Dean and Davy are circling the table like it's a battlefield.

"I'm sitting next to Des!" Dean declares, practically leaping over a chair.

"No, I want to," Davy argues, folding his arms with the gravitas of a tenured attorney.

"Dad!" They both yell at Tanner.

"Boys," Tanner says with a warning tone, wiping his hands on a dish towel. "It's a table, not a throne. Just sit down and eat before the lasagna gets cold."

I should intervene. I'm their fake stepdad now, after all. Unlike previous situations where two people have fought over me, this can't be resolved with a three-way.

"It's fine," I offer, trying for a diplomatic tone. "We can rotate. Tonight I'll sit next to Dean, and tomorrow I'll sit next to Davy."

Dean beams. Davy makes a face. Compromise. Beautiful in theory. Absolute garbage in execution.

As soon as I sit, Dean shimmies so close that we're basically sharing a thigh. He's mid-story about how he got in trouble for making fart noises during math when—*boom*—his elbow knocks over his glass of orange soda, which sails directly into my lap.

I suck in a breath as the cold citrus sticks to my jeans—or rather Tanner's jeans that I'm borrowing. They may not be the designer ones I'm used to, but they don't deserve to be covered in orange carbonated sugar.

"Dean!" Tanner barks.

"I didn't mean to!" Dean says, wide-eyed. "It was an accident!"

I hold up my hand, trying not to wince. "It's okay. I've survived worse."

Like the time I accidentally wore brown shoes with a black belt in front of a client. That haunts me more than it should.

"I'll get a towel," Tanner says, already heading toward the kitchen.

"Sorry," Dean mutters, staring at his plate.

"It's really fine," I tell him. I try a napkin to get out the orange tint in my jeans. The stickiness of the soda clings to my legs.

"Nice going, idiot!" Davy hisses at his brother.

"I said it was an accident!" Dean yells back.

Tanner returns with a towel and hands it to me. Dean intercepts it.

"Here. I can do it."

Dean's hand gets caught on my plate, though, and it sends a heap of hot leftovers onto my lap, coating the orange soda puddle with a savory layer of day-old lasagna.

"Shit!" I yell. Lulu's eyes go wide at the expletive. I made it a whopping two hours as a stepdad without cursing in front of the kids. Honestly, that's better than I expected.

"I'm sorry." Dean's lower lip trembles. After Lulu's previous water-works, I want to avoid another meltdown. So I take a deep-ass breath and pray my dry cleaner can handle these stains.

"It's okay," I say, thinking of my quiet, clean apartment right now. My happy place. Once upon a time, I used to eat sushi in silence while watching the sun set behind the mountains.

I pat down my jeans as I feel them clinging to my skin.

"You good?" Tanner asks.

"Other than being christened by neon orange soda? Never better."

———

THE WATER IS HOT, bordering on scalding, which is exactly how I like my showers. I scrub soda and ricotta cheese residue from my thighs and contemplate my life decisions.

Living in Tanner's house. With his kids. Pretending to be his husband.

What the hell am I doing?

I lean my head against the tile, eyes closed. This was supposed to be a smooth plan. No muss, no fuss. Sign some forms. Wait for Tanner to get a new job. Get the promotion from Stan. Resume bachelor life in my sleek city condo where my shower head has multiple settings. Tanner's shower has two settings: off and full power fire hose.

But now I'm standing in Tanner's phone booth-sized shower, wondering if I'm in over my head.

I towel off and wrap it around my waist. I go into Tanner's bedroom and pull on a worn T-shirt and soft joggers from his dresser. I get a little rush putting on his clothes. I inhale the fresh, springy detergent scent and it feels like he's hugging me.

As I step out into the hall, I hear Tanner's voice. Low, warm, soothing.

I follow the sound like a moth to a porch light and stop just before Lulu's door. It's cracked open.

Tanner is sitting on her bed, a hardcover picture book in one hand, Lulu tucked under his arm like a sleepy little burrito.

Tanner gives an award-worthy performance, utilizing multiple voices and sound effects. It makes me chuckle to myself.

He turns the page and continues reading. He gives her head a quick kiss, and she scrunches tightly up against him. My heart can barely take it. As chaotic as little kids can be, if you get to have this cute moment with them at night, is it really so bad?

Lulu yawns hugely, pressing her face into his side. His voice could lull me into a deep sleep, too.

"One more," she mumbles.

"Nope," Tanner says, planting another kiss on her head. "You'll turn into a pumpkin."

"I already am a pumpkin," she replies.

"Then you better sleep before someone turns you into pie."

She giggles, and I watch as he tucks the blanket higher up her chest, folding it like he's done this a thousand times. Which he probably has. His movements are automatic, practiced. But not rushed. There's a care to it. A kind of devotion I've never had to offer anyone.

It's intimate in a way that rattles something loose in me.

He turns off the lamp, slips out the door, and jumps when he sees me standing in the hall.

"Jesus, Des. You good?"

"I didn't mean to eavesdrop," I say. "I was just heading back to the couch."

He shrugs. "You can crash in my room, and I'll take the couch. You should get a good night's sleep. You're the one with the stressful job."

"You hate that couch. You said it's like a torture device out of *Saw* movie."

"That was very poetic of me."

"Why haven't you replaced it?" I ask.

Tanner leans against the doorway to his bedroom. "Oh, braces for

Lena...hockey clinics for Davy...a broken dishwasher that needed to be replaced..."

He could go on all night, but I stop him. Tanner needs his rest. My job is busy, but I see how wrangling kids is taxing on a whole different level.

"I'm fine," I say, walking toward the living room. "I've endured worse."

We start unfolding the pull-out bed together. I have a flash of PTSD at the scene of the family picture debacle. Tanner throws a fitted sheet on like he's racing the clock in a laundry competition.

He looks tired. Not physically—he always looks good, in that low-maintenance, easy charm way. But there's a heaviness behind his eyes. Something a shower can't rinse away.

"You okay?" I ask.

He pauses mid-pillow fluff. "Yeah. Just thinking."

"Dangerous," I tease.

"I'm worried," he says, finally. "About the kids. This whole fake-marriage thing... I don't want them to get confused or hurt."

I sit on the edge of the bed, the metal frame groaning beneath me. "You're not giving them enough credit. They're sharp, resilient."

"How resilient should kids have to be? They've been through so much," he murmurs. "Losing their mom. Me losing my job. Now this weird setup. I just... I don't want to make their lives harder."

I nod slowly. "They're going to be okay, Tanner."

He gives me a skeptical look.

"You know why?" I add. "Because they have you. And you're a great dad."

His face softens. "You don't have to say that."

"I don't say things I don't mean."

We sit in silence for a moment, the soft whirl of the dishwasher humming from the kitchen.

"How about you?" I ask. "How are you doing?"

He shrugs again, but it's different this time. Slower. Heavier.

"I hate not working," he admits. "Feels like I'm failing them. Like I'm not doing enough."

I chuck a freshly fluffed pillow at his face.

"What was that for?"

"For that baseless response. Not doing enough?" It's like Ina Garten calling herself an okay cook. "You're raising four kids, keeping a roof over their heads, being present. That's more than most people can manage. It took me a month to get around to scheduling an oil change."

"I was good at my job," he says. "It wasn't my passion like advertising with you, but I had a routine down. Without that routine, I feel so unmoored."

I can imagine how important routine is to a single dad struggling to make the trains run on time. "You'll find a new job soon, and you'll get your routine back. Until then, you have me."

He meets my gaze, something unspoken passing between us. I recognize the feeling. That quiet desperation to feel needed. Useful. Whole.

Sometimes, I lay awake at night worried about losing my job. There are always younger people with fresher perspectives coming into the field. Ad guys are always one bad campaign away from getting tossed. If this fake marriage doesn't get me fired, then bombing the Silq Cosmetics pitch will.

"You will find something. You've been unemployed for less than a month. Give it time. And don't beat yourself up, Tanner. The kids will be alright. I promise you that. They have a great father."

"And stepfather."

Weird to think that I'm a stepfather. I don't hate it as much as I thought I would. Orange soda and lasagna-stained outfit aside.

"That should do it." Tanner tucks in the last side of the pull out bed.

The silence stretches again, but it's not awkward. It's...peaceful. Tanner closes his eyes and smiles at something, like he's found Zen.

"I forgot how nice it is," he says, "when they're all asleep."

I smirk. "I didn't know silence could be this loud."

"It's kinda perfect."

He walks over to the thermostat, adjusts it slightly. "One last chance," he says, casual but not. "You sure you don't want the bed?"

"You hate the couch, Tanner."

"I'll live. Or...we could share the bed. It's a queen size." Tanner's cheeks flush for a moment. "Not like how you're thinking—"

"I wasn't thinking that," I quickly interject.

"I meant. There's room on there for both of us. We can put a wall of pillows if needed."

The idea of sharing a bed with Tanner sends a flicker of heat down my spine. I've never thought of him like that. Not really.

Okay, maybe a little. Like when he grins with his whole face. Or when he carries Lulu on his shoulders like she weighs nothing. Or when he says my name and it sounds like something he's always known.

I clear my throat.

"I'll stay here," I say. "*Saw* movies are underrated."

He smiles, half-laughs, nods. "Suit yourself. Goodnight, husband."

"Goodnight, husband," I reply, unable to help the way my lips tug into a grin.

He turns off the living room light. I lie back on the couch-bed, staring at the ceiling fan slowly turning above me.

A messy house. Loud kids. And a tortuous bed. What a fucking night.

And yet, I've never felt more settled.

11

TANNER

It's hard to fall asleep when I know someone in my house is tossing and turning. I have a preternatural ability to hear the faint sounds of a mattress shift or a general rustling in what should be a quiet bedroom. I am the princess, and each sound is another pea in between my mattress.

Tonight though, it isn't one of my kids refusing to join the land of nod. It's the adult man on my couch. The sound of a creaking mattress (not the fun kind of creaking) cuts through the silence like a leaf blower in a library. Again. And again. After trying to ignore it, I finally crack one eye open and glance at the glowing red numbers of my alarm clock.

1:33 a.m.

Every few minutes, Des rustles downstairs like he's in the final round of a wrestling match with the pull-out. A sharp huff, followed by a muffled curse. A squeak from the old metal frame of the pullout couch echoes up the stairs. One of the springs pings with the enthusiasm of a snapped violin string.

If this keeps going on, then the kids will wake up and nobody will get any sleep.

I push my blanket off and creep down the stairs in my sweatpants and Hershey Park T-shirt from an old family vacation. I find Des lying flat on his back, staring at the ceiling with all the despair of a man who's just learned that this is his life now—trapped in a zoo with four small, loud animals and generic coffee in the mornings.

"Hey. You good?" I whisper.

Des flinches, like I've caught him mid-internal monologue. He sits up, causing the pull-out mattress to release another yelp.

"Oh, just great," he says, rubbing his lower back. "This couch is a war crime."

"I warned you it sucked."

"Where did you get it from? The pits of hell?"

"Close. Marty's Discount Furniture." Despite being a store in New York, Marty dresses like a cowboy and will have customers celebrate their purchase by lassoing the floor model. At least he has a cooler of ice cream sandwiches for kids while the parents shop. Definitely not the type of store Des would ever step foot in.

"I think one of the springs dug so deep into my back it branded me." Des turns and lifts his shirt. He has a great back. Corded muscle and smooth skin. There's something about the prowess of a strong back for me.

I should be looking for mattress scars, not ogling my friend's back, though.

"No scars. It's all in your head," I tell him.

He lowers his shirt. My shirt. And jogger pants. My clothes look great on him.

"Jesus." His hair is sticking up in about twelve directions, a change from his usually well-coiffed style. Even chic bachelors get bedhead. It makes him look more human and less mannequin. "My mattress in my apartment is like sleeping on a cloud. It has individually wrapped coils."

"Do you even know what that means?"

"No. But the salesguy said it was important."

I snort a laugh. A beat of silence passes between us.

"You want to come share my bed?"

Des lifts an eyebrow.

"It's a queen. We won't touch," I add, perhaps a bit too quickly.

He looks at me. "You're serious?"

"It's either that or death by cheap mattress. You need your beauty sleep. You have a busy day of writing mustard jingles."

"I am executing brand strategies to maximize awareness and increase revenue." Somehow, Des makes corporate speak sound charming. "Will it be...weird?"

"We used to have sleepovers all the time in high school."

"I slept on the floor during those."

"I mean, you're welcome to sleep on the floor now." Just the thought of sleeping on the floor makes my back ache, and Des seems to have the same reaction.

He exhales. "Fine. But if you spoon me in your sleep, I'm filing for divorce."

I snort and turn, leading him upstairs. We shuffle quietly past the kids' rooms.

We don't say anything as we get into bed. I slide into my usual spot—left side, closest to the door—and Des takes the other side cautiously, still unsure on whether he should. I feel his weight sink into the mattress. It's an odd sensation seeing as nobody's been on that side of the bed for two years.

He pulls the blanket up to his chest and stares at the ceiling again.

"This is weird," he mutters. "But also much more comfortable."

"I'm a pretty still sleeper, so I'll stay on my side of the bed."

"You still sleep on your side? You don't sleep in the middle?" He turns to me, his eyes big and curious.

"Nah. This way, if I hear something from the kids' rooms, I can easily roll out of bed. Being in the middle, you have to shuffle in and out. Do you?"

"Oh yeah. I like my space. If I smack you in the face in my sleep, I apologize in advance." Des stretches out his arms and legs and does a snow angel in the sheets, making sure to whack me in the face at least once. The man may be suave and chic and wear designer clothes on the regular, but he can also be a total goofball.

I stifle a laugh, needing to stay quiet, just like in high school. Except now, it's not my parents we don't want to wake up.

"Just like old times," he says. "Although, you're missing all the stars."

Des nods up at my bare ceiling. My childhood bedroom had a glow-in-the-dark galaxy affixed on the ceiling, something I did when I was seven and left to be rediscovered by my fifteen-year-old self.

"I tried getting Lena and Davy to put stars on their ceiling, but they both refused. Lena didn't care about space, and Davy prefers to sleep in pitch black. I didn't bother trying with Dean and Lulu."

"They're missing out," Des says.

Silence descends for us again, and the quiet reminds me that I am *in bed* with another person. I should go to sleep, but I also want to keep talking. My body tingles with nerves.

"I loved those sleepovers," he says a moment later.

"Me, too."

"They were the best. I'd raid your fridge for leftovers. Your mom's spaghetti was out of this world, the garlic bread so soaked with butter it could kill a man." Des would crash at my place after games, or on Friday nights after we hit up someone's house party. "How do leftovers taste so good?"

"That's the magic of the fridge."

I turn toward him, but he's still staring up at the ceiling. His profile is outlined by the soft light leaking in from the hall—sharp jaw, messed-up hair, shadows under his eyes.

"Those nights fucking saved me," he says. "Anything to avoid being home."

I nod, knowing he can't see it, but hoping he can sense it.

"My home life was pretty shitty."

"You never talked much about it." Des would make jokes about his home life in high school. *I'm escaping World War III. I'm staying out of the line of fire.* When I'd try to ask him what was happening, he'd wave it off and list off how long until he turned eighteen.

"I wanted to forget them."

I'd wondered if I should've pushed back, asked for details. Even with close friends, there are lines you're afraid to cross. I took his jokes at face value, believing that if it was truly dangerous, he would let me know.

"My parents would fight about everything," he continues. "Money. Work. Whose turn it was to do the dishes. I think they were always kind of waiting for an excuse to explode. I'd lie in bed and hear it through the walls."

To the outside world, Des's parents put on a good front. They showed up at his games and participated in a few booster events, just enough so people wouldn't speculate on the state of their marriage. The few times I went over to Des's house though, I'd feel a chill. That sense of warmth you'd feel in a home was missing. No wonder Des wanted out as much as possible.

"Did it ever get..." A lump hits my throat.

"Physical? No. They were mostly passive aggressive and sniping toward each other. Very *Who's Afraid of Virginia Woolf?*"

I swallow. "I remember that one time, you showed up at my door at midnight."

"Fuck. I remember that. They were having one of their arguments about money that would go on and on. That night, my dad comes into my bedroom, which he would never usually do. He's pacing and still red-faced. I see him having a breakdown in real time. He says they only got married because he knocked her up with me. He told me how he'd regularly fantasized about a different life where he could go anywhere in the world, where he wasn't tied down."

"Des." My hand instinctively goes to his arm. "I'm so sorry." I can't imagine ever telling my kids that. That's something a child never forgets.

"When I came home the next morning, he apologized and said he didn't mean it. But, like, you said it, fucker." Des's parents got divorced less than a year after he graduated from high school and went off to college. "Your parents were saints. Your mom made me pancakes the next morning like I belonged there."

"You did."

He's quiet a long moment.

"I always thought if I had kids," he says slowly, "that I'd mess them up. That I'd turn into them somehow. I'd marry the wrong person, and the kid would be stuck in the middle. So I made a decision a long time ago that I wouldn't do it. That I wouldn't have a kid until I could guarantee I wouldn't be like my parents. And then the years passed, and I never got there."

I feel something in my chest shift—this tender ache that moves like a tide. Des never talks about his family. Not like this. Not with this much weight behind it. There's something about the darkness that's like a truth serum.

"Ever since I moved in here, I've been thinking about things. People loved to tell me that I'd regret not getting married and having kids. But I haven't felt that regret. I have an awesome life." His mouth twists as he searches for more words to complete this thought he's struggling with. "I never wanted to be in a situation where I told my kids they ruined my life. I never wanted to be like my folks."

"You're nothing like them," I say.

He snorts. "You don't know that."

"I do. You've been an amazing Uncle Des. You were there for them when their mother died. You show up." Des helped with little things like school pickups and grocery runs, but he was also this shoulder for them, for all of us. He'd take them on drives in his sports car with the top down and make sure they had a disgusting amount of Christmas presents under the tree.

He turns to me, his eyes shining slightly in the dark. "I don't know what I'm doing."

"You don't have to. They just need someone who cares."

"You think I care?"

"I think you're still here."

That shuts him up. For a moment, the only sound is the soft whoosh of the fan overhead.

"I used to be jealous of you, you know," he says suddenly.

"What?"

"In high school. Your house. Your family. The way your parents hugged you. The way they liked each other. It felt...like a different planet."

"They weren't perfect."

"Didn't need to be. They were *safe*."

He closes his eyes for a moment, then opens them again.

"I don't know how you did it," he says. "How you had kids. Got married. And then...lost Katie. You're a single dad to four kids. How are you not exhausted?"

"I'm definitely exhausted. That's par for the course," I admit. "Here's the thing: I don't know *how* I'm doing it, but it doesn't matter because I'm doing it. There are tough times, and I get through them. All those nightmare scenarios in your head right now—sick kids barfing on you, the grossest diaper blowouts you've ever seen, trips to the ER—they've happened, and they sucked, and I got through all of them. How did you get through cancer?"

"One chemo treatment at a time," he says.

"We're resilient, and so are they," I say, something I need to remind myself about constantly. I sit up, feeling a crease in my forehead. "But I still worry. All the time. Even though I know we can get through things, I still worry. I worry that I'm not enough."

The darkness truth serum has come for me, too, apparently.

"You're more than enough."

The words come out so fast I almost miss them. He doesn't look at me when he says it, like he didn't mean to speak it aloud.

"Thanks," I say softly.

A long pause stretches between us. Not uncomfortable—just... full. Like the kind of silence that means something.

"I used to think we'd grow up and live down the street from each other," I say. "You'd still be you, climbing some ad agency ladder. And I'd be the dad of four, waving from the porch."

Des smiles. "Instead, I'm sleeping in your bed and pretending to be your husband."

I laugh. "Plot twist."

He turns his head, looks at me. His face is relaxed now, free of all the tension he carries at work. There's something boyish in it, something familiar.

"Did you ever...think about this?" he asks.

"What?"

"Us. Ending up here. Like this."

I don't answer right away. I don't know how to. Because the truth is—yeah, I thought about it. When we were teenagers. When we were both buzzed off cheap beer and lying on our backs looking up at the fake stars, hands so close to touching I still got an electric jolt.

As Hank once noted, I am a slut for monogamy. I prefer long-term relationships. I had one girlfriend throughout high school. Des would sometimes have two girls in one night. Girls threw themselves at him, the cute, cocky, charming-as-fuck athlete. He was irresistible and he knew it. He wouldn't turn them away. A few closeted guys would slip him notes or give him loaded stares across crowded parties. He had them, too.

I was Des's safe harbor, a port among the storm of wild high school times. The reliable friend who was immune to his bullshit.

I cherish our friendship, but I wondered what it would be like if we were something more. I never thought of myself as gay because it was only Des who made me feel these things. It was confusing. I used to assume that these feelings were just really strong friendship feelings. It wasn't until recently, with the new vocabulary of the times, that I discovered I'm demisexual. I have to know the person before feeling attraction toward them. And for all of my life, that person had always been female. Des was the exception.

But Des always made it clear. He didn't want a family. Didn't want kids. I had way too much baggage. And I respected that.

So I kept it buried.

"I thought about you being around," I say carefully. "I thought... it'd be nice. To have you close."

He nods. "Same."

I feel it again—that urge. Like a magnet behind my ribs. I want to reach for him. I want to see what it would be like, just once, to pull him into a ravenous, passionate kiss—not a polite courthouse kiss.

But I don't. Because he's here as my friend. Because this is pretend. Because he said it himself—he never wanted this life.

Cancer almost took him from me. I can't risk losing him again. I know what it feels like to lose your partner. I've already gone through that hell once.

He shifts slightly, getting comfortable. His eyes drift closed.

"Thanks," he murmurs. "For everything."

"Of course."

"Night, Tan."

"Night, Des."

I lie there, eyes open, listening to the soft sound of his breathing. The fan spins overhead. A car passes outside.

And for the first time in a long while, I don't feel lonely in this bed.

Just confused.

And maybe...hopeful.

But mostly confused.

12

DES

The sun hadn't even cracked the horizon when I opened my eyes.

For a moment, I forgot where I was. The sheets were warm and soft, and the faint smell of ocean-scented shampoo clung to the pillow beside me. There was a solid shape in the bed—Tanner—facing away, breathing deep and slow, shoulders rising and falling in a rhythm that made me feel oddly...safe.

That's what threw me. The safety.

I was used to waking up alone. In silence. In my king size bed with my eight hundred thread count sheets in my sleek condo where everything matched and there were no sticky fingerprints anywhere. But here, wrapped in faded plaid sheets, the scent of childhood and chaos clinging to the walls, I felt like I'd crawled inside a photograph from someone else's life.

My late night conversation with Tanner brought up memories I'd spent years actively forgetting. A hellish home life. My dad confessing that I was the worst kind of accident. But it also reminded me of the warmth and security I felt sleeping on Tanner's floor, how we'd stay up until three bullshitting about school, life, the future, the universe.

People used to wonder how Tanner and I were such good friends when we seemed so different. He was pensive and sweet; I was a loud but lovable asshole. It worked in that weird way that peanut butter and jelly instinctively go together.

An impulse to turn and spoon Tanner shot through me, but I quickly tamped it down. I'd had those feelings for Tanner for nearly as long as our friendship. They would come and go. Everytime I broke up with someone, or suffered through an awkward morning after, I'd imagine us as a couple. How easy it could've been.

Y'know, if I was the relationship type. Which I'm not. Tanner only does serious, though. I think that's why our friendship works so well. We both know we're not good romantically for each other, so we've never blurred that line.

Even though it'd be quite yummy to do so. I've snuck a peek at him in the showers. He's got a great body, lean muscles padded with some dadbod softness, along with a nice rod.

Quietly, I slip out of bed lest my morning wood turn into actual wood. I don't want to wake him. He looks peaceful. The poor guy doesn't get enough sleep as it is.

I tiptoe out of the room, pulling the door closed with a whisper of a click.

The hallway creaks as I move, and for a half-second, I tense, waiting for one of the kids to pop out holding a Nerf gun or something. Nothing. Just the sleepy stillness of early morning.

Downstairs, the house is already lit with that faint gray light that makes everything look soft around the edges. I pad barefoot into the kitchen, expecting to have it to myself.

Wrong.

Davy, Dean, and Lulu sit around the kitchen table staring at me, like some pre-teen mafia waiting for their next mark.

"Morning, Des!" Dean chirps. He shuffles a deck of playing cards, then fans them out for me. "Pick a card."

"You're up early." I nervously take a card. Usually, Tanner is with me for kid coverage. But I am alone with a feeling of being thrown to the wolves.

"We're hungry," Davy says.

"Very hungry," Lulu adds. "Can we have pancakes?"

"Um...sure." I open the freezer door and sift through the heap of vegetables and ancient leftovers.

"We're out of frozen pancakes and waffles," Davy says. "And there's no more toast."

I open the pantry door. "Cheerios?"

"We don't like Cheerios," Davy informs me. End of discussion. "Dad usually does the grocery shopping today."

"I'm so hungry. I'm going to starve to death." Lulu doubles over holding her stomach.

"We don't want that. Is there any fruit?" I grab a banana from the counter. It's so brown and mushy that for a second, I worry it's something else. I chuck it into the trash.

"Is your card the nine of clubs?" Dean asks.

I flip it over. "Seven of spades."

"Hey, I was close!" Dean pumps his fist.

"No, you weren't, dumbass," Davy shoots back.

"Hey, don't use that language. Right?" I don't know where dumbass falls on the expletive scale, but this seems like a responsible adult thing to say.

"I guessed an odd number and a black suit. I was close. My telepathic powers are getting stronger every day, fartface." Dean flicks cards at his brother. Lulu giggles hysterically.

I breathe an epic sigh of relief when I spot the coffee. At least they haven't run out of that. It's a big tub of discount, generic brand coffee grounds that I would never drink unless I was in an emergency.

I immediately pour it into the coffeemaker and begin brewing. It's not the Nespresso I'm used to, but it'll do. I turn back and see my three charges blinking back at me.

"Hold up. Aha!" I pull a carton of eggs from the fridge.

"We want pancakes," Lulu says, tapping the table like a tiny executive.

"I don't know how to make those. But I can do scrambled eggs."

They were a go-to breakfast on game days growing up. "They're full of protein, a must for all athletes." I point at Davy.

"Can you do an omelet?" Dean asks.

"Yeah! Can we have omelets?" Davy seconds.

"I want an omelet, too!" Lulu shrieks.

"Uh, sure." I rub my face and move toward the coffeemaker like it was a life raft.

Tanner usually made them breakfast, I assumed. And judging by the expectant stares fixed on me, they thought I was stepping into that role this morning.

Right.

I could close a seven-figure campaign. I could pitch a rebrand strategy to a room full of skeptical executives. I once landed a client while bleeding from a paper cut the size of Texas.

But I had never—ever—made omelets for three children.

Wait.

"Where's Lena?" I ask.

"She's still getting ready," Davy informs me.

"She's putting on makeup so she can kiss her boyfriend." Lulu giggles, then doubles over with so-called starvation. "I'm so hungry."

"She has a boyfriend?" I ask.

"Matthias. He's cool. He appreciates the spectacle of magic," Dean says, whatever that means.

A pang hits me that I didn't know Lena had a boyfriend. And then a strange surge of fierce protectiveness comes over me. Who the hell is this punk?

"Omelets?" Dean taps his lime green watch. "The school bus is coming soon."

"Right. Omelets. Made with eggs." I pull a coffee mug from the sink and fill it with brew. It's bitter, but it's necessary.

"Is Dad okay?" Davy asks.

"Yeah. He's sleeping in." I pull out my phone and Google an omelet recipe. "What do you like in your omelets?"

"Eggs?" Davy looks to his brother for backup.

"Besides the eggs." I yank open the fridge door and bend down to find some kind of vegetable. I miss my Subzero fridge, where everything was magically at eye level. Hey now, what's this? Behind a mostly empty container of hummus, I find a red bell pepper.

A sense of victory fills my chest, similar to the ecstasy of scoring a goal.

"Look what I found!" I show it to my charges.

"I don't like that," Lulu says.

"You will." I find a cutting board and chop up the pepper. I put oil in a skillet and sizzle the vegetable, adding salt and pepper. Whatever cooking knowledge I had growing up starts to come back. Nights of having to fend for myself for dinner because my parents were who-knows-where. The salty aroma of the sautéed pepper fills the kitchen.

"I wanna help!" Lulu jumps down from her chair.

"Me too!" Dean follows.

"Absolutely not," I say, adding some butter to the skillet. "You can help by staying seated and not burning the house down."

"Boo," Dean mutters.

"Actually, do you want to crack the eggs. You know how to do that, right?" I ask the kids.

Lulu and Dean reply with an *are you serious?* look stamped on their cute faces. The answer is yes, apparently. But they grab a mixing bowl and crack some eggs for me. I pour it into the skillet. I don't know if Tanner lets them near the stove, but I'd rather play it safe than accidentally set one of his spawn on fire.

Davy finds a block of cheddar from the further reaches, and I have him grate it. The kitchen is humming with activity. The most activity my kitchen would get is pressing the Nespresso button. The mixing aromas of the eggs, pepper, and cheese fill the space, making all of our stomachs growl.

"Uncle Des?" Lulu asks.

"Yeah?"

"Did you and Daddy kiss yet?"

The spatula slips from my hand. "What?"

"You're married now," she says matter-of-factly. "Married people kiss. Like in the movies."

Dean snorted. "Ew, gross."

I tried to play it cool. "Well, not all married people do everything the same. Your dad and I... we're taking it slow."

She rolls her eyes. "You're so delusional."

"Do you know what that means?" I laugh, but her nonsensical comment sorta feels spot on. Called out by a five-year-old. Great start to the morning.

"Lena!" Lulu runs to her sister, who sweeps into the kitchen without fully clocking my cooking skills. She slips her backpack onto the counter.

"We're making omelets," I tell her.

"Nice. My ride is almost here." She gives the stove the minorest of glances before opening the pantry and grabbing a Pop Tart from the top shelf.

"We have Pop Tarts?" Dean asks, incredulous.

"Last one." She winks at him and opens it. She slides him a piece.

"You sure you don't want something more filling for breakfast? It is the most important meal of the day." Listen to me. I sound like a total...parent. When the heck did that happen? When I was her age, I treated breakfast as optional.

"Maybe next time, Uncle Des."

"Suit yourself." My omelet fold is A-plus work. It's almost so beautiful, I don't want to see it get eaten. I slide it over to Davy. I get to work making omelet number two for Dean.

I go to the cupboard above the counter for some more salt. I glimpse into Lena's backpack, and my eye gets caught on something. Under her notebook, I spot what I'm pretty sure is a vaping pen sticking out. I've walked past my coworkers vaping in parking lots enough times to know what a pen looks like.

Tanner comes downstairs—hair sleep-mussed, morning stubble on his cheeks—distracting me from my snooping. Morning stubble looks good on him.

He blinks at the scene in front of him. "What...happened here?"

"I'm a domestic god," I say, handing him a cup of coffee like a man who had just discovered fire.

"Clearly." Tanner laughs. "You made them omelets?"

"We were running low on Pop Tarts."

"Those look amazing. I didn't know you could cook."

"Neither did I. But your kids were hungry. I'll make you one, too."

"You don't have to." He takes a sip of coffee. He turns from the coffeemaker, landing flush against me. Our faces are dangerously close, enough to smell the ocean-scented shampoo that was on my pillow last night.

"Breakfast is the most important meal of the day." I shoot him a wink. "You need your energy."

He grins, and I feel something warm bloom in my chest. Approval. From Tanner. It means more than I expected.

He takes a seat beside Lulu, who immediately leans into his side. As Dean and Davy argue about which Pokémon was strongest and Tanner pours milk for Lulu—I lean back against the counter, sipping my coffee.

I hadn't expected to enjoy this. It was like being dropped into a movie I never auditioned for. Loud and strange and sweet.

Someone knocks at the door, breaking me out of this spell.

"That must be Matthias," Tanner says. Lena goes to meet this mysterious Matthias.

"What do we know about this guy?" I whisper to Tanner as I hand Dean his omelet. "Okay Lulu. You're next!"

A moment later, Lena and Matthias join us in the kitchen. She grabs her backpack. Matthias is tall, skinny, with the mophead hairstyle all the young guys are wearing that I absolutely hate but totally would've had. He wears a navy sweater vest over a blue button down shirt and clean pair of jeans, looking somewhere between a normal kid and a missionary.

He is the very definition of clean-cut. I eye him suspiciously.

"Good morning, Mr. Chance." Matthias shakes Tanner's hand. "Hey guys!" He waves to the other kids.

"Matthias! Great to see you." Tanner claps him on the back.

"How's your morning treating you?" Matthias asks. He takes the coffee pot and refills Tanner's mug.

He's polite and certainly more gregarious than most teens.

"Off to a late start, but we have omelets," Tanner says.

"I love omelets!" Matthias says with strong conviction. "The tomatoes are starting to come up in my garden. I'll have to bring some over next time."

"Please do. I wish I had time to garden," Tanner says wistfully.

I do another brilliant fold and slide Lulu's omelet onto a plate.

"I'm making omelets," I tell him. I hold out my hand for a shake. "I'm their Uncle Des. I'll be staying here for a little bit. Matthias, was it?"

"Uncle Des, it's great to meet you!"

I shake his hand firmly. He doesn't wince. Being close to him, I get a whiff of his very strong cologne. I forgot how insecure young men are about BO.

"How long have you two been dating?"

"Uncle Des!" Lena blushes, dead from the embarrassment of a single question.

"Four months," Matthias says, cool as a cucumber, one that he probably grows in his alleged garden. "Lena's a wonderful young woman."

"She is," I say, a hint of a threat laced in my voice. I doubt anyone under sixty calls their girlfriend a wonderful young woman.

"We need to get to school. Goodbye, Uncle Des. Dad." Lena waves at Tanner, then a big wave to her siblings. She grabs her backpack.

"Uncle Des, a pleasure meeting you!" Matthias gives me a salute. I reciprocate with another steely nod.

"I don't like him," I say as I watch them get into his car.

"You don't?" Tanner watches with me. "Matthias is a great kid. An A-student, runs a gardening club at school, always polite."

"I know. He's too perfect. No teenage boy is that good. He's every parents' wet dream, but wet dreams aren't real."

"What's a wet dream?" Lulu asks. Tanner and I trade looks. Davy looks down at the table, his cheeks glowing bright red. I guess he and Tanner had that talk already.

"Sorry," I tell Tanner. "At least it wasn't a curse word."

I get a feeling I can't shake, though. I've been around enough sleazy guys, and I was a quasi-asshole when I was his age, so I know the type.

"He was putting on an act. No teenager sounds that polished. And the sweater vest? That's just overkill. I have a weird feeling, Tanner."

I start to make an omelet for him, cracking the eggs and putting them on the sizzling skillet. I look up, and Tanner's smiling at me.

"What?"

"You don't like your daughter's boyfriend. You are such a dad."

Eventually, all the Chances eat their omelets and give me rave reviews. The kids scatter like caffeinated squirrels to different parts of the house to enjoy their last minutes before leaving for school. And then the house is quiet.

I start cleaning up—without being asked, which I hoped would earn me some kind of gold star. Tanner joins me at the sink, bumping my shoulder with his as we scrub plates side-by-side. It's so comfortable I could spend the next fifty years here.

"I was gonna let you sleep," I say. "Didn't expect the breakfast brigade to be waiting."

"They always are."

"Well, next time maybe I'll set an alarm and stockpile waffles."

Tanner smiles to himself, the gorgeous creases of his cheeks and crinkles around his eyes making him look ten times more handsome. "I can't believe you cooked."

We stand there in companionable silence, the hum of the dishwasher starting up behind us. I look over at him, at the way the morning light softens the lines of his face, at the ease with which he existed in this chaos.

"You do this every morning?"

"Pretty much."

"And then lunch. And dinner. And bedtime. And grocery runs. And broken crayons. And princess shoes."

"And lost library books," he adds with a groan.

I exhale. "Jesus."

"It's a lot. But you get used to it."

I shake my head. "You don't get enough credit."

"I don't do it for credit."

"I know. That's what makes it worse."

He nudges me again. "You did good today, Des."

And just like that, something settles in me. Like maybe I could belong here. Like maybe I'm not just faking it.

13

TANNER

There was something about dropping off the kids at school that always left me a little lighter on my feet.

Maybe it was the brief silence that followed. Maybe it was knowing they were safe for a few hours, learning about ecosystems and long division while I got to pretend—for just a second—that I had my life in order.

One of the benefits of not having a job is that I didn't have to rush through drop-off. I could indulge them (and myself) with extra hugs and hear about all the recess gossip.

This morning, as I watched Lulu strut into her kindergarten classroom in her glittery rain boots, hand-in-hand with a teacher she adored, I found myself smiling wider than usual.

And not just because I'd remembered to pack Dean's lunch *and* sign Lena's field trip form.

Des had made breakfast.

The omelets looked passable, edible. But my favorite part was the smile on his face, the same kind that Dean and Lulu get when they show off an *A* on a quiz. I couldn't stop thinking about the way his cheeks lifted and eyes widened with pride on his strong face. Even now, hours later, as I walked back through the school parking lot and nearly tripped over someone's forgotten water bottle.

It shouldn't have been so attractive. The way Des had held the frying pan like it was radioactive. The way he'd helped Lulu cut her omelet into bite-size pieces. The way the laughter of the chaos echoed on the walls. I miss hearing someone else's laughter.

Des was trying.

He didn't have to. This whole thing is a front—a strategy to keep jobs and medical coverage. But this morning, Des had been someone else entirely. He's playing the part, even though he doesn't have to.

And I liked that someone. A lot. Des as doting husband and harried dad. I could get used to it.

"Hey, Tanner!"

I turn and spot Russ waving at me across the parking lot, his crisp dress shirt remaining tucked into his also crisp dress pants as he jogs up to me. Right behind him is his portly husband Cal, wearing a *Golden Girls* T-shirt and cargo shirts, and a grin that made him look like he'd just won the lottery in someone else's name.

How these two ever wound up falling in love is one of the great mysteries of the universe. Even oil and water seemed to have more in common. They had wound up in a power struggle over leading their sons' scouting troop, which apparently was a form of extended foreplay.

It's always great seeing them. We gay dads need to stick together. Although, the urgency in Russ's march gives me pause.

"Tanner," he says.

"That's me."

Cal pushes past his husband and wraps me in a tight hug. "I heard about what happened." He leans in. "With the job," he whispers.

"I'll be okay, Cal." I pat his shoulder, wondering why I'm consoling him right now.

"I don't know what your company did, but I'm never patronizing them again."

"Thanks, bud."

"There may be an opening in my department, as a matter of fact," Russ says.

I offer a polite smile, wondering if our friendship could survive in an office where Russ is likely very meticulous. Working on school committees with him made me feel like Anne Hathaway in *The Devil Wears Prada* at times.

"Thanks for keeping me in mind," I say as diplomatically as possible.

"He's not going to work for you," Cal says.

"Why not? I'm a great boss!"

"And *The Hunger Games* is merely a fun competition." Cal raises his eye at his husband. "Sweetie, I love you with all of my bacon-saturated heart, but I wouldn't want to work under you either. Tanner's too nice to say that, so I am. Friendship and business shouldn't mix."

"Tanner can be the judge of that."

"I'll think about it. Thank you for thinking of me."

"I can see if there are any openings at my old grocery store," Cal says. When he married Russ, he quit to be a full-time voiceover artist. I love hearing his shapeshifting voice on commercials. Cal snaps his finger, a brilliant idea coming to him. "Oh! Okay, I know this is going to sound a little cray…"

Russ presses his fingers to the bridge of his nose. "Never a good sign when he starts a sentence that way."

"Have you considered Only Fans?" Cal offers the idea as if it's perfectly logical. "I know…crazy. But also sexy. And cool. I know people making good money doing it. You can set your own hours. And because of all the hockey sports you play, I'm sure you have a good body under there. You probably own a lot of jockstraps, too, which will come in handy."

Russ shakes his head, his ears red with secondhand mortification. "I am so sorry, Tanner."

"What? It's a legitimate career path. Sex. Work. Is. Work." Cal presses his finger into Russ's chest to emphasize each word.

"Who do you know who's doing OnlyFans?" Russ asks his husband.

"The gal who works behind the counter at For Goodness Cakes. I go in there every Friday for my weekly 'You Made It Through Another Week' red velvet cupcake. We got to talking, and it came up."

"It just came up?" Russ asks.

"We're both entrepreneurs navigating the ever-shifting digital landscape for creatives."

It's never a dull moment talking to Cal Hogan. He and Russ are like the Barbenheimer phenomenon brought to life.

"I'll give it some thought," I tell Cal with the same diplomacy as I used to brush off Russ's job.

Russ turns to his husband. "Have *you* been considering Only Fans?"

"I thought about it. But I prefer that you're my only fan, Russ." Cal winks at him, and despite their bickering, the fire burns bright between them. For a second, I think of the playful banter Des and I had while washing dishes the other night, how the purr of Des's smug tone can get me flustered in all the right (or wrong) ways.

"Since you're not currently working, we could use some more help at the Halloween carnival," Russ says. "I need volunteers."

"The school is putting on a Halloween carnival? Last year, we did a trunk or treat." I scratch at my head.

"Everyone does trunk or treats. They aren't special anymore. I'm envisioning a festival slash carnival, right here at the school. Hay rides, haunted house, possibly a ride or two." The blaze of ambition twinkles in Russ's eyes. He was never a man satisfied with the status quo when it came to school activities.

"That sounds like a lot," I tell him.

"It's going to be great," Cal gushes, nudging his husband proudly with his elbow.

"We'll see. I worry I'm over my skis a bit." Russ shrugs.

"You are not! If there's anyone who can orchestrate the first Sourwood Elementary Halloween Carnival, it's you. I believe in you." Cal leans up and sneaks a kiss from his husband.

"Are you helping out, too, Cal?" I ask.

Cal barks out a laugh. "No. For the sake of our marriage, I am staying away from all school volunteer gigs."

Halloween is something to look forward to, a nice distraction away from my job search and whatever is going on between me and Des. Why not?

"Sure. I'm in."

"Perfect. Our first meeting is this week. I'll give you a schedule," Russ says, already pulling out his phone.

"You don't want to check with the rest of your committee first?" I ask.

To that, Russ simply laughs.

He and Cal bicker all the way back to their car, and I stand there for a moment, chuckling as I watch them go.

Russ is a lot—loud, opinionated, and intimidating in a crisp-button-down way—but he has a heart under there. And Cal is the chaos gremlin that keeps him humble.

Katie and I had a solid relationship like theirs. Having four kids meant a sense of humor was needed to survive. I wonder if I'll ever find a connection like that again. Dating isn't on my radar. Yet those thoughts of me, Des, and the kids crowded in the kitchen, or struggling through the chaos of a family photo stir feelings in me that had long since been dormant.

And for the sake of my family, I need to tamp them down.

14

DES

The photograph was hideous. Truly, spectacularly hideous.

Lena was blinking mid-eye roll. Dean was sticking bunny ears behind my head. Davy looked like he was about to strangle his little bro. Lulu had her whole sticky hand wrapped around my tie. Tanner's mouth gaped open mid-yell at his sons. And I—forehead glistening with flop sweat, forced smile stretched like taffy—looked like a man being slowly devoured by four small, chaotic wolves.

But I couldn't stop looking at it.

"Cute picture," Craig says as he strides into my office, pencil behind his ear and notebook in hand.

I step back from the wall where it's hung—a perfect position so anyone walking by can see it.

Craig gets up close, studying each face. He snorts to himself. "Never thought I'd see you willingly surrounded by kids."

"It's the dawn of a new day."

"Is he giving the camera the finger?" Craig points at Dean's finger sticking up behind my head.

"That's an index finger. He was trying to give me bunny ears."

"Nice." Craig raises a fist in troublemaker solidarity with Dean.

Lisa, my senior copywriter, joins us in my office. Her wildly curly hair and boundless smile always help to put me in a good mood. She leans against Craig as she gazes at the picture. Craig is like a free-standing wall in that way.

"Aww. That's so cute!" She clutches her heart. "So sweet."

"I need to get a better one taken. That was a disaster, as you can tell."

"Looks about right," Lisa says. "We hired a photographer for family pictures. She shot for a half-hour, and we ended up with one usable picture where the kids were both looking at the camera and smiling." A flash of frustration, not unlike the one I felt the other night, crosses her brow.

"Yeah, that looks like every family picture we ever tried to take. My dad's face was so red one year because he'd been yelling at me and my brothers to shut the hell up," Craig says.

"I figure this is as good as we're going to get. We're going to hire a professional photographer for our holiday pictures." The lie comes out remarkably easily, but I tell myself I'm selling a story. This fake family is just like mustard or cosmetics. If we have to keep up this ruse by then, I think a family Christmas picture would make sense...and be nice.

The image was a disaster, sure, but it was *mine*. And it was real.

That was the part I kept coming back to.

It had felt real—everyone jostling to fit into frame, the exaggerated, rubbery expressions on the kids' faces. That tangle of noise and life. The way Lulu had wormed into my lap without hesitation.

"Oh, now this is a good picture." Lisa swipes the frame off my desk where I put mine and Tanner's shot, the one Lena convinced us to take.

"Cute couple," Craig says, easily peeking over Lisa's shoulder. "Never thought I'd see the day when Max Desmond would settle down."

"You're so smart for not doing a wedding. Six years later, my mother-in-law and I are still salty with each other over a fight about napkin rings." Lisa puts the frame back on the desk. "Married life suits you well, Des."

Craig slowly steps back from Lisa so that she doesn't collapse. He flops onto my leather couch, a spot where I've spent many a late night coming up with the perfect pitch. His legs are so long his knees bang into the coffee table. He is a man on stilts.

Tanner's big, blue eyes gaze back at me from my desk, his lips curled slightly with a smile trying to cut through the frustration. He has beautiful lips—full, soft. And that permanent five o'clock shadow is giving him major sex appeal.

I still haven't unpacked those feelings that've been coming up since marrying Tanner. Too many knots to tug on there.

"Enough mushy family talk. Let's get down to business. How can we win this Silq pitch? We need to talk through ideas." I pull a chair up to the coffee table, while Lisa joins Craig on the couch. "What've you got?"

As soon as I say that, I jump out of my chair. I can't brainstorm sitting down, never could. Motion is how I do my best thinking.

"Silq is animal friendly and vegan friendly. We can push that angle. You're not putting dangerous chemicals on your face," Craig says.

"That's not unique. Green is overdone." I wheel over a marker-board and jot down "green." Who knows what it could trigger in the future. "They'll be hearing that from the other agencies. We need to offer something more emotional. Makeup is personal."

I write "personal" and "emotional," then underline both.

"I'm all for being eco-friendly, but I will gladly put toxic shit on my face if it'll make me look younger and sexier." I love having Lisa in the room because she never shies away from honesty. She was working at a call center before deciding to go to night school. I took a chance on her, and it's paid off.

"Makeup is about being sexy," Craig offers.

"Not for everyone," Lisa rebuts. "Women of all ages wear makeup. We're forced by society, but we also like it. It's our special armor. It's something passed down from mothers to daughters."

Lena and Lulu pop into my mind, causing my heart to dip. They won't get to experience that tradition with their mother, and I hate the unfairness of that.

"Let's try a different tack," I say, still adding it to the board because there's no such thing as a bad idea. "Something more universal. Makeup allows you to feel beautiful."

"Or conceal."

Lisa and I both turn to Craig as a big light bulb flashes over his floppy hair.

"What?" Craig asks. "My girlfriend uses concealer to cover up breakouts. She's had me use it before, and that shit works."

"We use makeup to conceal. To cover up..." I add it to the board. The idea hangs in the air, our minds working to build it out.

"To put our best face forward," Lisa says, as the wheels spin in all of our heads.

We were hitting something here. Something bold and honest that Silq might actually bite on. If we landed this, I'd have Stan's vote for sure.

I was mid-sentence when the door swung open and Kyle walked in like he owned the place.

Which he didn't. Yet.

I flip the board to hide our brainstorm.

"Morning! I'm making a Starbucks run if you want anything." The more friendly Kyle's tone, the more suspicious I get.

"You've never asked for our Starbucks orders before," I tell him.

"I'm being nice. Don't be so paranoid."

"I'm good," Lisa says.

"Me, too," says Craig. The three of us trade a look, confirming we have each other's backs.

"Thanks for the offer, Kyle. If I were you, I wouldn't get an Americano. You don't want to have diarrhea in the office again. We weren't able to use that bathroom for a week."

"I got food poisoning from that kale salad, and it was very scary!" He sidles into my office. Were this caveman times, I'd pick him up and launch him into the hall. But I must be classy. He walks right up to my family picture. "Is this your new family?"

"Those are my husband and stepchildren, yes." I stabilize my breath as he continues studying the picture.

"How's it been? Big change, huh? Going from zero to four?"

"It's been great," I say simply.

"I'll bet you miss that swanky condo. And is your half-naked friend doing okay?"

My jaw tightens. I resist the bait. I check my team to see their reactions, and they just roll their eyes. Luckily, Kyle has spewed so much bullshit that they aren't phased.

Kyle tilts his head. "Must be hard, though. Getting used to their routines, their likes and dislikes. Allergies, bedtimes, favorite snacks…"

Still not taking it.

"We're making it work," I say.

He smirks. "Well, let me know if you need any pointers. I have three of my own."

The room is dead silent. Kyle shows no signs of leaving.

"Interesting that this is the first time you've ever had a family picture up in your office, and right on a spot where everyone can see." He looks over his shoulder at the direct line of sight into the hall.

"I'm a proud stepdad," I say flatly.

"This framed picture doesn't mesh at all with all the artwork you have hanging on this wall. As someone so into aesthetics, it seems off." He chuckles to himself. "But what do I know?"

"Not much," I shoot back.

"And it's funny that this is the only picture you have of them, and it looks like it was recently taken."

I dart my eyes to Craig and Lisa and see if they're being swayed by Kyle's questions.

"Have you ever tried wrangling a family photo with four kids, Kyle? I can barely get my two kids to sit still for one. This is a miracle," Lisa says.

"And I like the picture more than the douchey art," Craig says.

I whip my head to him, and he immediately turns red.

"Cool douchey art," he tries to explain.

Lisa and Craig's defenses have given me a spring in my step.

"We're good on Starbucks, Kyle. Thanks anyway." I shoot him a wink.

Yet before Kyle can go, he's blocked by Stan, who can never turn down a chance to chitchat with coworkers.

"Nice picture." Stan wears a tan suit with red bowtie and that ever-curious expression stamped on his joyful face.

He steps inside without waiting for an invitation and glances at the framed photo.

"Is that the family?"

It was happening. The test. Would this work on Stan? I smiled like it didn't hurt. "Yep. The whole crew."

"Looks...lively."

"That's one word for it."

"I can't wait to meet them. You should bring the brood by!" Kyle suggests. Whenever people would bring their kids to work, I'd hole up in my office to avoid the shouting and eventual crying.

"They have school," I say, hoping that's correct.

"That reminds me." Stan turns and, without missing a beat, says, "I'll be coming over Tuesday night for dinner."

My heart dropped into my shoes.

"This Tuesday?" As in six days from now.

"Mm-hmm. If the offer still stands."

"Yeah. Of course," I say, the only acceptable answer.

"I want to meet the family, see how you're balancing things. If this promotion's going to put you in charge of a whole team, I need to know you've got support at home."

Support at home. As if emotional scaffolding was an itemized expense report.

"Of course," I said with the calm of someone white-knuckling a plane crash. "We're excited to have you over."

Stan gave me that genial, terrifying smile. "Great. I'll bring a bottle of wine. Your husband drink red or white?"

"Red," I said, the one fact I recited today that wasn't a lie.

Kyle, who's been watching this conversation with bated breath, claps his hand on Stan's shoulder. "Stan, what if my family joined on Tuesday? Make it a fun group work dinner for all the higher ups to get together."

My eyes want to bulge out of my head. It takes all of my professional training not to yell "what the fuck?"

"It'll help create team unity. I remember you and my dad would have family barbeques together. I always loved those times. Your hamburgers were delicious." I can see Kyle fighting past his flop sweat in real time to sell this pitch. The man was born with the ability to kiss ass. "Plus, I'd love to meet the man who finally took Des off the market."

"That does sound nice. I don't want this race for creative director to become ugly. We're all family here. Des, would that work for you?" Stan asks me.

"I love that idea," I say, the only acceptable answer. "But Kyle, don't you need to check with your wife?"

"We're free Tuesday night," he says without missing a beat.

"Perfect." I plaster on a smile. No amount of makeup can conceal the venom I want to spew Kyle's way.

Once they leave, I find myself turning back to the family picture. God help us.

———

THAT EVENING, I arrive at the ice rink still half-full of caffeine and rage. It's only a practice night. I hope my teammates will love me in the morning.

I find Tanner near the benches, lacing up his skates.

"You look like you aged a decade," he says, handing me a helmet.

"Stan's coming for dinner, along with Kyle," I mutter.

"Kyle?"

"And his whole family." I've bitched about Kyle enough times for Tanner to be familiar with his level of annoyance.

"How'd that happen?"

"Kyle is onto us." Tanner's face sinks for a moment, probably images of skyrocketing insurance premiums dancing in his head. I reach out for his hand. "We're not going to let him find us out."

"He invited himself to dinner?" Tanner asks, yanking his laces tight.

"Fucker. Now we have to worry about Stan and Kyle and I'm trying to work on this pitch for Silq." I rub my temples. I'm so ready to smash a puck into a net. I might blow a hole in the rink.

Tanner blinked. "When is this dinner happening?"

"Tuesday."

His eyebrows shot up. "That's in six days."

"You can count. Great. Maybe you can explain to Dean that dinner guests don't usually bring magic tricks to the table."

Tanner shoves my stick into my hand, panic sliding onto his face. "So we'll be hosting your boss, who will be deciding your job, and your coworker, who is actively trying to expose us."

"Party time. Excellent," I deadpan.

"Well, today my postman congratulated me on my marriage. Apparently, he's friends with Cal and Russ, who've been letting it slip about us. And I can't tell them to keep quiet because then they'll ask why, which will just lead to more lying. I don't even know how many people know at this point."

We both stare at each other for a second, then simultaneously groan.

"Want to work out our rage by destroying some hockey pucks?" Tanner offers.

"God, yes."

We join our teammates on the ice and immediately swoop up the puck.

"Hey, we're about to do some drills," Bill says.

"We gotta work out some life rage for a few minutes," I tell him.

Tanner and I pass the puck between us for a while, no real form or finesse. Just fast motion and clean slaps of rubber on ice.

"You know," Tanner said between breaths, "if you'd told me a month ago I'd be fake-married and doing line drills with you to cope with anxiety..."

"You would've what?"

He laughs. Even when upset, his laughter is pure and clean. "I probably would've believed you. But I wouldn't have believed I was enjoying it."

I send the puck flying into the net with a satisfying *thwack*.

"Yeah," I admit. "Same."

We pass the puck a few more times, our movements syncing up almost unconsciously. It reminds me of high school—those post-practice moments when it was just the two of us on the ice, sending the puck back and forth until the janitor kicked us out.

"Hey, save some for the rest of us," Griffin says. He and Hank join us on the ice.

"Are you guys ready to drill?" Bill asks. As the captain, he runs a tight ship.

"Sorry. We had to get out some bullshit coursing through our systems." I pass the puck to Bill.

"We may be in too deep with our lie," Tanner says. "Maybe it's time to come clean. I hate lying."

I can't let that happen. I'd lose my promotion, probably my job, too. My career would be over. But the fear that bubbles up more than those is somehow losing Tanner in all this. Like if this ruse collapsed, would our friendship recover?

"We're not confessing," I say with renewed dedication. "Look, we just have to get through one dinner. Stan will make his decision by December, and you should have a new job by then. We'll be in the clear before we know it."

"But what about if you do get this promotion? You're going to have to pretend we're married for a long time."

Why don't I hate the sound of that?

"We'll figure it out." I hit his helmet, reminding him to keep his head in the game.

"We'll help you, too," Hank says. "Wherever you need. We got your backs."

"Hank's right," says Griffin. "You've already started this crazy idea. You have to keep going."

"I will tell my brother and brother-in-law to shut up," Derek says. "Lovingly. I'll tell them that you guys want to share the news on your own timeline, for the sake of the kids."

"Thank you." Tanner makes prayer hands and aims them at Derek.

"Okay. Enough with the spiraling. Let's play some hockey," Bill says.

The instant we cross the blue line, I can feel Tanner in my periphery, like a magnetic pull. He doesn't call for the puck; he doesn't need to. I know exactly where he'll be, and when I thread the pass through, he's there like he was waiting just for me. He flicks it back without even looking, trusting I'll be where he wants me, and damn if I'm not. Out here, it's more than hockey—it's the way we move together, like my body already knows his rhythm, like we've been practicing for something bigger than the game.

"You're good at this," Tanner says.

"I grew up with nothing *but* this."

He nods.

I'm not sure what makes me say it then, but the words come anyway.

"I'm glad it's you."

He looks over, eyes dark and serious. "What do you mean?"

"I mean...this whole mess. If I had to do it with anyone, I'm glad it's you."

He doesn't say anything for a moment.

Then he passes the puck back to me, smooth as glass.

"Me too," he says.

15

TANNER

The job interview was a bust.

Another polite smile, another stiff handshake, another "We'll be in touch," that meant absolutely nothing. I walked out of the office lobby and into the too-bright sunlight, already pulling off my tie before I hit the sidewalk. I hated how these things chipped away at you—the performance of professionalism, the pretense of being someone who's not desperate but also not *too* aloof, just the right amount of hungry. Exhausting.

I believed in monogamy in my professional life as well as my romantic life. I was at my previous company for nine years before I was canned. I could've spent my whole career there. Not because it was the dream job. But it was a fine place to work. I was comfortable. I didn't have a drive to climb the corporate ladder like Des. Something stable and pleasant enough allowed me to focus on my family.

I'd rather be a slut for monogamy than go through this job search hell more than necessary.

By the time I get home, all I want to do is crawl into bed and sleep for a week. But as soon as I pull up to the house, something stops me cold.

Davy and Des playing hockey in the driveway.

Des is still in his work slacks and a white dress shirt, sleeves rolled up, sweating a little under the low golden sun. He's holding Davy's hockey stick in one hand, trying to coach him through footwork, but Davy keeps tripping over the cones they'd laid out in a lopsided pattern.

I crack my window to hear their conversation.

"Keep your knees bent! You're not herding goats, bud."

Davy laughs so hard he snorts. "Why would I herd goats with a hockey stick?"

Des puts a hand to his heart. "Blasphemy. All true hockey players know how to herd goats. Gretzky? Goat herder."

"Wait—seriously?"

"I don't know. Who knows what they do in Canada. I had to do a million of these drills when I played in high school, and they actually helped me be more agile on the ice. When I was more agile, I could get around opposing players and get more chances to score. Let's try it again." He tosses the stick to Davy.

Davy weaves through the cone course on his roller blades, dipping in between each cone with grace. Des cheers him on like he's at an Olympic trial.

"Yes! That's what I'm talking about!" Des shouts. Their hands come together in a loud, proud high-five.

I bite back a smile and lean on my steering wheel, just watching. There's something surreal about it—the way Davy looks up at Des with this effortless trust, the way Des crouches down to fix the Velcro on Davy's shin guard. I wasn't sure when the shift happened, but Des was starting to look...comfortable here. Stable. Like maybe this could be a fine place to stay for the rest of his life.

Eventually, they see me.

"Dad!" Davy waved. "Des is teaching me goat herding!"

"Useful skill," I say, joining them on the driveway.

Des grins at me, flushed and proud. "I ordered pizza. Cheese and bread are part of a balanced diet, right?"

"I appreciate that," I say. "And the goat herding."

Davy grabs his stick and skates inside to get water. Des turns to me, his eyes flicking over my face. "How was the interview?"

I hesitate. "Short."

He gives me a sympathetic wince and opens his arms for a hug. I don't even think twice; I step into him and let myself rest there for a beat longer than I mean to. His shoulder smells like sweat and that cologne he wore to work. Strong, clean, expensive.

"Pizza's on the way," he murmurs. "Pizza solves everything."

"Thanks."

We go inside, and the chaos picks up again like someone hit play on a sitcom. Dean and Lulu argue over control of the TV; Davy gulps down water, letting his hockey gear fall to the floor; Lena texts away in her armchair.

I go upstairs to change out of my interview outfit. I hear the doorbell ring, and Des yells out "PIZZA!!!" and my kids chime in. The noise could shake the house. I can't stop smiling to myself, the stress of my job hunt lifting away temporarily.

When I return downstairs, Des hands out paper plates like a man on a mission, and it's adorable how seriously he takes it. "Okay, two slices each to start. No hoarding dipping sauces."

Des hands me the first plate. The hot, greasy pizza beckons. "Since you had a rough day," he says.

"Daddy and Des are married and love each other very much," Lulu recites. Des gives her a thumbs up.

"I did a little Stan dinner prep with the kids." Des bites his lip, feeling caught. "Am I psychologically damaging your kids?"

Well, nothing Lulu said was a lie, at least not for me. I don't have a suitable answer, so I take a bite of my dinner and flop onto the couch.

The doorbell rings again, and I wonder if it's more pizza, when Lena races to the door. Matthias steps inside.

"Hello!" He gives all of us a big wave. "Happy Friday!"

"Hi, Matthias." I wave back, too tired to get off the couch.

"Dad, is it okay if I go bowling with Matthias tonight?"

"They just waxed the lanes, and I want to try a new spin move," he says.

"What time will you be back?" Des asks before I can give my okay. He gets up close to Matthias, flexing the few inches of height he has over him. Matthias's lower lip trembles.

"Is ten okay?" Matthias asks, looking back at me for confirmation. I nod yes.

"Which bowling alley are you going to?" Des crosses his arms, not letting up.

"Empire Lanes."

"Where's that?"

"Off Maple?"

"They serve alcohol at bowling alleys. If I looked in your wallet, would I find a fake ID?"

"No, sir." Matthias holds out his wallet. "You're welcome to check."

"Are you giving me lip?"

Lena is crimson from embarrassment, and I'm almost there with her. I hop up from the couch and put my hand on Des's shoulder, like telling an attack dog to stand down.

"Des."

"Just making sure these kids follow the rules."

"Sir, I don't drink alcohol, and I'd certainly never drink in the presence of Lena." His Adam's apple bobs in his throat like a Geiger meter.

Des leans into Matthias and sniffs. "You wear a lot of cologne, Matthias. When I was in high school, I used to douse myself in cologne to cover up anytime I smoked. Or I guess it'd be *vaping* now."

Lena seems about ready to fall into a pit. I fear a stern phone call from Matthias's parents in a little bit.

"I don't smoke, sir. I just sweat a lot when I'm nervous. Like now," he says, his voice cracking.

Des just nods. I cut in between this interrogation.

"You kids have fun." I kiss Lena on the cheek, which she seems to find as mortifying as Des giving her boyfriend the fifth degree.

"Thanks. Bye." She pulls Matthias out the door with her.

"Whoa! Don't mess with Uncle Des!" Davy says.

"It's Daddy Des now," Lulu tells him.

Des raised a skeptical eyebrow. "You sure about this guy?"

I narrowed my eyes. "What?"

"He's taking Lena bowling on a Friday night? What next? The malt shop and a sock hop?" Des cocks an eyebrow.

"Kids go bowling," I say, returning to the couch. "We went bowling in high school."

He leans in to my ear. "First, we got high in the parking lot. Well, not you. But some of us did."

"No wonder I always beat you."

————

AFTER PIZZA, the kids decide to have a movie night. Through multiple rounds of negotiation, we all agree on *Wall-E*, which Des has never seen. We dim the lights, drag out the sleeping bags and blankets, and fire up the movie. Lulu immediately worms her way into Des's lap, curling up like a baby kitten.

Dean wedges himself between us and demands to be the guardian of the remote. I help Davy make stovetop popcorn while Des deals with Lulu wiping her hands on his slacks.

He doesn't even flinch. I'm afraid to ask what part of Italy those pants are from. "I'm gonna assume this is grape juice and not blood," he says.

"You're so delusional!"

Halfway through the movie, the kids finally settle. My arm brushes against his every now and then. It's just light, casual contact, but every time it happens, it lights something up in me I don't want to look at too closely.

"I'm confused," he says.

"By *Wall-E*?" I ask.

"If the adults are all super fat, stuck in their chairs, and don't communicate with each other, how are they able to make babies?" He points to the screen where a classroom of babies on the spaceship are learning their ABCs. "Were Buy N Large customers artificially inseminated without their knowledge and consent?"

"Ew." Davy squirms on the blanket on the floor.

"What's Daddy Des talking about, Daddy?" Lulu asks me.

"Oh, nothing. Daddy Des really likes the movie," I say, hoping that suffices.

"Disregard," Des tells Lulu. "Sometimes adults say silly things."

He looks at me over Lulu and Dean and mouths "I'm sorry." I don't think I'll ever be able to watch this movie in the same way again, but apology accepted.

Des's face splits with a lazy smile that zaps me right in the belly. Then he reaches up, absentmindedly, and runs his fingers through my hair. My breath hitches.

"You've got popcorn in it," he says softly.

"Oh." My voice cracks. I clear my throat and look at the screen, trying not to think about how starved I've been for adult touch.

Des doesn't stop. His rough fingers make circles in my hair. I sink into the bliss of his impromptu massage. I run my hand up his thick arm and begin rubbing his beefy shoulder. He lets out a low groan that I want to record and play on repeat until the end of time.

His fingers dip from my scalp down to my neck in an effortless move that lights me up. Back and forth he goes from my neck to my head, fingers slinking up and down, electrifying me. One finger caresses the top of my ear. How the heck is that an erogenous zone? One of the perks of playing the field is that Des is efficient when it comes to his hands. Or so I assume. I let it all happen—even lean into it.

I don't know how long I sit there before I realize I'm getting hard.

Shit.

I shoot off the couch like it was on fire. "I'm gonna grab some water."

Des blinks up at me. "You okay?"

"Yeah. Just...hydration. Important."

I duck into the kitchen and lean on the counter, breathing hard. My heart is thudding like I'd just sprinted across the rink.

This wasn't supposed to happen.

Des is my best friend. We are playing house. There are rules. There are *kids*. This is a temporary fix, not a...a romance.

So why did my skin burn everywhere he touched? Why did my mouth ache with the need to kiss him?

I run a hand through my hair and force myself to breathe slower.

I *can't* fall for him.

Even if I already am.

16

DES

Post-*Wall-E*, I help wrangle the kids to bed. My storytime skills are massively improving. I've ventured into doing voices when reading Lulu the latest Elephant & Piggie book. Her laughter is the greatest sound in the world.

Lena came home at 9:45 p.m. She went straight to her room without talking to me. I suppose I deserved that, although my suspicions about Matthias are still there. I just know it was him who gave Lena that vape pen. Sweater vest and volunteering, my ass.

The house is quiet now, that rare kind of quiet that only exists when four kids are finally asleep. The TV is off, the dishes are done, and no one needs anything from me. It's a kind of earned silence I'm not used to, but I'm beginning to crave. It settles in around me like a soft blanket.

Tanner turns off the hallway light and gives me a sleepy smile as we head toward his bedroom. Our bedroom, I guess, for now. I'm still not used to that either.

"Long day," he says, stretching as he walks. His T-shirt rides up a little, and I catch a glimpse of the taut skin at his waist. I look away.

"Yeah," I say. "I think I pulled something trying to keep up with Davy in the driveway."

He laughs under his breath, flipping the comforter back. "Kid's a machine."

"When're his tryouts?"

"In a few weeks."

"He's going to crush it," I say confidently. The kid works hard.

The bed stares back at me. Just as I was getting used to sharing it with Tanner, I now feel nerves tangle in my stomach at the thought of being so close to him. I couldn't keep my damn hands off him tonight. I loved the tickle of his hair under my fingers, of his warm skin. Tonight, I made holes in the dam keeping my non-friendship feelings at bay. If I don't watch myself, the whole thing could blow.

Tanner scratches his stomach, showing off its flatness. I may need to do something I haven't done since high school: masturbate in the shower.

But isn't it just as bad if I think about him while jerking off?

"Des? You coming to bed?" Tanner asks as he slides under the covers.

We get into bed without talking much more. I figure the less I talk, the less awkward I can keep things.

"Good night," I say.

I roll onto my side, back to him. I close my eyes, but the sleep doesn't come. My mind is racing with no chance of slowing down. There are those nights when I know instantly I won't be sleeping. Tonight is one of them. (Sadly, they've gotten more frequent in my forties. Is insomnia part of the aging process?)

I turn onto my back, close my eyes again, and do all my mental tricks to fall asleep. I count sheep. I count backward. I imagine myself on a beach sipping blended cocktails. Anything that can help me forget about the man next to me, my fake husband who I can't help but imagine being my actual husband. Even though I told myself I never wanted a husband.

Tanner rolls to my direction. His eyes are closed, lips slightly parted. He looks peaceful. At least one of us will sleep tonight. He can get up with the kids tomorrow and make them breakfast. God, I'm already thinking like a parent.

I have my hands on my chest, but as a touch of sleep hits me, my hand falls to the side...and brushes against a part of Tanner that is most definitely not asleep.

I shift my hand closer to him to confirm what I felt.

Yep. My man is rock fucking hard.

His eyes bolt open, causing me to jolt back and gasp out a silent scream.

"Sorry," he says. "I can't sleep."

I should've realized his eyes were squeezed shut too tight.

"Same. And, uh, sorry." I nod southward. "My hand fell by accident."

Tanner shuffles back. "Sorry. That, uh, happens sometimes. Some guys get morning wood. I get evening wood. Or both."

"So you're just horny all the time." I'm impressed he can feel horny after managing four kids.

"Maybe?" Tanner isn't as frank about sex as I am, so the fact he's even admitting this is a big deal. And Tanner talking about being horny is making me horny. My silk pajama bottoms begin to tent.

"Tanner, can I ask you something? When was the last time you got laid?"

"If we're being honest..."

That's never a good sign.

"It was my wife."

"Your late wife? Who died two years ago?"

He sheepishly nods yes.

"Tanner, you're telling me you haven't had sex in two years?"

"Maybe a little bit more."

"Tanner!" I whisper-yell. I sit up in bed. "Buddy, that's a medical condition."

"I do masturbate. But..."

"It's not the same."

"It's not." He throws his head into his pillow.

"What's going on?" We spent last night talking about my fucked-up family, when we should've been addressing this, which is more pressing. "Are you still in mourning?"

"No! I mean, yes I am. I'll always miss Katie. But that's not why I haven't had sex. I've done a little bit of dating since she passed, but no relationship ever got serious enough to get to that point."

"Dude, we're not talking about dating. We're talking about fucking." My balls ache just thinking about going two years without sex. "There are apps out there. Hell, you could walk down the street and probably pick someone up."

"I don't want to have sex with a stranger. I have to know the person."

"Right." Tanner is demisexual. He has to have a connection with someone in order to be sexually attracted to them; whereas a connection is the one thing I steadfastly avoid in choosing my sexual partners.

"I'm trying to find someone. Believe me." There's a vulnerability in his voice I don't often hear. Tanner is steady. He keeps things in control—for his kids, for everyone. But now, in the dark, in this shared bed, he's not hiding. "Dating with kids is hard."

"So is your dick right now. If you're hard all night long, it might be an emergency."

As an ad man, I get ideas all the time. In order to be a working creative, I have to allow myself to be open to any ideas that pop into my head. Most of them are bad, but some are good, and it's hard to tell the difference in the moment. Bad ideas can lead to good ones. And sometimes good ones can go off the rails and become bad ones. It's an art.

All this is to say that an idea pops into my head in the moment, and before I can determine whether it's good or bad, I say it out loud.

"What if I gave you a helping hand tonight?"

Tanner teepees his eyebrows at me in utter confusion. "What?"

"You obviously need a release. You're not getting to sleep with that thing, which means I won't sleep. I can help you out, make sure we both get some rest."

"You're seriously suggesting this?"

"Uh-huh. I doubt we're the first two friends to help each other in this department. Look, man, if you roll over, you could send yourself to the emergency room."

Tanner snorts out a laugh.

"You need an emotional connection in order to get off. Would friendship work?"

He doesn't answer right away. I can feel the war inside him—guilt, probably. Uncertainty. But also something else. Need. Hunger, even if he hasn't felt it in a long time.

His eyes snap to mine in the dim light. "Des..."

"I mean it," I say. "You've been carrying a lot. Maybe you don't have to tonight."

"Isn't this weird for you? Why would you do this?" he asks finally.

"Because I care about you." I pause. "And we're best friends. We've done a lot of weird shit over the years. What's one more?"

His breath catches. The weight of my proposition hangs between us. Then, slowly, Tanner nods.

I move closer and let myself greedily fist his hard cock through his boxers. I pull back the front slit of his underwear and maneuver his cock out. He's thick and warm. The tip is already coated with precome.

I don't rush. I touch him like a secret I've been keeping, something I finally get to share. He lets out a shaky breath as I guide him back, as my hand wraps around him, careful and sure.

It's quiet, save for his breathing, the subtle creak of the bed. He tenses and relaxes in my grip. My thumb slicks over his cockhead, and I feel him shiver.

His fingers clench the sheets. His head tilts back.

There's something holy about this. After everything he's been through, the fact that he trusts me with this moment. The fact that I'm the one here with him now.

I dip lower, kissing the hollow of his throat.

"Des," he breathes.

"Just relax," I whisper. "Let me take care of you."

With a tender hand, I slip my fingers under the waistband of his boxers and push them down to his knees. The soft hairs of his thighs brush against my palm. His cock springs up, ready to be drained.

I run my mouth down his chest and stomach until I reach it. His cock. Literally staring me in the face. A layer of friendship about to be unlocked. Or decimated. Here goes nothing.

Tanner cries out in utter, heartbreaking relief the second my mouth makes contact. I drag my tongue up his shaft to his bulbous head. He trembles underneath me. He's salty and warm and for tonight, all mine.

I won't think about how long I've dreamed of this. I'm here to lend a helping hand—and tongue. Tanner deserves a world-class blow job.

I swirl my tongue against his head, licking up his precome. I slide back down his shaft and lick his balls. He hisses out tight breaths, as the rush of ecstasy almost seems too much for him.

"You okay, bud?"

"Yes. Please keep going. Please don't stop." Even his dirty talk is polite. He's practically begging.

I pull all the tricks I've learned through my years of being a proud man slut. My tongue and fist traverse the whole landscape of his cock. I stroke his shaft while circling his cockhead with my tongue as it slowly disappears into my mouth. Down I go, taking all of him until his heat fills me up.

He puts a tentative hand on my head, seemingly unsure about whether to push. I take his hand and thread it through my hair. I'm all his. Take me for a test drive, I communicate to him with my eyes.

His legs clench and release with waves of pleasure as I bob on his dick. I grip his muscular thighs, breathing in the dank, manly smell of his balls. I've admired Tanner from a distance, making sure to keep my feelings at bay. Tonight, I get to indulge.

My dick is a throbbing hammer pressing against my pajamas, dying for touch. I rut against the mattress, trying to give myself some kind of release. Yet I am not the focus tonight. It's all about Tanner. My guy needs this. I can wait for the shower.

I look up and find his lower lip quivering as he gasps for breath.

He is even more sexy, more beautiful than I realized. Maybe I'm part demisexual because I can feel myself moving to a higher plane with him. Our connection, our years and years of friendship, is elevating us.

"Des," he cries out between strained breaths.

"What is it? What do you need, Tan?"

"You." His voice crumbles into a desperate whimper. "Kiss me."

"Baby." My face hovers over his. His cheeks are flushed, his eyes big and wild and needy, lips pouting. He is vulnerable and eager and scared and so fucking beautiful. When our lips meet, it's magic. It surpasses every dream I had about this moment. Our mouths tangle with need. He slips his tongue past my teeth.

Tanner reaches into my pajamas and strokes my achingly hard cock. I moan into his lips, possessed with a carnal need for my best friend. I pull my pajamas down, giving him better access. I reach over him and fist his leaking cock. We jerk each other in unison, our lips never parting. I rub his slicked-up cock against mine, giving him lubrication.

"You fucking needed this," I say against his lips.

"So did you." He spits into his palm and returns it back to being wrapped around my dick.

Our lips mash together just like our cockheads farther south. I can't fucking believe I'm making out with and jerking off my best friend, the guy who's always been there for me more than my own family. My body tenses, ready to explode from Tanner's touch.

"I've wanted this for so long...I've wanted to know what you tasted like," I grunt out.

He groans into my cheek, the orgasm so strong that he can't kiss anymore.

"Come for me, baby."

He falls apart quietly, chest heaving, his hands fisting the sheets. His come shoots up, soaking my fist. Some even splashes onto my cock, sliding down my shaft. His heat coats me.

When it's over, he lets out a long, trembling breath.

Tanner doesn't stop jerking me off. He is a dutiful friend. He takes some of his own come and uses it as lube. He slicks up my cock, and it doesn't take much. My balls draw up. I grab his neck, forcing us to lock eyes as I blow my load.

I lie next to him, listening to the sound of his heart slowly steadying. Neither of us speaks.

Eventually, Tanner turns his head toward me. His voice is hoarse. "That was…"

"Yeah," I say softly. "It was."

He watches me in the dark. I can't read his expression. Not fully. I grab a washcloth from the bathroom to wipe us off—the icky part of sex that somehow only adds to the intimacy between us. The clean up doesn't break the spell we're under.

"We should probably talk about this," he says.

"We will," I promise.

But not tonight.

Tonight, I pull the blanket up over us and settle into the silence again. It's not empty this time. It's full of something else.

Something real.

Something more.

17

TANNER

I wake up to the smell of coffee and the feel of my boxers tightening all over again.

Des is already out of bed, which I should've expected. He's not the type to linger in messy moments. Especially ones that involve...whatever that was last night.

We made a glorious mess. I've never come that hard, as if Des reached inside me and pulled the orgasm out with his bare hands. I've gotten by with my own hand for the past two years, but nothing compares to the touch of another person, especially one who cares about you as they're giving you pleasure.

I stare at the ceiling, my chest heavy in a way I can't quite name. It wasn't just a blow job, or a hand job, or kissing. Oh God, the kissing. I always suspected Des was a good kisser. Girls would gossip about it in school. And the ladies were right. Those full lips were forceful but generous. Des took lead but made sure it was good for both of us.

Flashes of last night cut into my vision. It was Des—*my best friend*—touching me like I was something delicate and important. His hands were careful. His mouth reverent. And I—

I liked it too much.

And that's the problem.

Because I know Des. He doesn't want this. Not *this*. He doesn't want four kids and school drop-offs and PTA meetings. He wants martinis, award-winning ad campaigns, and expensive decor. He wants space, freedom. Control.

I'm the opposite of control. I'm junk drawers and noisy dinners and couches with food stains. I'm exhaustion and compromise and still trying to figure out who packed the wrong lunch into the wrong backpack this morning.

Des isn't built for this life. And he's made it clear, over and over again, that he never wanted it.

Which means last night...was a blip. A lapse. A one-time thing. The thought of being Des's husband is becoming less of a farce and more of a dream scenario to me. But if I tell Des that I have these feelings for him, that each second I see him with my kids and each time he flashes me his confident smile my stomach flips like a hammock, he'll panic. Because that's not what he wants. I don't want to lose him.

I push the thought down and get out of bed. In the shower, I run through the hot footage of last night and jerk off as fast as I can before one of my kids starts looking for me.

I get dressed and check my phone. It's quieter now. No more frantic work emails and Slack messages. An email from an old coworker Rodrigo who was also laid off. He informs me there's a job fair happening today. Oh, right. On top of fighting through feelings for my best friend, I'm also trying to get a job so my kids don't go hungry.

Downstairs, Des pulls waffles from the toaster and distributes them to plates for the kids. Dean helps Lulu butter toast, while Lena and Davy cut up fruit. Des wears an apron over his black sweatshirt and jeans, a casual Saturday outfit that his aura still manages to make seem chic. I want to kiss him so badly.

"Waffle?" he asks.

"Yeah. I'll take two."

"I have to go into the office for a few hours today to work on that Silq Cosmetics pitch with my team. I'll be back by the afternoon." Des drizzles syrup over waffles and hands them to Dean.

"My coworker emailed me about this job fair today. I don't know if I should go." I shuffle to the coffeemaker and pour myself a mug.

"You should. When I get back today, I'll watch the kids and make them dinner. I actually found a recipe for slow cooker tacos I'm curious about trying." His eyes go to the slow cooker sitting atop the fridge amid half-empty boxes of water and juice and old art class projects from the kids.

"You know how to use a slow cooker?" I ask.

"You just dump a bunch of stuff in there and hit cook. If I can handle omelets, slow cooker tacos will be a piece of cake."

I admire his confidence. I love using the slow cooker, but getting tasty meals in there can be deceptively hard sometimes.

"Okay. Tacos sound good."

"Great. So you'll hang with the kids in the morning, and I gotcha covered for the afternoon." Des pulls my waffles from the toaster and drizzles them with syrup, making deliberate concentric circles. He puts them on the kitchen table then whips off his apron.

"Sounds like a plan."

"I gotta run to the office." He hangs the apron on a hook in the pantry and grabs his car keys from the counter.

Without thinking, my lizard-brain self taking control, I give Des a quick kiss on the lips. "Have a good day. See you later."

It's quick, effortless, one of the millions of moments that make up a marriage.

"Wish me luck with cracking this Silq pitch." Des calls out to the kids.

"Good luck!" The kids yell back.

"You should get Skibidi Toilet to be the brand's mascot," Dean shouts and flicks a blueberry in his mouth.

"Who's that?" Des asks.

"Don't ask," I warn him. I truly believe kids should be banned from using the internet until they're thirty.

———

THE JOB FAIR is being held in the gymnasium of the MacArthur Community Center, which some people have taken to calling the Bea Arthur Community Center.

I love the center, but I hate it here.

I've got my résumé printed on decent paper, my blazer is only a little wrinkled, and I've practiced saying things like *"I'm pivoting back into the workforce with leadership experience and strong problem-solving skills."*

But no one's biting.

One recruiter looks at my résumé and frowns. "You don't have a master's?"

"It's not required for my field."

"Mmhmm," she says, already sliding my résumé into a pile I know she won't revisit.

The next guy doesn't even ask a question. Just glances at me, sees my age, sees the graying hair at my temples, and says, "You may be too overqualified for currently open positions."

I plaster on a smile and thank him for his time.

By the time I leave, my feet hurt, my jaw aches from all the fake grinning, and I feel like someone's stapled "TOO OLD, TOO LATE" across my forehead.

I need to find a job. My kids deserve to see their dad working. Katie was the ambitious one in our relationship. She used her grit and drive to make partner at her firm. She quickly began outearning me, and I never flinched. I never had that toxic masculine insecurity. I was flipping proud of my wife. She was a badass, and I was happy to be on her team.

I'm not built like her or Des. I don't have their ambition. I strive to be content. I wanted to be a dad with a good job. I wanted to make enough to give my family a solid life; I never longed for a mansion. I wanted to be the little league coach, the one who taught them how to ride their bikes, the one who'd ride the roller coasters with them. I'm the one who encourages their passions and whatever ambitions they may have.

Being an anonymous office drone worked because it allowed me to have that balance to be a dad. But now I'm jobless and fighting in an awful employment market.

I can't slack on ambition. I have to do this for my kids. Finding a new job while in my forties is going to be a challenge. Ageism is real and it sucks. But that just means I have to fight harder. I sit in my car and close my eyes, trying to summon the ambition of my late wife and current husband.

The day gets better once I get home. Des greets me with a quick, effortless kiss that immediately washes away all the unpleasantness of the job fair.

"How'd it go?" Des asks.

"I'm not one for cursing, so I'll just say not well."

"Don't worry. You're going to find something." Des pulls me into a hug and rocks us. It melts my stress away, as does looking into those swoony eyes of his. "Send me your resume. I'll look it over."

"Yep." I pull back before I let myself get lost in his warm hug forever. "Davy! Time to go to practice!"

Davy hops up from the TV. He's got his hockey bag and is ready to go. The dad locomotive never stops.

He's all wiggly excitement in the backseat, chattering about the new hockey moves Des taught him.

I let his energy wash over me. It helps.

Practice is at Summers Rink, the same place where The Comebacks play. It smells like old skates and freeze-dried sweat. I love it. Familiar. Predictable. I watch Davy push onto the ice to join his teammates.

Griffin waves from near the penalty box, dressed in his referee gear. He's been volunteering at practices for a few months now. Before we made him join The Comebacks last spring, he hadn't touched a hockey stick or an ice skate in over twenty years. He lost his eye in a pivotal high school game and had to kiss his NHL dreams goodbye in an instant. But now that he's rediscovered his love of the game, he's wanted to get more involved.

He might be blind in one eye, but sees all on the ice. The kids and coaches don't second guess his calls. The eye patch and grizzled bear and hulking frame make him one intimidating ref.

I walk over and lean on the boards beside him.

"Hey, man. Davy looks good out there."

Davy swooshes around the ice with excitement and energy, each push-off from his skate fortifying him. He loves hockey in a way I don't know if I ever did.

"He's been working hard. Doing drills with Des afterschool."

"Is he trying out for the traveling team?"

"Yep." I refuse to think about the added cost of competitive hockey. I'll find a way to afford it.

"In my unbiased opinion, I think he has a great shot at making the team. He's great out there. Fast, determined."

"He gets that from his mom."

We watch in companionable silence for a moment before he clears his throat.

"How are things going with your husband?" he asks with a smirk. "Are you guys ready to clobber each other?"

"Actually...I hooked up with Des."

Griffin turns slowly, his thick eyebrows raising. "*What?*"

It's probably something I should keep to myself, but I'm dying to discuss with someone, and Griffin isn't the gossipy type.

"Last night," I say. "After movie night. We were sharing the bed, and...it just happened."

"You're sharing a bed? How seriously are you taking this?"

"My couch—it's a long story. We were just supposed to share the bed, but stay on our side."

"Holy shit." Griffin whistles.

"I feel insane."

"I hooked up with a twenty-something shithead hockey player, so I'm no better." He cracks a smile. That shithead is his wonderful boyfriend Jack, and the two of them are adorable together, even if it's hard to imagine the words "Griffin" and "adorable" in the same sentence.

"It's a little weird. Do you think Des is freaked out about what happened?"

"Nah." Griffin answers with such ease I do a double take.

"You think so?"

"He'll be onto his next conquest very soon," Griffin says. "We've always wondered if you two would eventually hookup. You know, such good friends and all that. To be honest, I didn't think he had it in him."

"What's that supposed to mean?"

He shrugs. "I mean, Des is Des. Mr. Bachelor. Mr. Cool. You've seen the people he dates—sorry, *hooks up* with. They're like...baristas who model on the side. Personal trainers with six-packs and no interest in talking about feelings."

I rub a hand over my face. "Yeah, I know."

"You're not his usual type."

"I'm not *anyone's* usual type," I mutter.

"Hey." Griffin's tone softens. "That's not what I meant. I just... I'm surprised Des would cross that line. I guess he figures you're cool with it."

"Yeah." I gulp a lump back in my throat.

"Des doesn't *do* family."

I know. God, I *know*. But it still stings hearing it out loud.

Griffin bumps my shoulder. "Look, if it was good and you're still cool, then no harm done, right? He probably thinks it's fine. You know, casual. No big deal."

That's Des. Mr. Casual.

I force a smile. "Yeah. Right."

But something inside me curls up at that.

Because it was a big deal. To me, at least. And maybe I hoped—just a little—that it was something more to him too.

———

"THESE TACOS ARE AMAZING," I say.

Des beams with pride as he stuffs another hard shell taco for his plate. The six of us sit around the dinner table. The kids gobble up dinner. Davy talks about practice and tryouts. It's chaos. It's messy. It's loud. But it's home.

I find Des above the din. He looks like he belongs here.

And it's killing me that I know he doesn't think he does.

Because when I picture something real, something long-term and rooted and warm, I picture this. I picture *him*. And that's a problem.

Because the more I try to push the feelings down, the more they come clawing back to the surface.

"What did I tell you?" Des takes another bite of his homecooked meal and moans with exaggerated glee. (A different moan than the one from last night, thankfully.) "I told you to trust me."

He winks at me.

And for a second—just one—he looks at me like maybe he's wondering the same things I am. Like maybe it *did* mean something to him, too.

Then he looks away, and the moment passes.

But I still feel it in my chest. Like the echo of a shot that almost went in. And I'm scared as hell it's gonna cost me more than just the game.

Yeah, I trust him. But I don't know if I can trust myself.

18

DES

I t's been barely a day since the night Tanner and I crossed a line.

And now there's this...*thing* between us.

Not a wall, exactly. More like fog. A thick, quiet haze that follows us from room to room, softening the air between us, making it hard to tell what's normal and what's *changed*.

He doesn't bring it up, and I don't ask.

Because it was just a favor, right?

And if I can't stop replaying the sounds he made in the dark—his breathing, the way his hand gripped my arm—well. That's just a side effect. Muscle memory.

Right?

He needed release. He hadn't touched anyone since his wife passed. I'm a good friend. That's all. There are guys who give kidneys to their friends in need. I merely went with another body part.

Saturday night, we go to bed in silence. The kids are finally down, the dishes are done, and I climb into Tanner's bed like it's any other night.

Except it's not.

Now I know what he sounds like when he falls apart under my touch. I know how he feels—hot, strong, trembling—how he tastes.

After nearly thirty years of friendship, I got to discover new parts of Tanner. That's not the kind of thing that goes away.

We lie on opposite sides of the mattress, not touching, not talking. The silence is heavy, loaded with everything we're not saying.

There will be no heart-to-hearts or good friend blowjobs. I'm great in a room. I can schmooze and pitch and persuade with the best of them. But in this small, cramped room with creaky ceiling fan and dusty nightstands, I feel out of my depth.

I stare at the ceiling and listen to him breathe.

I don't sleep well.

––––––––

SUNDAY MORNING, we suit up for our recreational hockey league game. I'm grateful for it. At least on the ice, things make sense. There are rules, boundaries. Structure.

In the locker room, Tanner pulls on his gear beside me, his eyes cast down, focused on lacing his skates. His jaw is tight. I want to say something—make a joke, break the tension—but my throat is too dry. Everything I come up with sounds too risky, too honest.

Our teammates mill about us, seemingly unaware of the tension.

"Charlie thinks we should start a book club," Mitch says as he laces up.

"At the bar?" Griffin asks. Mitch owns our favorite bar in town, the Stone's Throw Tavern, which he runs with his husband Charlie.

"He says it could pull in more female patrons." Mitch shrugs. If he had his way, there would be no evolving the business. Stone's Throw would serve beer and nothing else.

"Isn't it too loud to host a book club?" Bill wonders. "Don't you need quiet?"

"You should do a book club with male strippers," Hank says, totally serious.

"I'll run it by Charlie." Mitch arches an eyebrow. "So who are we playing today?"

"The Special Deliveries," Bill says, slathering war paint under his eyes. "They're a bunch of UPS drivers."

"We can take 'em." Hank puts on his goalie gloves.

"Hank, these guys can hurl seventy-pound packages onto your doorstep. I'd take them seriously," Griffin says as he tapes up his hockey stick. He looks up at Derek rubbing his eyes. "You okay, buddy?"

"Yeah. Jolene and I were up late. There was a meteor passing through the sky at 2:45 in the morning. It was pretty cool." Derek's teenage daughter is big into astronomy and even secured a part-time internship with the local college's observatory. I'd love to watch a meteor shower with Tanner. Holding hands as the sky lights up. Maybe Lulu sitting on my shoulders.

Damn. I should be dreaming about a hot chick's legs resting on my shoulders, not a precocious five-year-old.

"Des, you're quiet. You actually nervous?" Griffin asks. I feel everyone look at me, including Tanner, aka my teammate, my best friend, my husband.

"I don't get nervous. I'm mostly concerned about the state of my packages when we wind up kicking their asses. I might need to switch to FedEx."

The guys chuckle at my comment, throwing off any suspicion of weirdness. Unlike Tanner's bedroom, this is one room where I feel at ease. These are my guys.

"You good, Tanner?" I turn to him, try not to get bowled over by his big, sweetheart eyes.

"Yes. Just trying to get into the zone," he says. Fortunately, Tanner's pregame ritual is to be very quiet and pensive, so the guys think he's acting himself. They can't sense the I-got-sucked-off-by-my-best-friend weirdness that I can feel coming off in waves.

I bounce my knee against his thigh. "You good?"

"Uh. Yeah."

"Tan..." I force him to meet my eyes.

He stands up and is the first one to throw on his helmet. "I'm good. Let's get out there."

On the ice, I don't know what to expect from my fellow offense man. Bill, our center, wins the puck drop. He passes it to me. I take a quick breath and pass to Tanner, hoping this game isn't a flaming disaster.

The second the puck hits my stick, *everything* shifts.

Because this? This is ours.

This is where we're most us.

From the opening whistle, we fall into our usual rhythm. No, not our usual rhythm. Better. More in sync. Like we share the same damn brain. It's uncanny. Tanner and I move like two parts of the same body—passes gliding between us without a word, instinct taking over. Tanner cuts left, and I'm already there. I drive forward, he drops behind, scooping up the rebound like he *knew* I'd miss just a hair too high.

We're art out there. Fluid, fast, unstoppable.

The play unfolds before I even think about it, like Tanner and I drew it up in secret. He cuts left, I drift right, and the defense scrambles, chasing shadows. I send the puck across the slot, trusting he'll be there, and of course he is—he always is. One touch from him, back to me, and it's like the ice clears just for us. I don't even see the goalie, just Tanner's grin flashing in the corner of my eye as I bury the shot. The crowd roars, but all I hear is the quiet certainty between us—that perfect, wordless connection, as if we've only ever shared one brain.

By the second period, we've scored three goals between us. The rest of the team is feeding us the puck like it's automatic.

By the third period, we're laughing. *Laughing.*

Whatever fog was between us—gone. Melted away by sweat and speed and the solid thunk of blades carving ice.

He slaps my back after we score again. "That pass was disgusting." He grins.

"You're welcome, husband," I mutter, catching my breath.

He laughs and bumps his helmet against mine. "Guess this marriage has *some* benefits."

It's ridiculous how good that makes me feel.

After the game, we head into the locker room. Steam rises from the showers. The guys are all chatter and towel slaps, stretching and hydrating and catching up like Sunday warriors do.

"That wasn't just a victory out there. That was domination!" Bill yells.

"Best game you guys ever played," Mitch says nodding at Tanner and me.

"MVP! MVP!" The guys shout in unison, their voices echoing against in the small quarters.

Tanner grabs my hand, and we lift our arms in the air, soaking in the acclaim.

Bill Crandell is not one for showing emotion. A half-smile from him is as happy as he gets. He's gruff and serious and has no intentions in changing that, not even after falling in love with his assistant last year. He is the only guy that love hasn't turned into a softie. But he's positively glowing. I don't know if I've ever seen his face more animated. "You guys were on fire out there! Holy shit! Your passing was freaking poetry. We nearly shut them out."

"It was all Tanner," I say.

"No. It was all Des," he zings back. "That shot in the second quarter was a thing of beauty."

"Only because of your cross-ice pass through the legs of that other player. That pass needs to be hung in the Louvre."

"You can stop sucking each other off," Griffin says.

I fumble my stick out of my hands, sending it bumping into the head of Hank, seated in front of me.

"Ow!"

"Sorry, Hank."

Tanner lets out a laugh, but I detect the red lingering on his cheeks.

"You did great out there. Don't let it get to your head. Next Sunday is a blank slate," Bill says as he walks his bare ass into the showers.

"Hey." I hold out my fist to Tanner once the other guys go back to getting undressed and heading into the shower. "We did good."

He gives it a pound. "Dynamic duo pounces again."

"Are we, uh..."

"Good? Yeah." There's a definitiveness to his nod. Tanner wouldn't be able to lie about something like that. But it seems all it took was a little hockey to fix the weirdness.

He peels off his pads, tugging his shirt up and over his head.

I don't mean to look. I *really* don't.

But.

There's a moment when the shirt sticks, and his torso flexes as he yanks it free. The stretch of his arms. The curve of his back. That thick scar above his hip from where he slipped fixing the roof years ago.

My mouth goes a little dry.

I am an admirer of the human body—Tanner's especially.

I look away and continue undressing. I yank my sweaty under-shirt off, then my pants. I love hockey, but am so ready not to smell like a gym sock anymore.

Then I look back.

Because he's standing there in nothing but compression shorts, damp curls stuck to his neck, his skin flushed from the game, and my brain short circuits. Completely. *Spectacularly.*

Is he...?

Wait.

Is he looking at me too?

I catch him, just for a second, glancing over.

Not a long look. Not obvious.

But his eyes sweep over me—over my chest, my arms, down to the towel slung around my waist—and then dart away like they weren't there at all.

Except they were.

And I know it.

My stomach flips.

I head to the showers, hoping the hot water can cool the thrum low in my gut.

But the whole time I'm under the spray, I'm wondering what would happen if I turned around, if he came in, if we forgot all this bullshit and *did it again*. Throwing Tanner against the shower wall, kissing the salty sweat off his neck, hearing that goddamn moan again.

I shake the thought loose and scrub shampoo through my hair like it can wash away the desire.

This is stupid.

We're not together. We're pretending to be married. For *insurance*. There is nothing less sexy than insurance.

I'm not built for permanence. I grew up watching a marriage rot from the inside. I swore I'd never get tied down. Never do to a kid what was done to me.

But...Tanner's different. Always has been.

And I don't know how much longer I can pretend that's not what's driving me absolutely insane.

———

WE DRESS IN SILENCE, except this time, it's different.

There's no awkward fog. No tension.

Just...awareness.

Every time he brushes past me, my skin sparks. Every time he looks at me, I feel *seen*. It's all charged. Alive.

We say goodbye to the rest of the team and walk to the car, side-by-side.

He unlocks the doors. "You hungry?"

"Starving," I say.

"Burgers on the way home?"

"Only if I get fries."

He snorts. "You always get fries."

I grin. "Yeah, but this time I want extra."

He smiles back, and the way he looks at me—

It's not just friendly.

It's not just nothing.

And as I slide into the passenger seat, sweat-damp and sore and stupidly content, I realize something else.

I might be falling for him.

For real.

And I don't know if I can stop.

————

AFTER A LUNCH of drive-through burgers and fries, we relax at home and watch some football. Despite the pullout mattress being a form of torture, Tanner's actual couch is shockingly comfortable. It's so easy to sink into the cushions and rot for a few hours. Lulu dozes off against me during the third quarter. My heart swells as I watch her sleep, her small body an accordion filling and emptying with breath.

As the sun sets, Tanner gets to work on dinner. I offer to help, but it's decided I'll clean up and take out the trash after. The kitchen smells like garlic and butter. Tanner's doing his usual wizardry with spaghetti and sautéed zucchini, humming some off-key tune.

On game days, my appetite is insatiable. I have two servings of spaghetti and meatballs. I probably could've eaten more, but there are five other humans who need dinner. We sit around the dinner, Davy regaling us with highlights from today's game when Tanner and I made magic on the ice. I keep looking over at Lena, moving spaghetti around her plate, only half-listening. The way she keeps looking down, it's obvious to me she's stealthily reading her phone.

"Lena." I clear my throat. "No phones at the dinner table."

"Sorry." She puts it in her pocket.

"She's probably texting with Matthias." Dean turns around and mimics making out with extra-loud kissing noises.

She turns red, which possibly means her brother's right. Are they arranging a time to meet up to smoke, do drugs, have sex. All things I did in high school that now make me break into a cold sweat.

Once I'm done cleaning up the kitchen post-dinner, I knock on her bedroom door. She sits on her bed, scrolling her phone.

"Hey. Can you help me with bringing out the garbage and recycling?"

She glances up, warily. "Sure."

Can she smell the ulterior motives already? Teens are scarily perceptive.

"Thanks." I keep cool and have her follow me outside. We each roll a bin to the end of the driveway. In my apartment, there's a convenient trash chute, so I never have to smell this putridness.

The start of a fall chill hangs in the air. I dig my hands into my pockets. "So, I wanted to talk to you about something."

"Oh." She tenses slightly, hands fixed at her sides. "What?"

I can feel myself entering a new level of dad. My stomach twists, but I'm already here. "I wasn't snooping. I want to say that first. But I accidentally caught a peek inside your backpack the other day. And I saw a vape pen."

Her eyes widen, then narrow just as fast. "Seriously?"

"Seriously," I say, glancing back at the house to make sure her siblings didn't follow us out here.

"It's not mine," she says, automatic.

I raise an eyebrow. "Lena."

She shrugs, brushing curls out of her face, something she did as a little girl, too. It's wild that I once held her newborn self in my arms. "It's my friend's. She was freaking out because her parents would kill her if they found it, so I said I'd hold it for her."

"That's altruistic of you." It would be mean of me to call bullshit. She would shut down. I have to tread lightly. "Um, I've noticed you've been wearing your perfume extra thick recently."

"I've been wearing too much? I thought it smelled nice..." She hangs her head and sniffs her forearm.

Fuck. Insulting my faux stepdaughter is not the best foot forward.

"It does!" I say. "It just seems like you want to cover up the smell of smoke."

"I'm not."

"Uh-huh." I fold my arms, leaning against the mailbox. "Did this alleged friend really have nowhere else to hide a vape pen? Maybe this friend is actually...Matthias."

I keep my eyes on her to gauge her auto reaction. Is this where she gives up that Matthias is actually a pot-smoking, cocaine-snorting, drunk-driving, sex fiend?

Yet she doesn't get cagey. She doesn't get still. She bursts out laughing. "Matthias?"

"Yeah. Mr. Goody Two Shoes Boyfriend. I know his deal."

She laughs harder. "Matthias?"

Is she laughing too hard? Like she's trying to cover up for her bad boy, bad influence boyfriend?

"He's the variable. You weren't stashing vape pens before he came around."

She scoffs. "Oh my God. Matthias doesn't even drink soda."

"People who don't drink soda are the ones you have to *really* watch," I mutter. "Come on, Lena. I'm not trying to catch you in a lie. I just want to make sure you're okay. That you're not being pressured. That you're thinking for yourself."

Her eyes flash. "I *am* thinking for myself."

"Good. Then think about this: if your dad finds this first, it's not going to be a conversation. It's going to be a house lockdown, no phone, and one of those serious, soul-searching dad lectures that lasts three hours and involves *feelings*."

She rolls her eyes. "I doubt that."

Her dismissiveness throws me off for a beat.

"I'm giving you the chance to be honest. That's all. You want me to believe it's not yours? Cool. But I'm asking you—off the record— what's really going on with Matthias?"

She hesitates. Something flickers in her eyes—defensiveness, maybe, or just hesitation—and then she fires back with something I *don't* expect.

"You know what I want to know?"

I blink. "What?"

"What *your* deal is with my dad."

I go still. "My—what?"

She stands up straighter, crossing her arms. "You guys say this marriage thing is fake. But you sure don't *act* like it's fake."

"I—I don't know what you mean."

"Yes, you do. You're living here. You make breakfast. You're sharing a bed."

"Only because your pullout couch sucks."

"You two do all this weird silent eye contact thing. So what's your plan? Are you going to get together for real?"

I stare at her. She stares right back. And for once in my entire adult life, I don't have a preloaded answer. Not even a slick one-liner.

"I..." I clear my throat. "That's...not what this is."

"But it *feels* like it is," she says, voice softer now. "I've seen my dad. I know when he's just getting by. He's been just getting by for a long time. But lately...he smiles more. Laughs. I haven't seen that since Mom died."

I look back at the house. In the front window, I can make out Tanner playing with Dean and Lulu, his smile beaming all the way out here.

"I care about him," I admit, quiet.

"Do you love him?"

My stomach drops. She watches me with those sharp teenage eyes, not letting me look away.

"I don't know," I say. And it's the truth.

We each soften our stances and silently call a ceasefire. It's no fun getting interrogated.

"If you ever hurt my dad," she says, tucking hair behind her ears. "I will make your life a living hell."

I smile despite myself. "Fair enough."

As she heads for the house, she pauses and turns back. "Des?"

"Yeah?"

"You're not half as slick as you think you are."

19

TANNER

We are twenty-four hours away from The Dinner. Des says this get together with Stan is the most important meal since the Last Supper. I personally disagree, but I keep that to myself.

After filling out more job applications in the morning, I spend the afternoon cleaning up the house. I do a deep clean that is months overdue. Scrubbing layers of dust off the shelves. Vacuuming in between the couch cushions. Wiping off dust that accumulated atop the ceiling fan blades. Mopping—not Swiffering—the floors. With what little energy I have left, I dump something edible into the crock pot for the kids and run to make a PTA meeting for the fall carnival.

Des and I have a boisterous dinner with the kids where we go over our embellished backstory once more. *Uncle Des and I were friends for a long time but recently realized that we love each other very much.* Uh, where's the embellishment on my end?

Once we put everyone to sleep, I collapse on my own bed with a basket full of laundry needing to be folded. The laundry never ends. The kids are asleep, the dishwasher hums faintly in the kitchen, and I'm left alone with my thoughts—and the mountain of stress sitting on my shoulders.

And yet, all I can think about is the way Des looked at me earlier.

The soft edges of his smirk when we nearly bumped hips in the kitchen. The quiet, lingering way his gaze settled on me when he thought I wasn't paying attention.

I'm still sorting laundry when he pads into the bedroom in an old Vertical Horizon T-shirt clinging to life and flannel pants that somehow still make him look unfairly good. His hair's damp from the shower, curling slightly at his temples. I like seeing Des with shaggy, uncombed hair, a natural version of himself that he rarely lets the world see.

"House looks great," he says, pulling a pair of socks to fold from the basket, the tip of the laundry iceberg. "Didn't know you were gunning for a job with a cleaning service."

"I'm trying to make sure your boss doesn't think I'm raising these kids in a dumpster." I snort, folding the last pair of Dean's shorts. If he had his way, he'd wear shorts all year round. It's a three-round negotiation getting him to switch to pants in the winter. He's totally going to be one of those college guys wearing flip flops to class in January.

Des falls onto the bed beside me, his knee brushing mine, warm even through the fabric. It takes him a few tries to fold one of Davy's T-shirts.

"Do you do your own laundry?" I ask him.

"Laundry service and dry cleaning. I ship it out. They do their magic."

"I hate you." The day we brought home Lena from the hospital, the laundry went from a once-a-week occurrence to a nonstop part of life. I think I've developed callouses from all the folding.

"One of the great joys in life is paying someone to do something you don't want to do."

"Do you miss being in your luxury apartment? Do your leather couches and impressionist wall art cry out for you?"

"I write them postcards." His eyes travel around the bedroom, one of the only rooms I didn't deep clean. I doubted Stan would be in here, unless he really wanted proof we were playing house. But a sweet, wistful smile crosses Des's face as he takes in the room's imperfections. "I don't know. I think this house is growing on me."

"That's just a fungus."

He snorts a laugh, and it's music to my ears.

"One of the benefits of unemployment is having the time to clean. I may clean the fridge tomorrow."

I create piles of sorted clean clothes on the bed. Des quickly catches on.

"How's the job search going?"

"Nothing yet."

"You'll find something soon."

"Yeah." I can't meet his eyes, instead choosing to stare intently at a pair of my boxers.

"What kind of jobs are you applying to?"

"Ones similar to what I had been doing," I say, hearing the mumble of shame in my voice.

"But you weren't crazy about that job. What is your dream job? What would you love to be doing?" Bless him, his eyes light up.

Des is ambitious. He has lofty career goals and the fire in his belly to make them happen. I'm realizing more and more that I don't. My lofty goal is a job that pays the bills, keeps my kids fed, and provides health insurance. Des would reel in horror if I told him that, though.

He'd never fall in love with someone who didn't share his drive. *Four kids* and *a dad who lacks career ambition?* No way.

"I'm wiped. I'll fold the rest of this tomorrow." I put the folded piles into the basket and bring it to the corner, where it can sit atop my hamper.

Des pulls back the covers. He pats the empty space next to him. That lazy, slightly smug smile beckons. I feel that stupid jolt of awareness again—the one I've been trying to bury since last night.

And yet, once I fold myself into bed, and Des wraps his arms around me, all the chatter in my head stops. There is no heated blanket or body pillow that can mimic the comfort and warmth of cuddling with another person. It is nature's anti-anxiety remedy.

In his arms, everything will be okay. I don't even know what "everything" or "okay" actually means, but...everything will be okay.

"Oh shit. Let me know if you don't want me on top of you." Des pulls back, shifts to his side of the bed.

"No. I don't mind," I say, a lump thickening in my throat...and my dick thickening in my pants. *Please touch me* is probably too forward. "How is it sharing a bed with someone?"

"Good." His voice drops an octave when he whispers it in my ear, making me shudder with want.

He returns to prime cuddle position, pulling me against him, his arms clamping me in place. We're...strengthening our intimacy in preparation for the dinner tomorrow. We're...just two middle-aged guys trying to sleep well on a queen-sized bed.

I close my eyes and sink into his touch. I want to be his little spoon for life.

My dick tents my boxers. It's going to be a challenge getting to sleep. I wiggle myself to get comfortable in my tightening under-wear. I shift back and feel something thick press between my cheeks.

"Shit. Sorry," Des says. He laughs into my shoulder, breaking the awkward tension of the moment. "I feel like a fucking teenager. I don't know what's wrong with me."

"I'm no better."

Des reaches over and feels my boxers. "Good God."

"I'm sorry."

"Your boxers are so tight you're going to cut off circulation." He opens the front slit and frees my cock.

"What are you doing?"

"You're like ridiculously hard. There's normal hard. And then there's this." He gives my dick a stroke, sliding a thumb over my engorged head. "Your dick is whatever metal the Terminator is built out of. Do you feel light headed?"

"No." I laugh so hard I might cry. It's that kind of laugh that you try to stifle but only makes you laugh harder. I try to stay quiet, but Des is practically giggling into my shoulder, making this all the more hilarious. "I told you it'd been a long time."

"I think you still need a helping hand." His thick hand fists my cock, gingerly sliding up and down. I'm laughing and shivering and horny and having a great time with my friend.

"I thought we weren't going to do that again. It'll make things weird."

"You snuck a lead pipe into your marriage bed. That's weird."

I let out a moan in between laughing fits. Des continues his rhythmic pumping of my dick. Between his hand and the warmth of his chest, I am drowning in desire for this man.

"What's weird shit between friends?" He says in a low voice right in my ear.

"Would it be weird if we did this again?" I close my eyes, asking this question as much to the universe as to him.

"It's been two years, Tanner. One blow job is not enough to make up for your drought." He pushes my boxers to my knees. I want Des to take me, manhandle me, give me two years' worth of sex tonight.

I greedily rub my ass against his stiffening dick.

"You want it so bad." He kisses along my neck, sending shivers down my spine.

Des strokes me with assured pumps of his fist, making my balls tighten and tingle with anticipated release. I dip my head back and gaze into his glassy, heat-blanched eyes as our lips connect. His mouth is hot and minty and all mine.

"How does this feel, Tan?"

"Good. So good." I rub my ass against his dick, alive with curiosity about what comes next. The thought of having sex with a man wasn't something I thought about. But having sex with Des would be incredible. Hearing him moan? Tasting his kisses? Feeling his thick cock inside me?

"Someone's horny." He lightly snickers in between kisses.

"Two whole years."

He smears the precome I'm leaking around my cockhead, slicking me up. I reach between us and wrap my hand around his girthy dick. He lets out a deep groan against my lips.

I writhe under his touch, stroking his cock and pressing it harder against my ass.

"God, you're beautiful, Tanner," he whispers. "I can't stop thinking about you. Being your husband."

"I love being your husband." My soul soars as the connection between us goes from strong to unbreakable.

But deep down, I know these are things being said in the heat of the moment. It's the flip side of dirty talk. Romance talk. Love cosplay. The truth is Des doesn't want a husband or a family. And yet...my heart can't tell the difference. I let myself believe him, just for tonight.

I drift my hand farther south and cradle his balls.

Ball.

My hand freezes, and I yank it back, like I was caught in the cookie jar. The moment stops cold. Des rolls away from me. My back hits the cold sheets.

"I'm sorry," I say, turning to face Des.

"Don't be. I may have one ball, but I'm going to make you come so hard you'll swear I have three." He winks at me, and I can tell this is a line he's used before with lovers. A way to ease the awkwardness and stay in control when someone discovers their suave one-night stand has one testicle.

Des doesn't have to be brave with me. I held his hand during chemo, and he let me collapse into him when I lost my wife.

I bring my hand back to his crotch, holding his gaze. I cradle his ball and give him a nod that has thirty years of friendship behind it.

"What does it feel like?" he asks.

"Sexy." The strangeness fades away, and I'm left with Des, same as ever.

"When I'm with other people, I usually have them avoid...that area. And I still can make them come." His confident smirk slips for a beat. "People are either curious or horrified. Or they feel bad for me. I don't like people feeling bad for me."

"I like it. It's strong. Powerful. Virile." I slink down and lick down his shaft to his scrotum. I play with it, soaking in the salty taste of him. "It's proof that you beat cancer. You're still standing. You fought back the cruelest disease on the planet and won. You're full of power."

I swirl my tongue around his ball. It's another chapter in the story of Des, a tome I wish to keep reading. He lets out the guttural moan of someone finally able to enjoy an old sensation again.

"What does it feel like for you?" I ask.

"I don't notice anymore. My sac has tightened up. Sorry if that's graphic."

"It's not."

"I'm still able to perform. Oddly enough, having one has made me much hornier. Maybe because I know I could lose it at any moment, so I have to keep using it."

"Live every moment. Bust every nut."

"I only think about it when other people notice. So I do what I can not to make them notice."

I kiss along his scrotum. "I like noticing. I like knowing everything about you."

We trade one of those silent looks that speaks volumes. Love and gratitude emanate from him. I travel back up his shaft and take his cock in my mouth, letting its heat and bitterness envelop me.

"You know you're giving a blow job right now?"

"Mm-hmm."

"First time you're doing this."

"Mm-hmm," I say through strokes and slurps. "How am I doing?"

"You're going to receive an effusive comment card afterward. How does it feel giving head for the first time?"

"I like it," I say, smiling against his thick cock. I like that it's Des's cock I'm sucking, that we are closer than ever before.

Having a dick in my mouth doesn't feel as strange as I expect because it's Des. We're best friends. And friends do weird, unexpected shit with each other and can laugh about it after. I bob up and down on his thickness while Des runs a gentle hand through my hair, very gently guiding me. Electricity crackles between us.

"Yes. Oh baby." He twists and moans under my touch. Des arches his back to push his cock farther down my throat. "Keep doing that."

I stroke and suck him, just thinking about what I would like. Just wanting all of Des, wanting to do anything to make him utter those sexy sounds.

He pulls back, and my mouth feels sad and cavernous without his dick.

"What's wrong?" I ask.

"Nothing. I want to join in on the fun."

"You're not that flexible."

He sits up and adjusts me to lay parallel to him on the bed. His cock is shiny and hard and sticking up in the dark of night. He spins his body around to put us in prime sixty-nine position.

"Two orgasms with one position," he says. At this angle, I can rake my eyes over his muscular chest and flat stomach. He has the slightest gut, but also the faintest abs, as if he's standing on the pinpoint edge of middle age. His body has an overall thickness to it—some fat, some muscle, some that just comes with age.

"Hey, my cock is down there," he says with a wink.

Before I can say another word, his mouth is on me, sucking my still insanely hard cock. I go back to burying his cock down my throat. I see if I can fit the whole thing in my mouth. Doing that makes him groan against my cock, sending scorching vibrations of need through my body.

My body tingles with the feel of his hot, wet mouth sucking me off. The orgasm begins to crest in me, surging through my balls.

"Taste so damn good," he utters with heavy breaths.

I pray that all of my kids are deep in a REM cycle because I don't know if I'll be able to stop before I come. Des has so taken possession of my body. His bitter precome soaks my tongue. I graze my fingers over his muscular, tree-trunk thighs.

I rock my hips to thrust inside his mouth while my tongue circles his firm cockhead. Des drags a finger to my ass, opening up electrifying new sensations for me.

I can only hold out so much. I want this to last forever. I want to continue giving this man pleasure, all the pleasure he can handle. My legs shake with impending release; his thighs tense under my touch.

"Come for me," I say.

"Baby. I want to taste you so bad."

I shake with lust and heat as my balls draw up and empty themselves into Des's mouth. He thrusts his cock inside me as he shoots come down my throat. I swallow all of it.

We collapse back on the bed, catching our breaths, finding center. I am completely spent. I gave everything I had to my husband.

My husband. I love calling him that.

The silence stretches, comfortable but charged. The air hums with everything unspoken.

I stare at the ceiling long after the lights are out, after we cleaned ourselves up and put on our pajamas. Des returns to the position that started all of this mischief: spooning me. Pulling me so close I can feel the faint thump of heartbeat against my back.

I listen to the rhythm of his breathing beside me, wondering how long I can keep pretending my heart isn't completely tangled up in him.

20

DES

I've closed multi-million dollar clients. I've presented at global conferences. I've handled screaming clients, impossible deadlines, and over-caffeinated artists. But none of that, not a single moment of my career, has prepared me for the level of stress that is family dinner night.

Correction: not just *any* family dinner—*The* Dinner.

Quite possibly the last supper I'll ever have if I fuck this up.

The dinner with Stan.

Stan, my boss. Stan, the guy whose recommendation basically determines whether I get to call myself creative director or end up working under that smug pile of nepotism known as Kyle.

Tanner's house smells like lemon cleaner and mild panic. He's been in a whirlwind all day, wiping down every surface, even the ones no human eye will ever see. I keep refreshing the time on my phone, wondering if maybe—just maybe—an unexpected blackout will hit the block and save me from this catastrophe.

I line up Tanner and his kids in the living room and strut in front of them like a drill sergeant.

"This is a make-or-break night. I need us all on our best behavior.

No fighting with each other. Keep the volume at a moderate decibel level. No burping the alphabet."

"Why are you looking at me?" Dean asks as a burp escapes his lips. "That was a coincidence."

"Mr. Stan is a good guy, but he's perceptive. He's very observant. The man may be seventy-five, but he can spot an uncentered image from across the room." I turn on my heel and pace back down the line. "What this means is he has a very strong BS detector. He has to believe that my marriage with your dad is real, that me living here with you is real. That we are an imperfect, but real, family. Can we do that?"

Lulu's hand shoots up. "What's BS?"

Tanner dips his head into his hand.

"It means bullcrap," Davy says. "Except instead of crap, it's–"

"It means something that isn't real," I explain. I'm enlisting a five-year-old for subterfuge. The depths to which I have sunk. I glance back at Tanner. Tanner, who I held in my arms last night, who begged for my cock, who found my imperfections beautiful and sexy. It's not just a promotion. It's his family in the middle of this.

We can't mess this up.

Tonight may be the toughest pitch I ever have. Stan's daughter is grown, and she lives in Seattle. He sees his grandkids a handful of times per year. He's not used to being in kid chaos.

The doorbell rings, and my soul briefly leaves my body. Through the front window, I spot Stan waiting at the front door.

"Fuuuuudge. He's early. Should I have him wait outside? No, I can't do that."

Tanner claps me on the shoulder, his bright eyes conveying worry, but also a dash of confidence.

"We got this," he whispers.

Tanner pulls the door open. "You must be Stan!"

Stan holds a bottle of wine and wears a red polka-dot bowtie and blue suit.

"Evening!" Stan booms, stepping inside.

"Stan. Welcome." I step past Tanner to shake my boss's hand.

Then I realize I need to start projecting husband and dad energy from the jump, so I throw my arm around my fake husband. "Come on in."

"I hope you don't mind that I'm early. I thought there would be traffic, but I managed to hit all green lights."

"The universe wanted you here," Tanner says, shutting the front door. Stan doesn't rely on Google Maps after one experience where the app had him almost drive into the Hudson River.

To my utter relief, the kids remain in their line in the living room, making an excellent first impression. Orderly, calm, quiet. I stop and watch them for a quick second, and it hits me how adorable they all look.

"This is the family," I say. Every ad campaign depends on a singular image. Tanner and I stroll behind the kids and put our hands on their shoulders. One big, happy family. Take that, Norman Rockwell. "We have Lena, our oldest. She's a fantastic student."

"Nice to meet you," Lena says with a perfectly friendly smile. She steps forward and shakes Stan's hand. Hopefully her siblings follow her lead.

"Pleasure, my dear."

"And this is Davy. He loves playing hockey, just like his dads." I tussle Davy's hair.

"How's it going, big guy?" Stan gives his hand a hardy shake. "What position do you play?"

"Left winger. Just like my dad. Uh, that dad." He points at Tanner.

"A real chip off the old block." Stan elbows Tanner.

"You betcha!" I exclaim, for probably the first time in my fucking life.

I give Dean's shoulders a massage, praying he keeps things in check. "And this is Dean, our resident magician."

Dean steps forward, but instead of holding out a hand, he whips out a deck of cards from his back pocket. I knew I should have searched him earlier.

"Pick a card." He fans them out.

"Mr. Stan doesn't have time for a trick," I say.

"Of course I do!" Stan rubs his hands together and hunches down to Dean's level. "Hmmm which one should I pick? I'll go with this one." He hugs it to his chest.

"Remember it. Now put it back." Dean looks away as Stan slides the card back into the fanned out deck, both of them hamming it up. "Excellent."

Dean shuffles the deck, then massages his temples. I feel my heart pound in my chest hoping that Dean gets this right. He has a confidence I have no choice but to admire. He taps the deck twice, and flashes the top card. Seven of clubs.

"Is this your card?"

"Nope."

Dean flashes the next card. "This?"

Stan shakes his head no.

"This?"

"Incorrect."

Stan's excitement fades with each card. I can feel my promotion and job slipping away.

"This?"

I step between them. "You'll get 'em next time, buddy."

"It was the eight of clubs," Stan tells him.

"That was the next card in the deck!" Dean holds it up, but too little too late.

"And this is Lulu, our youngest."

Stan bends down and holds out his hand like he's meeting a princess. "Charmed, madam."

Lulu points to the opposite wall. "Is that picture centered?"

Stan wrinkles his brow in the confusion we're all experiencing. He follows her finger to a framed picture of the kids at the beach.

"Uncle Des–uh, Dad–says that you can spot an uncentered image from across the room."

Tanner muffles a laugh behind his hand. I internally curse myself for not watching my phrasing more carefully.

"He did?" Stan lets out an amused laugh. "What else did he say?"

"We don't have to—" I start.

"That you have a great BS detector." She signals for Stan to lean in. "BS means bullcrap," she whispers.

Stan turns back to me. I throw up my hands and emit the most pitiful laugh known to man. "Kids stay the darnedest things!"

"Why don't you have a seat, Stan? We have some cheese and crackers out. Dinner's almost ready." Tanner leads Stan to the couch. "I can open this bottle of wine. Would you like a glass?"

"Yes please." Stan lowers himself onto the couch—and the unmistakable *Pfffffttttt!* noise of a loud fart echoes through the living room.

Tanner's eyes widen. I brace for impact. I dart my eyes to Dean. Even his face goes white.

Stan pulls the whoopee cushion out from under him and examines it.

My career flashes before my eyes. It was good while it lasted.

But Stan throws his head back and *laughs.* "Good one," he says, patting his knee. "Reminds me of when my brothers and I were little."

I release the breath I've been holding since sunrise.

"I'm a magician *and* comedian." Dean beams, victorious. "I got more tricks, wanna see?"

"Maybe after dinner," I interrupt, trying to regain some control. Tanner comes back to the living room with two glasses of wine. He hands one to Stan, and one to me, which I chug.

"You've got an energetic brood," Stan says.

"Kids, why don't you go play outside until dinner is ready," Tanner says in a genius move. I could kiss him. I flash him a sigh of relief.

Davy, Dean, and Lulu gallop through the living room to the glass sliding door. They're probably as excited to burn off their energy as I am. I find myself standing a bit taller, more relaxed.

Lena pours herself a Sprite and sits on the couch arm.

"Lena made the honor roll all through middle school. I suspect she's going to do the same in high school." Tanner tucks a lock of her hair behind her ear.

"That's great. Good grades will open up so many doors for you. Opportunity awaits," says Stan.

"I love school." Lena shrugs, nearly on the cusp of laying it on thick. "Des always talks about how important school is. He always talks about making good choices. I know it's corny to say, but he's a great role model."

Stan looks over at me and winks.

"I'm lucky. These are great kids. Parenting has its challenges, but it's so worthwhile." I pour myself another glass of wine and promise myself that I'm cut off after this one.

"Des is the best stepdad ever," she declares, all wide-eyed sincerity. "He makes sure I don't have to babysit my siblings every second anymore. And he said if I make the honor roll this semester, he's going to buy me a car!"

Tanner chokes on air. I stare at her like she's sprouted another head.

"I—what?" I manage.

"You said you'd think about it," Lena counters, smirking just enough to make me suspect blackmail is her love language. "I think Lulu needs help on the swing. A big sister's job is never done."

I watch her stride into the backyard. Did I just get played?

Stan chuckles warmly. "Well, sounds like you've settled into family life, Des."

I plaster on my most convincing, definitely-not-panicking smile. "You know me, all about stability."

Before I can unravel any further, the doorbell rings again. Enter stage left: Kyle, his glamorous, Botoxed wife Marissa, and their trio of miniature private-school diplomats. The boy wears a blazer and tie, while his younger twin sisters wear matching dresses. They look like they stepped off a yacht where they were getting family pictures taken. Why didn't I think to have the kids dress in color-coordinated outfits?

"Salutations!" Kyle bellows louder than he needs to, announcing his arrival. "This must be the mysterious Tanner. The man who finally tamed the wild and crazy bachelor."

"Nothing is impossible," Tanner says. He's classier than me and shakes Kyle's hand, whereas I want to pounce on this putz.

"This house is so cute." Kyle takes a look around, the word cute drenched in all kinds of acidity. He lives on a cul-de-sac in one of those bougie gated communities. When he had coworkers over for a Memorial Day BBQ one year, he gave tours of his house on the half-hour. "Probably a rough adjustment from your swanky riverfront condo, Des."

He pokes me in the rib with his elbow. And again, I resist the urge to put him in a headlock.

Kyle's family all gets in line as if on cue. "This is my wife Marissa."

"Stan, a pleasure as always. We need to have a pickleball rematch." Marissa shakes his hand, then flops her hand in Tanner's almost like she expects him to kiss it.

"I'm game." Stan mimics some pickleball moves.

Kyle points to his oldest spawn. "My son Wesley, currently top player on his lacrosse team."

Wesley steps forward and gives Stan a hardy shake. He looks about Davy's age, though his hygiene seems much better. "Good to see you again, sir."

"And my twins Cayleigh and Brynleigh."

I half-expect these girls to say "Come play with us, Danny." They look about seven or eight. They take a step forward in unison, doing little to dispel their *Shining* aura.

"Hi, Mr. Stan." Also said in unison. They turn to Tanner. "Nice to meet you, Mr. Tanner."

Fear crosses Tanner's face. He's a scaredy cat when it comes to horror movies and possessed doll movies.

"Y-you, too," my husband says. I squeeze his hand. "My kids are playing in the backyard. Why don't you join them?"

"We'd love to," Wesley says. He takes a hand of each of his possessed doll sisters and they nearly skip out the sliding door.

"Don't worry. They're gone. They can't hurt you," I whisper to Tanner, who stifles a laugh.

Kyle watches his children of the corn with a twinkle in his eye.

"I love 'em. It goes by in the blink of an eye. But you know all about that, Stan," Kyle says.

Tanner and I get the adults their cocktails as the pre-dinner chatter flows. Kyle's already circling like a shark, zeroing in on Tanner and me with predatory interest.

"So..." Kyle sips his drink. "The whirlwind romance. How did you guys meet?"

"High school. I was new and when I joined the hockey team, this player loved pranking me." Tanner shoots me a wink. "What he didn't expect was that I could prank back just as good."

Tanner may seem all sweet, but the man has a dark talent for team pranks. He could be a total savage when he wanted to.

"I wasn't sure what to make of you at first. Once we got out there on the ice, I thought, this guy's okay. It's like he can read my mind. Our passing is so quick and in sync, people think we have a secret language." A nostalgic feeling pulls at my stomach.

"'I can tell that about you, Tanner," Stan says. "It's always the quiet ones."

"It's always the quiet ones what?" he asks.

"It's just always the quiet ones." Stan laughs into his drink.

"I second that." I clink my glass against Stan's.

"Hockey is a very violent sport," Marissa says in between cocktail sips.

"Aggressive, not violent," I say.

"So, are you divorced, Tanner?" Kyle asks as he spreads cheese on a cracker and shoves it into his mouth.

"Widowed."

I cock an eyebrow at Kyle. *That's what you get for trying to stir shit.* He shrugs it off in stride.

"So you've been friends for a while. And then you just realized you were meant to be husbands? Romantic," Kyle says, with no feeling.

"It was," I reply smoothly, but Tanner cuts in before I can spin corporate-level PR.

"We've known each other forever," Tanner says, his voice steady, easy. "Sometimes, it just takes you a while to see what's right in front of you."

I glance at him, startled. There's a softness in his eyes I didn't expect—a quiet warmth that feels too genuine, even for this elaborate performance.

"And you...decided marriage was the logical next step?" Kyle probes, fishing for inconsistencies.

"Wasn't about logic," Tanner answers, still smiling, hand brushing casually along the small of my back.

"I don't know. I mean, it's sweet and all. But you have small children. To suddenly marry...how are they handling it?" Kyle asks in his most concerned voice, the kind politicians use when they talk about wanting to protect the children.

"Our children are doing just fine," Tanner says, a sheet of ice behind his tight grin. "They've known Des since they were born. He held each of them in his arms before they were a week old. He's always been a part of this family."

"Lena peed on me. I still won't let her live it down." A wistful pang floods through me. I can't believe those tiny peanuts I once held are running, thinking, talking children. The time really does pass quickly.

"Imagine having twins. I thought I would get buried under dirty diapers," Marissa says, her voice softer. She's not trying to compete, but commiserate.

Kyle ignores her and turns back to me. "So none of this felt rushed to you?"

I want to yell at him to shut up already, but Tanner stops me from saying anything.

"I can't speak for Des, but it's funny how natural this all felt. Usually going into a relationship with someone, there's an adjustment period. It's two lives meshing. But we didn't have that. Des just fit like Cinderella's glass slipper when he married me. For years, we were always friends and that was that. And then when we started to see each other as more, that also felt weirdly natural. Like it was something always meant to happen." He looks up at me, his eyes the slightest bit wet. He's so beautiful I don't know if I can breathe. "I know it's fast and unorthodox, but nothing has ever felt this right. They say the best decisions are made in the blink of an eye."

I take his hand and massage his palm. "I agree."

Damn. He's good at this. Too good.

I feel the ground tilt slightly, not because we're lying, but because suddenly, part of me wishes we weren't.

I open my mouth to contribute when a bloodcurdling scream from the backyard shatters the evening.

21

TANNER

There's not much my kids can do that phases me anymore. I've seen it all. Or so I think until we follow the screams into the backyard.

We run outside to find Davy putting Wesley in a headlock. Meanwhile, my three remaining kids are holding the door to their plastic playhouse shut, trapping Kyle's twins inside, who are screaming for dear life to get out.

Before I yell at them to stop, my hand flies to my mouth. Every parent dreads the day when their children get in a skirmish on the playground and they have to do the awkward apologizing to show the other parents that they know what they're doing. There is no rulebook for your kids terrorizing party guests.

"Oh my babies! My babies!" Marissa screams.

"Davy! Get off him!" Des marches forward and stands over my son.

"My girls! They're going to suffocate in there!" Kyle cradles his wife, who looks on the verge of collapse. While they have every right to be upset, their reaction seems just a tad histrionic.

"What are you doing?" I race over to the playhouse and shove my kids out of the way.

The twins burst through the plastic door just as Davy relin-
quishes his headlock. The three perfect angels in their matching
yacht wear run into their parents arms, crying. Again, I'm taken
aback for a second at how hysterical they are. I know Davy would
never willingly hurt Wesley. My kids aren't monsters.

But by the way Kyle and Marissa glare at me, they sure think so.

"What happened?" Stan asks.

"Des's kids...they..." Kyle strains to catch his breath. "Sorry, my
children's lives just flashed before my eyes. They attacked my kids,
Stan."

"What the hell were you guys thinking?" Des barks. We all jolt for
a second, not used to him using such a stern tone.

"They started it!" Davy yells. "They were teasing Lulu, and they
took Dean's magic hat." He turns to me, his eyes wide with fear and
the retreat of adrenaline.

"You don't turn to violence. If there's a problem, you call an adult
over. You don't settle it like this." For being a new parent, Des sure has
the stern dad voice down pat.

"I wasn't trying to hurt him. I just wanted him to give back Dean's
hat." Davy looks down at the ground.

"I asked to play with it, and then he clobbered me," Wesley yells
to his parents, immediately falling into sobs.

"We asked to play in the playhouse," says one twin.

"And then they locked us in!" exclaimed the other. I'm too on edge
to remember their names.

"We only put you in there so you'd stop pinching my sister," Lena
says, the calmest one of all.

"Lena, you should know better," I say.

"We only put them in there so they'd chill out. They started
screaming out of nowhere."

"Because they were trapped. That's false imprisonment. That's a
crime." Kyle points a finger at my daughter. Rage pulses through me
so hard I want to snap that digit off. "Des, how could you let your kids
do this?"

Des turns to him with a stone cold grimace. "My kids said they didn't start this. And I believe them."

I silently cheer. Des gives each of them a tense nod of support.

"Let's let cooler heads prevail," Stan says, stepping into the middle of the fracas like a wrestling ref. "I think playing just got out of hand."

"I don't want to paint over this with a euphemism. My poor kids were attacked." Kyle hugs his brood tight. "I'm going to get them checked out by a doctor."

"I'll do the same for mine," Des shoots back.

"I just want peace!" Marissa dabs at her eyes.

"Daddy, I think I have trauma!" cries one of the twins.

"Kids." Stan claps his hands, getting all of their attention. "Now, are any of you physically hurt?" Stan gives them that teacher look, making it hard to lie. He stares each of them in the eye. The kids eventually shake their heads no. "Alright then. Just a little rough-housing."

"A little roughhousing?" Kyle guffaws. "I think we're gonna go."

"It's okay." Des squats down and checks in with Lulu and Dean. He picks up Dean's hat from the ground, places it back on his head.

"We're sorry. Did we ruin your job?" Dean asks with a trembling lip.

"No. Are you all okay?" Des caresses a hand down Lulu's hair. Despite the embarrassment of this moment, I can't help but be swept away by Des's warmth.

I go back inside the house and check on dinner. It's staying warm in the oven. Well, it looks like we're going to have a lot of leftovers. Through the kitchen window, I glare at Kyle's family as they make their way to the minivan. Kyle hands each of his kids a five-dollar bill before sliding the door shut.

"Stan, I am so sorry about this. I don't know what happened," Des says back in the living room.

Stan chuckles to himself. "Des, welcome to fatherhood. Being a parent means watching your best laid plans go to shit over and over again."

"I'm realizing that." Des pours himself a glass of wine. He offers me one when I rejoin them in the living room, but I decline. I probably shouldn't consume alcohol mere minutes after watching my kids falsely imprison little girls in a playhouse.

Stan signals for Des and me to come closer. "Between us, Kyle's kids give me the creeps."

"It's the Stepford vibe," I say.

"Exactly. Des, I like this one." Stan claps me on the shoulder. He heads to the door.

"Did you want to stay for dinner? We have plenty." I let out a weak laugh.

"It's probably best that I go and let everyone's nerves settle."

We huddle by the door, Stan pulling on his coat. Perhaps we came out of this disaster without burning everything to the ground.

But then Stan pauses, looking between Des and me like he's working out a puzzle.

"You two have been so polite tonight," Stan says, smoothing down his sleeves. "Almost too polite. You didn't even..." He gestures vaguely between us, a wry smile curling his lips.

"Kiss?" I ask.

"You're not holding back just to keep an old man comfortable, are you?"

My stomach dips. Des stiffens beside me. I can practically hear the PR machine spinning in his head, trying to spin this moment.

Stan chuckles softly. "Listen, I've been in love, I've been married a long time. I know when people care about each other. And I also know when they're holding back."

Des glances at me, something unspoken passing between us— panic, maybe, or...something else.

Stan waves a hand. "Don't be shy on my account. I'd hate to think my old-fashioned ass scared you two into acting like roommates."

There's a beat where neither of us moves.

And then Des surprises the hell out of me—he steps closer, hand curling gently around the back of my neck, tilting my face toward his.

His eyes search mine for a split second, like he's asking permission—and I give it, leaning in.

The kiss starts soft. Careful.

But somewhere in the space between Stan's chuckle and Des's grip, it deepens. Des's lips mold to mine, firm, steady, like this isn't fake at all. Like this has been years in the making.

And maybe... it has.

We break apart slowly. My pulse is hammering in my ears.

"That better?" Des asks Stan, his voice a little lower than usual, his thumb brushing along the edge of my jaw. "Are you still an ally?"

Stan laughs, satisfied. "Des, I'm impressed at how quickly you can go from a romantic to a sarcastic son of a bitch. Night, you two."

———

THERE'S plenty of dinner for everyone, but naturally, the kids mostly filled up on cocktail snacks. By the time we wrangle the kids to bed, put away all the dinner leftovers in Tupperware, and stumble into our room, I can still feel the ghost of that kiss lingering.

Des untucks and unbuttons his shirt, avoiding my gaze in a way that's distinctly *not* like him.

I climb onto the bed, stretching out, watching him. "That kiss..." I start.

He hums noncommittally, pulling off his watch, eyes fixed anywhere but me.

"It was good," I say carefully. "Really good. Better than good."

"We sure sold it to Stan."

"Yeah," I say, though Stan was the last guy I was thinking of currently.

We get into bed. I cuddle close to him. It's our new routine, and my body craves his touch.

"Can we..." I swallow, pushing past the nerves. "Could we maybe... pick up where we left off the other night?"

His shoulders tense. I've known Des long enough to sense slight shifts in his demeanor. He seems just a touch too stiff. Perhaps he's still coming down from the stress of dinner.

"I've been thinking lately...about what it would feel like to have sex with you. To feel you inside me." My breath hitches as these images flash in my head.

Here is the part where Des would hold me in his arms, or say something incredibly charming about how badly he wants that, too.

But instead, I'm met with silence.

I sit up straighter, the mood shifting, cold creeping in around the edges. "Des?"

He finally turns, face carefully neutral, walls going up brick by brick.

"Tanner, you are so gorgeous, but...I can't," he says quietly.

I blink. "You...can't? Or you don't want to?"

He rubs the back of his neck, frustration simmering just under the surface.

"Is it because of the dinner? We sold Stan on our family. Fight aside, it went great."

"It was a success. We sold everybody." His face is pensive when I least expect it, another side of Des to wonder about. "It's not that I don't want to—Jesus, Tanner, you felt what I felt the other night." His voice softens. "But this thing with your kids, this house, this whole... life. Things are moving really fast."

An old ache settles in my chest.

He breathes out, heavy. "I'm already in deep pretending to be this perfect husband and stepdad. And I can't tell when I'm pretending and when I'm not anymore. If we keep blurring the lines—if I...slip— it'll screw with my head. And yours. And the kids."

My jaw clenches. He's probably right. But it doesn't stop the sting.

"I don't want to hurt you, Tanner." His big, dark eyes bore into me. They break my heart.

"Okay," I say finally, lying back down, keeping my voice steady. "I get it."

Des shifts under the covers. The distance between us feels cavernous, even though the bed's not that big.

I stare at the ceiling for a long time, listening to his quiet breathing.

It's the safest, most dangerous place I've ever been—lying next to him, knowing exactly how close we could be, and how far apart we still are.

22

DES

Three weeks after The Dinner, I'm nursing a Sunday afternoon martini at Mitch's bar Stone's Throw Tavern after a strange game. We lost by one. It happens. You can't win 'em all. But why we lost is something I keep thinking about. Tanner zipped a pass my way, and I totally missed it. That doesn't happen. No matter the stress or weirdness of life, we've always been able to put the world in a box and focus on the game.

But maybe that power has its limits.

The weirdness that started when I turned him down in the bedroom continued to linger on the ice. In our first game after that awkward sexual moment, Tanner and I began to show cracks in our dynamite offense. Playing against a team we should've easily dominated, we only won by a single goal. The following week, our foundation crumbled some more. Two of my passes to him got scooped up by the opposing player; if it wasn't for our stellar defense, we would've gotten clobbered.

Today was one of the worst games Tanner and I had ever played. Missed passes. Missed goals. Missed cues. It was almost like we were strangers out there. At home, we weren't much better. I was having flashbacks to growing up, when an undercurrent of tension laced every interaction between my parents.

Did I make the right call turning Tanner down? My dick says no. And so does my heart. My brain, keeper of logic, says it's for the best.

Tanner didn't join the team for a post-game drink. He had to take Dean to a birthday party, and he seemed grateful to have that excuse.

If I was a responsible parent and husband, I would've gone home. But I'm neither, no matter what the paperwork I got from the court-house says.

I don't say much over drinks. After going over the loss in detail, a favorite pastime of Bill's, the conversation shifts to lighter topics. Bill talks about the struggle of moving in with his boyfriend Tate, while Derek fills us in on the remodeling his boyfriend Cary is doing to their home. Mitch floats around his bar to visit regular customers. Eventually, most of the guys go home, while I work on martini number three.

"You take martini drinking very seriously," Hank says. He and Griffin nurse what little is left of their beers.

"It's a drink for serious people." I swirl the olive around the rim of the glass. When I was in my early twenties and had no idea what to do with my life, I'd see rich guys sipping martinis at happy hour and tell myself that was the life I wanted. This drink represents every-thing I've accomplished. I have everything I want in life: great job, great apartment, great friends, freedom.

So why the heck aren't I smiling?

"What are you guys still doing here?" I ask my friends.

"We don't let friends drink alone." Griffin purses his lips in concern. His eyepatch gives him instant gravity. "Are you good?"

"Yeah I'm good."

"Because you haven't seemed like your asshole self tonight," Hank says. He takes a sip of his beer, but keeps his lips closed, as if he's an actor on set going through the motions.

"Tonight? More like for the past month," Griffin says.

"If you shitheads are going to stay with me until I finish, the least you can do is get another beer instead of pretending to drink. My tab is still open." I wave them off to the bar, not needing their commentary. Am I being an asshole enough for them now?

"He has a point." Griffin doesn't need to be prodded to drink. He's at the bar in a flash.

"So bossy. I never thought I'd say this, but I think I like you better sober." Hank gets up and shuffles to the bar.

A few moments later, they're back with fresh pints, yet the concern on their faces has remained.

"It's a loss. It's not the end of the world," I tell them. Their mood is tampering the joy of my well-made martini.

"You missed Tanner's pass. You never miss a pass from Tanner," Griffin says. "I have one functioning eye, and even I could tell something was off."

"It happens."

"Not to you and Tanner," he pushes.

"What's going on with you guys?" Griffin asks, staring me down. I can even feel his left eye studying me from behind his patch. "The last few games, you guys have been like...well, it's like you've never been teammates before."

"We won two of the last three games we played. Relax." I roll my eyes as I feel them getting closer and closer to hitting a nerve.

"Yeah, but...it's just not the same." Griffin looks like he's going to say something else, but can't seem to find the words.

"Trouble in your marriage bed?" Hank snorts at his own joke as he gulps his beer.

Instead of laughing, my stomach twists into a tight knot.

"Holy shit. *Is* there trouble in your marriage bed?" Hank's eyes widen. He looks to Griffin, wondering if his joke went too far.

"Tanner and I..." I press my martini glass into the cocktail napkin, leaving an imprint. How the fuck am I supposed to fill them in? "We...have been intimate."

"Whoa." Hank's big eyebrows jump. Griffin doesn't flinch.

"Tanner told me," Griffin says.

Hank turns to his teammate and lets his eyebrows leap up his forehead again. "He told *you*? I feel so out of the loop."

"He did?" I ask. Griffin, to his credit, never gave away that he knew. He's not the gossipy type, and probably knew better than to publicly give us shit about this. "How did he seem when he told you?"

A knowing smile emerges on his lips. "Electric."

I feel myself swell with hope, while at the same time, a foreboding pang aches in my chest. It's a clusterfuck of a reaction that usually happens when I get something I want and don't know what the hell to do with it.

Hooking up with Tanner *has* been electric, but it can't last. This fake marriage feels wobblier than a house on stilts.

"Crap." Hank leans back in his chair, almost pissed off, if he was ever the type of guy to get that angry.

"What?" I ask.

"We all suspected you two were hooking up. I should've made us put money on it. I could've bought myself a new power drill."

"We were that obvious?"

"Yes," Hank and Griffin say at the same time.

"You two have always seemed close," Griffin says, more diplomatically than Hank would have. "Like you two speak this special language. The passing on the ice. But even off...sneaking glances at each other. Laughing the loudest at each other's jokes."

"And didn't you guys used to have sleepovers in high school? Just the two of you?" Hank arches an eyebrow.

"You think we were giving each other hand jobs at these sleepovers?"

"Yes," Hank and Griffin say at the same time.

"For fuck's sake. Nothing ever happened at those sleepovers except sleeping." However, we talked. We talked about anything and everything. Those conversations in the dark were more intimate than any physical act. Tanner's always been there for me.

"There it is again. That dopey, dare-I-say lovestruck grin." Hank points at my face. "You're thinking about Tanner, aren't you?"

"Fuck off, Hank."

"I will do no such thing." He crosses his arms, victorious.

"Tanner is my best friend. We've been through a lot of shit in our lives. That's why we're so 'close,'" I say, using scare quotes. "You know why we got married. It wasn't about romance."

"For all this non-romance, it kinda seems like you two are having your lovers quarrel play out on the ice." Hank shrugs his shoulders to his ears.

"We're...things are in a weird place, okay? We're just pretending to be husbands. It's not real."

"Then why are you fucking?" Griffin doesn't mince words, but boiling down what happened to merely fucking sends a flare of rage roiling in my chest.

"Don't use that word."

"Fine. Then why are you copulating? Fornicating? Initiating intercourse?" Griffin's bearded face lifts into a gotcha smile.

"I believe the proper gay term is breeding each other," Hank says.

"Stop!" I bang my fist on the table, letting my frustration spread through me.

Hank turns to Griffin, both of them having a fucking ball. "All this talk about bodily penetration is hitting a nerve."

"I love him, okay!" I yell, getting stray looks from neighboring tables.

That shuts my friends up. It shuts me up, too. But damn, it felt good to say.

"I love him," I say, this time quietly. "This was supposed to be a sham marriage for insurance. We didn't plan to be intimate, it just happened. All of this just happened, like this insane plan was the most natural thing in the world. We've been *intimate* a few times now. And he wanted to keep going, but I...I couldn't. I mean, I could have. I have zero problems in that department. Things were solid steel down there. But something held me back. And now things are weird."

Enough nursing. I down my martini like I just held my breath for a minute.

"Why didn't I keep going with Tanner? I wanted to. But it didn't seem like the right thing to do."

My friends aren't laughing anymore. Concern rings their faces.

"Because Tanner doesn't fool around," Hank says softly. "Whether you planned it or not, the first time you climbed into that bed with him, things got serious."

"Single parents don't fuck around. Trust us," Griffin says. He and Hank share a knowing single dad nod of solidarity. "Anytime we even flirt with someone, we're thinking about how this will affect our kids. We're wondering how this person will fit into our lives. We're doing the mental calculations about whether this person would be worth upending our family."

Hank chimes in, "I guarantee you Tanner has been doing this since the moment he agreed to marry you, even if this marriage was a so-called sham. And if it was a total sham, then I'd like my Third Eye Blind CD back." Hank takes a breath. I'm not used to seeing him so focused when not in goal. "Tanner is a serious, thoughtful guy. Deep down, you know this, Des."

"Griff, how did you know it was okay to introduce Jack to your girls?" I ask him. Last spring, he began dating fellow hockey player Jack. Whenever I see Jack with Griffin's young daughters, he seems like a natural fit. Despite their massive age gap, they're madly in love.

"It happened by accident. I was taking them to a pottery activity, and we ran into Jack. He wound up spending the whole day with us. He clicked with Annabelle and June right away. All those fears I had about introducing a new partner to them faded away without a thought. When it's right, it's right."

I've known these kids since they were born. To me, uncle isn't a strong enough word for my relationship to them. Getting to spend so much time with them has made me see how thoughtful and inter-esting they are. Dean's wonderfully creative, and Lena's struggling through the hell of adolescence. I love Davy's drive and seeing how Lulu perceives the world through her five-year-old brain.

"Fuck." I lean back in my chair, things more clear and yet more confusing. Even when we just fake kissing and giving each other hand jobs to relieve stress, I suspected this meant more to Tanner than it should have. He doesn't mess around. I've barged into the lives of Tanner and his kids. Even though I didn't mean to, I've been playing with his heart. "I can't keep being with him."

"Unless you want to. Papa Des has a nice ring to it," Hank says.

I rub my hand wildly through my nicely combed hair. Those kids have fucking grown on me. "I am not meant to be a dad. I am not a family man."

Griffin cuts in, calm but firm, like a therapist who's known me too long. "You like him. It's scaring the hell out of you."

I shrug, eyes flicking toward the bar TV looping silent hockey highlights. "I like martinis and my promotion. This...this is different."

Hank wiggles his eyebrows. "Different like how? Butterflies? Daydreams? Can't-stop-thinking-about-him energy? Or the classic Des spiral where you think you've caught feelings, panic, and blow up your life?"

I hate how well they know me.

I sigh, leaning back against the booth. "Tanner's...he's Tanner. He's been my best friend since high school. He's the guy who made sure I didn't flunk algebra, who picked me up when I'd drank too much at a party no matter the time. I never thought..." I trail off.

Griffin raises a brow. "You never thought you'd fall for him."

"I never thought I'd get this domestic," I admit, the words foreign on my tongue. "Family dinners, helping with homework, grocery lists. I told myself this fake marriage was logistics. Paperwork. Now I'm..." I drag a hand down my face. "I'm looking forward to bedtime stories and accidentally staying for movie nights."

"Those Pixar films are really freaking good," Hank adds helpfully, waving for another round.

Griffin ignores him, leaning in, tone serious. "Look, I get it. It's terrifying. You've built your life to avoid messes like this. But Tanner's not a one-night stand. And those kids? They're not accessories."

I nod, throat tight.

"If you keep going down this road, you can't just...disappear when it gets complicated," Griffin continues. "You can't play house and bail when it stops being convenient. You do that to him—after everything he's been through—you'll break him. And probably those kids, too."

Hank, for once, sobers. "You can't half-ass this, Des. You either keep your distance, or you're in. All in."

The weight of their words settles over me heavier than expected. It's one thing to joke about falling into this chaos. It's another to hear it laid out plain.

"I'm not the family guy," I murmur. "I've never been good at the whole...commitment thing."

"Maybe you weren't," Griffin says evenly. "But people change. Life changes."

I picture Tanner's smile—the one he hides behind when he's worried. The way Lulu curls up in his lap for stories. Dean trying to wrestle me for the best seat at dinner. That damn sticky kitchen table. All of it, messy and loud and nothing like my sleek condo or carefully constructed life.

And yet...it's the first thing that's felt real in a long time.

Hank raises his glass toward me. "So? You gonna stop being a coward, or are you running?"

I hesitate, the answer knotting in my chest. "I don't know."

Hank gives me a soft pat on the back. "Maybe it's time for that fourth martini."

23

TANNER

The arena is too bright.

Fluorescent lights hum overhead, casting long reflections over the scraped-up ice. Kids lace up their skates with trembling hands and hopeful eyes, the smell of rubber mats and cold metal thick in the air. Parents line the bleachers, coffee cups clutched like lifelines.

I might be as nervous as Davy.

He's been practicing for weeks. Slept with his stick beside his bed. And now we're here. Tryouts for the traveling team, the most elite hockey program in the region.

I'd never seen him want something this badly.

I've been trying to stay focused on it, and not the odd dynamic currently marinating between me and Des. Our own hockey playing has been off, and that's been the least of our problems. I knew this fake marriage would be a bad idea, even if, for a short window, it was pure magic.

"Go, Davy!" I call when the coach waves him onto the ice.

He doesn't look back. He's all nerves and focus, his expression carved in stone.

I grip the edge of the bleacher so tight my knuckles ache, but

Davy's out there flying, and for a second I forget to breathe. He's got the puck on his stick, weaving past kids bigger than him, faster than him, like he was born out here. My chest swells, pride and relief tangling together, and I catch myself grinning like an idiot. He's holding his own. Hell, he's shining.

Then it happens.

A stumble, a tangle of skates, and the puck slides away like it never belonged to him. He sprawls across the ice, arms flailing. The moment lasts for years in my head, but in reality, he's back up less than five seconds later. And yet I can see how he's begun to unravel, how everything he built in those first few minutes is slipping through his little hands.

He tries to get back his confidence, but his movements on the ice get jerky, desperate.

And then they get sluggish with resignation. It's over. It's all over.

I want to run down there, scoop him up, shield him from the eyes watching, judging. Tell him it doesn't matter, that one screw-up doesn't erase his brilliance. But I can't. All I can do is sit here, heart breaking for my boy who's fighting tears he won't let fall.

Around me, the other parents keep clapping and cheering—encouraging murmurs and polite applause—but it feels miles away. My hands go numb. I want to storm down there and pull him off the ice, wrap him in a blanket and tell him he never has to try anything scary ever again.

But I can't. This is his.

And I know the second he skates off the ice—head down, trying to stay tall but visibly crumbling—that he knows. He didn't make it.

Coach confirms it gently after the last group finishes. "He's got hustle," he tells me. "Good attitude. Just not quite ready this year."

I thank him. I shake his hand. I nod like it doesn't feel like someone kicked me in the chest.

Davy is sitting in the locker room, his helmet still on like he doesn't want to face the world without it.

"Hey, bud," I say, kneeling next to him.

He doesn't answer.

"You were really brave out there. Most kids wouldn't have gotten back up at all."

Still nothing. He's gripping his stick like it's the only thing keeping him upright.

My throat is tight. "I know this hurts."

He shrugs, but his chin wobbles.

"We'll work harder. Try again next season."

His voice is so small I almost miss it. "Maybe I'm just not good at anything."

God. Watching your kid hurt is worse than heartbreak, worse than loss. It's helplessness in its rawest form. He is crushed; I am completely and utterly flattened.

I wrap my arm around his shoulders. "This doesn't define you."

He doesn't answer.

We drive home in silence. I watch him in the rearview mirror the whole time. His face pressed against the window, eyes dry but far away. I want to fix this. I want to snap my fingers and make the pain disappear.

When we walk through the front door, Des is in the kitchen chopping vegetables. Even though the state of our fake marriage is in a weird place, he still insisted on making dinner tonight.

He sees our faces immediately.

"What happened?"

Davy just walks past him, straight out the sliding glass door into the backyard. Des looks at me.

"Didn't make the team," I say, rubbing a hand over my face. "He's barely said anything since we left the rink."

Des sets the knife down. "I got this."

He doesn't ask. He just walks out the door.

I lean against the frame and watch.

Des approaches Davy slow, like he's approaching a spooked animal. He says something I can't hear. Davy doesn't respond. Then Des goes into the shed, pulls out an old aluminum baseball bat, and hands it to him.

Points at the maple tree standing mightily by our back fence.

At first, Davy just stares at him like he doesn't understand.

Des nods again. "Hit it."

Davy takes a hesitant swing.

"This hurts. Let it out, Davy," Des says, his voice calm, supportive, firm. Overflowing with love for my boy.

Davy pulls back the bat, then smashes it against the tree. A chunk of bark spews out. For the first time since tryouts, life returns to his face. He bashes the bat against the tree again. Then again. Then again. Harder and harder.

I hear the *clang* of metal on bark as he starts yelling with each swing. Not words. Just sound. All the rage and frustration of a ten-year-old with a broken dream. Tears pour down his cheeks.

And Des is right there, the whole time. Steady. Unmoving.

Until Davy drops the bat. He's sobbing now, full-body heaves. He crumples into Des, who catches him instantly. Wraps him up tight.

And holds him.

I press my fist to my mouth.

It's like something cracks open in me. Because I've always known Des was smart, funny, sharp as hell. I've always known he was a good friend.

But this?

This is something else.

He didn't hesitate. He knew exactly what my son needed. Not a speech. Not a fix. Just space to feel it and someone strong to catch him when it got too big.

I watch them from the doorway—my son, cradled in the arms of the man who was supposed to just be my friend. The man who's become so much more without either of us saying it out loud.

And I think: I'm in love with him. God help me. I really, truly am.

But I'm in love with a man who ultimately doesn't love me back, not in the way I want him to. I'm in love with a man who sees this marriage as what it is: fake. Soon, Des will find out about his promotion, and all this playing house will be over. Just like that.

Tears fall down my face as I watch Des comfort my son. The more Davy cries, the tighter Des holds him.

For today, though, we can pretend we're a family.

————

A FEW NIGHTS LATER, after a final PTA meeting going over logistics for next week's Halloween carnival, my phone rings as I pull into my driveway.

"Hello?"

"Hi, this is Ellen from MedTech" a bright voice says.

MedTech...MedTech. I filled out so many job applications, I can't keep them straight.

"I got your resume from Elise Shyer. She's a good friend, and when I told her I needed someone on my team, she raved about you."

"Elise!" I loved working with her. Warm, friendly, always brought in the best home-baked treats. She had a vast array of plants on her desk, and their branches would fall over my cubicle wall, making me feel like I was in a walled garden. Elise was one of many people who asked for my resume and would keep their ear to the ground for me. And she actually came through. "Elise is great. She makes the best chocolate chip cookies."

"I know! Because of her, I gain ten pounds every Christmas. Anyway, MedTech is a medical device supply company, and I have an opening for a senior project manager on my team. You'd be liaising with our suppliers and keeping the trains on time as it were. I can send you more about the company and the role."

"That sounds great. I'm very organized and meticulous..." I go into robot mode reciting my best qualities and experience highlights. I can feel my soul leave my body.

"Excellent," Ellen says. "I need to hire for this role fast as we have a lot coming down the pike. Usually we do a screener interview first, but Elise's word is good enough for me. I'd love to bring you in for an interview as soon as possible."

"That's...wonderful," I manage, but my heart's not in it.

I look toward the house. Through the window, I see Des on all fours being ridden by Lulu while Dean lifts a foam sword and chases them.

If I get this job...we won't need to be married anymore. He'll go back to his bachelor life. His sleek apartment. His late nights. His hookups.

He won't be tied down by me. We can go back to how things used to be. We don't have to worry about blurred lines, crossed boundaries, and scary questions about what this all means.

I wouldn't have to worry about whether Des loves me or not.

I clear my throat. "Does Thursday work?"

24

DES

A good night out for me was going to a hot new restaurant followed by a nightcap at a swanky martini bar. It didn't involve cotton candy or Tilt-a-whirls. But that is where life has brought me tonight, to the Sourwood Elementary Halloween Carnival.

And I'm low-key excited.

The smell of funnel cake and sounds of gleeful screams deliver a nostalgic punch. The lights and sugar high are even strong enough to shake Davy from his funk for the night.

The Ferris wheel creaks overhead, the bright bulbs spinning in slow, hypnotic circles. The smell of kettle corn and fried dough fills the air, mingling with the distant sound of kids shrieking on the spinning teacups. I shove my hands into the pockets of my jeans, trailing a few steps behind Tanner and the kids as they weave through the crowd.

I spot Griffin and Jack at a game throwing baseballs to knock over wooden pins. Garish, large stuffed animals hover above, tantalizing Griffin's two young daughters.

"You call that pitching?" June, Griffin's highly opinionated seven-year-old, yells at the two large men. "Put some oomph into it. There's an Olaf stuffed animal on the line."

"This is harder than it looks," Jack says, breaking a sweat.

"So is long division, but you don't see me complaining." June crosses her arms. She's got a lot of spirit. I'm secretly scared of her.

Griffin briefly makes eye contact with me. His eye flits between me and Tanner, which elicits an eyebrow raise from him. *Are you shitting or getting off the pot?* His expression asks me.

"Dad! Focus!" June yells.

I turn back to the kids.

I shell out what feels like a month's salary on ride tickets and refreshments for everyone. The kids gobble down enough fried Oreos and cotton candy to make their dentist a very rich man.

Tanner hands Davy and Dean a handful of tickets before they run off to join their friends. The boys hold out their hands like hungry goblins. Lena decided to skip the festivities to hang with Matthias and her friends. I asked her to elaborate on what "hang with" meant. She said they were all studying for a test. Before I could call bullshit, Tanner approved. He told me he trusts her. I should do the same. She's a good kid. But the image of the vaping pen sticks out.

Lulu is talking a mile a minute, giving us a rundown of her itinerary as she holds each of our hands. "First, I want to ride the carousel. Then the bumper cars. And the train ride. Can one of you win me a bear?"

"Let's take it one thing at a time," Tanner says, with a crinkle in his cheek.

"This is nicer than any school carnival I went to," I say, surprised at how big the whole thing is.

"Russ runs a tight ship. I'll give him that."

Lulu slips from our grip and runs to a flying airplane kiddie ride. So much for her itinerary. My hands graze against Tanner, who pushes them back in his pockets.

It's been awkward between us since...that night.

The night I turned him down.

It wasn't supposed to be like that. I wasn't supposed to feel this tight pull in my chest every time I look at him, wasn't supposed to catch myself watching the way his hand grazes Lulu's shoulder or how his eyes crinkle when Dean makes another dumb joke. I wasn't supposed to want more.

So, yeah, I pushed him away. And now things remain complicated.

We've been living in this weird gray area that's new for us. We're not the kind of friends who leave things unsaid. I want to be with Tanner, but I'm terrified of breaking his heart—which would mean breaking the heart of four wonderful kids, too.

"Daddy, can we go to the ring toss?" Lulu tugs at Tanner's hand, her face sticky with remnants of cotton candy.

"Sure, sweetheart." Tanner's voice is easy, but his eyes flick to me for a brief second. It's subtle, but the tension's there, hanging heavy between us. He adjusts the collar of his flannel shirt, trying to act normal, but I see the faint strain in his jaw.

Like many parents in shaky marriages, we smile for the kids, though.

Tanner tries his hand at the ring toss while I cheer him on with Lulu on my shoulders. I pat his back here and there for support. Tanner wins her a little Smurf stuffed animal that feels like a gold medal at the Olympics tonight and will gather dust by tomorrow.

"Hey." Tanner turns to me in a brief moment. "I have some good news," he says with a heavy cloud over him. "I have an interview with this company next week. MedTech. They seem very excited about having me."

"That's great!" I muster partial enthusiasm, but it feels so out of place against the seriousness in Tanner's voice. "Is it a good job?"

"Yeah. Seems like a nice place to work. The woman I spoke with who'd be my boss seems nice. So if I get this job, it means I can put the kids on my insurance plan once I start."

Oh. That's the other shoe dropping.

"We can get our marriage annulled in maybe a month. Have things go back to normal." Tanner pats my shoulder, the most bro-y, platonic move two men can do.

"Great," I say.

"I know it's abrupt. We said this was just until I could get a new job. We can keep things quiet until Stan makes his choice for creative director."

"Yeah. Of course. We knew this was coming. And I'm glad it is." I nod at my friend. "Congratulations."

If all goes according to plan, in a month, our marriage will be over. All this, this whole life of chaos will be done. No more carnivals and making breakfast. No more sharing a bed. No more messy, cluttered house.

But I can tell that this is what Tanner wants. He wants his life back, and I guess I do, too. I'm not going to put a damper on tonight and give Lulu a shitty core memory. The big thing I've learned about being a parent is smiling through the pain.

"Where to next?" I ask Lulu, squatting down to her eye level. She's currently ensconced with her Smurf.

"Hmmm." She lets the Smurf whisper into her ear. "We want to go on the flying airplane ride."

"Awesome!" I give her and the Smurf a high-five. "I'll catch up with you."

I let them drift toward the booth while I hang back, trying to breathe through the noise and chaos. My phone buzzes—work emails piling up, more pressure about the Silq Cosmetics pitch coming up—but I ignore it. For once, I need to focus on this...fake family...that doesn't feel so fake.

I scan the crowd, eyes drifting toward the rows of tents and booths. That's when I spot him—Matthias. Lena's boyfriend.

Or supposed boyfriend.

Shouldn't he be hanging out with his girlfriend?

He's by the edge of the school grounds, half-hidden between two food trucks. He's talking to some tall guy in a hoodie, the kind of guy who looks like he either sells burner phones...or something worse.

My stomach tightens.

The guy hands Matthias a wad of cash, which he quickly counts and stuffs in his back pocket. Matthias pulls a brown paper bag from his backpack and quickly hands it over. The guy darts out of sight.

I knew it. That sweater vest didn't fool me for a second.

I'm moving before I can think about it, cutting between families and booths, my heart pounding. If this kid is dealing drugs at a freaking elementary school carnival, I'll—

"Hey," I say sharply as I approach, grabbing Matthias by the arm. "What the hell was that?"

Matthias jumps, his face immediately turns pale. "Whoa—Mr.—uh—Des...Hey—"

"What were you just doing?" I snap, stepping closer. "What did you give that guy?"

"It's not what you think—"

I level him with the kind of look I reserve for junior copywriters who miss deadlines. I fist his sweater vest and pull him close. "Don't lie to me. I saw the exchange. I won't have my stepdaughter dating a drug dealer. You don't fool me, Matthias."

Sweat beads stream down his face. Matthias swallows hard and reaches slowly into his backpack. I steel myself, wondering if he's going to pull a gun on me. But instead he takes out... a comic book in a plastic folder.

I stare at it. Retro Spider-Man. Ready to save the day. Whereas Matthias looks ready to shit his pants.

"You're selling comic books?"

"Vintage comics." Matthias holds it up like proof of his innocence. "Jimmy wanted a special limited-edition Spider-Man comic. I forgot to bring it to school today. He's volunteering at the carnival, so we decided to meet up."

His face flushes with embarrassment, his light skin getting translucent.

I blink, exhaling slowly as my pulse starts to settle. "Jesus. I thought you were..." I shake my head. "Never mind."

"No! I don't do that stuff. Any of it. Not even the stuff that's technically legal." Matthias fidgets, shifting his backpack from shoulder to shoulder.

"What's your deal? Are you really like this?"

"Like what?"

I take a good look at Matthias. His sweater vest. His eager to please demeanor. The nervous pitch of his voice. I see now what's undeniable: he really is this squeaky clean. It's not an act.

"Why aren't you hanging with your girlfriend tonight?" My stern look reminds him that he better not lie to me, though now I'm certain he won't.

Matthias's ears turn pink. "Um. About that..."

"What?" I narrow my eyes.

"We're not really dating," he admits, voice low. "It's a cover. She asked me to pretend."

I freeze. "What do you mean, 'pretend'? You're her fake boyfriend?"

Matthias runs a hand through his hair, glancing nervously toward the carnival crowd. "I don't know if I should say."

I take a step closer. "Now you definitely should say."

"Lena's been hanging with some upperclassmen. Some sketchy kids. I don't know all the details, but she figured if she had a 'nice boyfriend,' it'd keep things chill at home. Not like her dad even notices anything she does."

I wince at the comment, even though it wasn't directed at me. There's no time to fight back against that accusation on Tanner's behalf. I need to keep digging.

My chest tightens. "Sketchy how? Like...vaping?"

Matthias nods.

"Is it just nicotine, or is it pot?"

He nods, too nervous to elaborate.

I clench my jaw, memories flashing back to finding that pen in her backpack, the way she flipped the questions back on me, asking about my intentions with Tanner. She's smart. Too smart for her own good.

"What else? Drinking? Drugs?"

He stares down at the ground and nods again. "I'm sorry."

"Why did you agree to this?"

"I thought...maybe if we spent more time together, she might actually want to be my girlfriend."

Matthias crumples, a bigger hunch in his back as he comes to the sad realization that he and Lena won't be happening. My heart goes out to him.

"Where is she tonight?"

"I can find out," he says. "I'm sorry. I didn't mean to do anything wrong."

Said anyone who's ever been in a fake relationship.

I run a hand over my face, sighing heavily. "Okay," I say finally, my voice firm. "Thank you for telling me. If I find out you're lying, or that you're part of the rough crowd? We're gonna have a problem."

He holds up his hands. "No problem. I'm the most boring guy you'll ever meet."

I almost smile. Almost.

———

I TEXT Tanner that I had to leave. Work emergency. I Uber back to the house, get my car, and drive to a woodsy area on the edge of town. I march down a muddy trail, destroying my new sneakers, until I reach a clearing.

I spot her through the haze of cigarette smoke and the glow of someone's car headlights. Lena, perched on the hood of a beat-up sedan, surrounded by kids who are all at least two or three years older than her. The kind of kids with too much eyeliner, torn jackets, and the simmering energy of people looking for trouble.

It's not like I belong here either. I stick out—pressed shirt, nice jeans, the faint lingering scent of fried carnival food still clinging to me.

She looks so much younger out here than she does when she's rolling her eyes at me across the dinner table. Her legs swinging off the car. Her hoodie sleeves pulled down over her hands.

I step closer, my shoes crunching over gravel.

One of the older guys notices me first—skinny, wiry, with a vape pen in his mouth, a beer bottle dangling from his fingers, and a look that says I'm not welcome.

"Lost, old man?" he sneers.

Lena's head snaps up at that. Her eyes go wide. "Des?"

The whole group quiets. They watch us like it's a showdown.

"What are you doing here?" She turns red, an avalanche of embarrassment. I get that. I'd feel the same if my parents showed up at a party to drag me home. But now that I'm on the other side, I don't care.

"I could ask you the same thing," I say evenly. "But let's not do this in front of your...friends."

The group mutters among themselves, amused. One of the girls giggles, her hand curled around a bottle of pills.

"We're just having a good time, old man," the wiry guy says, his eyes glassy. I doubt it's just tobacco in his vape.

"Do you know what one of the benefits of being an old man is? Having other adult friends. Like my good friend, the chief of police. Should I call him and ask if he wants to join?"

The wiry guy backs away, hands up. "Narc," he mutters.

Yeah, I am. And again, as an adult, I don't care. Being in your forties means everything aches, but it also means I don't give a fuck if some pissant teenagers think I'm uncool.

"Why don't you guys get the hell out of here," I tell them.

Lena slides off the car.

"You're joining the narc, Lena? Forget him." Wiry guy grabs her ass to pull her back, spiking a bout of rage in me I didn't know I was capable of feeling.

I grab him by the collar, yank him off the car and throw him to the ground. I squat down to his eye level. Panic sets in for him, the scared boy shining through his wannabe bad boy facade.

"What's your name?" I ask.

"Tyler."

"Tyler, here's the deal: if you so much as talk to Lena again, I will find out." I inch closer, my jaw tighter than a steel blade. "And I won't be happy. I play hockey, which means I have no problem beating the shit of people."

I stand up. I might be a quarter-century out of high school, but I've still got it.

Lena keeps her distance but starts walking with me toward the edge of the lot, away from the cluster of headlights and smoke. I don't push; I just walk beside her until we're far enough that no one can hear.

She shakes her head. "I'm going to kill Matthias."

"In his defense, I didn't give him much of a chance to cover for you."

"You embarrassed me."

"Believe me, suffering a little embarrassment is worth avoiding whatever path you were headed down back there." I stop, trying to remember what it felt like when I was her age, when I so desperately wanted to experience all the world had to offer. "Look, I'm still new at this dad stuff. But even you know those kids are trouble considering you enlisted a fake boyfriend to hide them."

"You know all about fake boyfriend shit."

"Watch your language." Words I never thought I'd ever utter. I think I just aged myself a decade.

She crosses her arms. "It's not what you think."

I cock an eyebrow. "Really? Because what I think is that you're fourteen and hanging out in a parking lot with kids who all look like they failed out of a CW casting call for bad decisions."

She groans, tilting her head back. "God, you sound like such a dad."

"Yeah, well, fake stepdad duties apparently come with the lectures."

Lena scuffs her shoe against the pavement. The streetlight overhead flickers. She looks small again, the hard edges falling off her.

"What are you doing here with these idiots? You know better."

"You never went to parties?" She cocks an eyebrow, thinking she's got me.

And she kind of does.

"It was different," is all I can manage. They seemed a lot less shady than whatever was going on in this parking lot. Though maybe that's just my recollection.

"Let me guess. Because you're a guy, they were fine. But because I'm a girl, I have to be saved."

"I...I know what those guys are like. I wouldn't want Davy here either. One of the benefits of being older is seeing what happens to these types of 'friends.' Spoiler alert: it's not anything good. You don't want to end up like them."

"You don't know anything about them."

"That's because you never brought them around the house, which means you don't even think they're good people." Internally, I pump my fist. Point Des. "Why did you lie? The vape pen. Using Matthias as your shield. Sneaking out to secluded parking lots with a bunch of sketchballs. This isn't you, Lena."

"Why can't it be?" she yells back, her voice breaking. Her cool, detached teenage facade drops, revealing primal emotions.

"Hey, talk to me."

"I'm supposed to be the responsible daughter, and that's all I am to him." She sucks in a shaky breath, shoulders hunched. "Dad treats me like I'm the built-in babysitter. Like I'm always fine and I have it all together. He doesn't really care how I'm doing, just so long as I don't give him another thing to worry about. But I'm not fine."

The crack in her voice hits me square in the chest.

"I...I miss my mom," Lena adds, quieter now. "I miss her so much. Every day, I wake up and have this thought that maybe the last two years were a dream, and she's going to come into my room. It lasts for a second or two before my brain kicks on, and I have to remember that she's gone all over again." Tears roll down her face.

My throat tightens. For a second, I picture the version of myself that was fourteen, angry and lonely in my parents' house, wishing someone would just notice I wasn't okay. All I want to do is pull her into the tightest hug possible and make this better. But this isn't Lulu wanting the last strawberry Fruit Roll-Up. There is no patented dad solution.

I take a careful step closer. "You're allowed to be angry, Lena. And sad. And all the other crap feelings that come with losing someone. But this?" I gesture toward the parking lot. "This isn't you. You're smart. You've got your whole life ahead of you. You don't need to play at being reckless to prove anything."

She sniffs, silent.

"And for the record," I add, "your dad? He's hanging on by a thread, trying to keep it all together. It doesn't mean he doesn't care. He just...he thinks you're stronger than him half the time."

Lena lets out a weak laugh. "He's such a mess."

"Yeah." I smile faintly. "But he's your mess. And mine, apparently. I'm going to talk to him about finding a different babysitting option for practice nights."

She looks up at me, eyes puffy but sharp. "I didn't want him to know about this, but also...I wished he would've been suspicious like you."

"He was blinded by the sweater vest. Your dad was a nerd like Matthias in high school. A nerdy hockey player. He defies stereotypes. He's going to be so heartbroken when he discovers you and Matthias aren't dating."

She lets out the quickest laugh, letting me know I haven't lost her.

We walk back toward my car, through the muddy trail that destroys my sneakers even more. She keeps pace with me, quiet, thoughtful.

"I'm grounded, huh?" she asks eventually.

"Oh, absolutely," I say, unlocking the door. As she slides in, I catch her glancing at me, smiling for the first time tonight.

"Hey," she says before closing the door. "You don't suck at this dad stuff."

I look up at the stars blanketing the night sky for a moment. Maybe I don't suck at this dad stuff. Maybe, against all my better judgment, I've found my place. I just hope there's still time left to save it.

25

TANNER

I come home from the carnival ready to crash. I shared cotton candy with Lulu and a bucket of fries with Dean, and all the sugar and salt is clouding my head. That, and the fact that Des left so abruptly. He said he had a thing he needed to take care of and would meet us back at home.

Did he have to go back to the office? His Silq Cosmetics pitch is coming up soon, and more than anything, Des cares about his career. Despite how my heart beats for him, he's not going to give that up for this manic collection of kids and one harried dad.

The kids are crashing from the copious amounts of sugar they had at the carnival, as well as the general high of rides wearing off. I make them brush their teeth, and after that, it's easy getting them into bed.

Des's car is in the driveway, but I don't find him in the bedroom. He isn't upstairs. Did he have a coworker take him to the office? Is he pulling an all-nighter? Before my mind can do its favorite thing—spiral—I hear the faint sounds of music coming from outside. My bedroom window is cracked open.

The roof.

Moments later, I join Des up there. Some '90s rock is playing softly from his phone as he stares out on the rows of cookie cutter homes before us. The view can't compare to the one he gets from his riverfront condo.

"Hey. How was the rest of the carnival?" he asks.

"I won Lulu a Paw Patrol stuffed animal, which she's currently hugging in bed, even though she doesn't watch Paw Patrol. Dean is pumped that he won the ring toss game. And I think I ate my weight in cotton candy and deep-fried foods. It's a shame you had to leave early."

"I'm sorry about that. Sounds like I missed a good time." I know Des well enough to sense a tiny shift in him from earlier tonight. His eyes are ringed with heaviness.

"Is everything okay?"

"Yeah." He pats the roof next to him. I take a seat, and we stare into the suburban abyss together. Des feels tense beside me. I'm always the first to sense when his cool demeanor begins to slip.

Worry seizes my stomach.

"Tanner, I hope you get this job. But I also know what it means." He turns to me, eyes big and serious. Worried. "It means this ruse is over."

I gulp back a lump in my throat. "We can wait until you find out about your promotion. To keep up appearances and all that."

"Uh-huh. And you think this is for the best?"

Against every impulse in my heart, I nod yes. "This was only supposed to be temporary. We don't want to...confuse things any longer."

"Confuse things?"

"Yes. This isn't real. You have an exciting career and an exciting life to get back to." It takes all of my strength not to buckle and break down. This dream life with Des as my husband wasn't built to last.

"Maybe I want this life." His voice quivers with emotion. "Being in this house is messy and chaotic and loud. So freaking loud. And I've never been happier. I spent my whole life outrunning a crappy home. But being here with you and the kids, it makes me feel like I'm part of a team." He takes my hand, squeezes it tight. "I belong here. And I think...I don't suck at the dad stuff."

Before I can object or say anything, he leans in and kisses me. His lips fill me with new life. It's been way too long since we last kissed, and I don't know how I survived.

"I don't want to be your fake husband. I want to be your real one."

"But I thought...when we were in bed, and you pulled away..."

"I got scared. All of this started to get serious. You have a whole family to think about, Tanner. I couldn't continue to hook up with you and then freak out and push you away. I'd hurt you and those kids. But I realized that this is what I want. You. Me. Kids. Family pictures that end in tears. Pop Tarts for breakfast as we're running out the door. Going to sleep every night with you cuddled in my arms. I want all of it. I'm not running."

I have to catch my breath as I take this all in. He is saying everything I've wanted to hear. My soul gets so light, I might just float away.

"I thought you were a proud bachelor."

He shrugs. "People change. I thought you were straight."

I snort a laugh. "I tried to talk myself out of falling for you so many times, and it never worked."

"You're falling for me?" Des asks.

"Uh-huh. Are you falling for me?"

"No." He smooths a hand over my cheek. "I'm already there."

Des has always been my friend. We've been there for each other through everything. I never thought I'd develop feelings for him, but here they are, and they are as natural as the wind.

He takes my hand and twists the ring on my finger. "You really like wearing that ring."

I blush. "Old habits."

"Can I borrow it for a second?" He gently tugs the ring off my finger. "I'd get on one knee, but I'm afraid of falling off the roof."

"We can pretend."

"Perfect. Okay, I'm on one knee." That salesman twinkle is in his eye, though I don't need to be sold. "Tanner Michael Chance, will you marry me for real?"

"Before I say yes, you're aware that I come with four kids, which you will also be responsible for? There will be fights, and punishments, and throwing up, and forcing them to do their homework, and probably more throwing up, usually on your favorite outfit."

A huge grin slides onto his face. "Sign me up."

He slides the ring back onto my finger.

I shuffle over to him for another earth-shattering kiss. He swallows me up in a hug, and we sit there making out in the moonlight, ready for the next stage of our lives to begin.

After a few minutes of romantic tranquility, Des's hand slips down to my crotch, which is just as excited about the nuptials as my heart.

"Should we pick up where we left off?" he asks.

"Definitely."

"Technically we're already married, so we don't need to wait until the wedding night."

"We're having a wedding?"

He pleads the fifth by kissing me hard and quick, priming both our pumps. We make our way back into the bedroom and fall back on the bed.

Des, on top of me, those soft lips kissing down my neck. Our cocks rub against each other through our pants. I can feel how hard he is. Hard for me. I melt to his touch.

"You're wearing too many clothes. Let's do something about that." Des takes his torturous time unbuttoning my shirt. His warm hands glide over my chest, across my light dusting of hair.

He kisses between my pec muscles down my stomach. My cock strains against my underwear and pants, begging to be free.

"Daddy."

I jolt up. It's not Des calling me daddy. It's one of my actual kids.

"Daddy, my tummy hurts," Lulu whines.

The doorknob twists open, and I work in record fast time to button up my shirt. Des sits on the edge of the bed, his legs crossed, face red from what must be a tight squeeze.

Lulu shuffles in, half-asleep. I pull her onto my lap.

"What's wrong, sweetheart? You have a tummy ache?"

She nods yes and crumples into a sob. I hug her to my chest while Des rubs her back.

"I think you ate too much junk food at the carnival. Didn't I tell you that eating all that cotton candy would give you a tummy ache?"

She doesn't answer, but continues crying. She hasn't fully grasped that her actions have consequences. Though to be fair, neither have most adults.

"Maybe some ginger ale could help settle your stomach," I say. I rock her in my lap. "How does that sound?"

"Okay," she says into my chest.

"Uncle Des will get you some."

Des holds up the one minute finger. He points to his crotch, apparently wishing ginger ale could settle that, too.

"Don't worry. Uncle Des is going to go real soon to get you some ginger ale."

Lulu whines in pain. She looks up, her big eyes all red with large tear drops. "Daddy, can I sleep with you tonight?"

I swivel my head to Des, and we silently commiserate. Looks like sex is off the table for tonight.

He hops off the bed, jeans nice and flat. "One ginger ale coming up."

"Could you put it in my Bluey cup? With a straw?" Despite being horribly sick, Lulu still remains a girl who knows what she wants.

"Are you sure you still want all this?" I whisper to him.

He winks at me, a security blanket if I ever needed one. "Oh yeah."

26

DES

I wake up the next morning on the downstairs couch. Wake up is a generous word for the shitty sleep I got. It was more like long stretches of closing my eyes. Lulu got sick in Tanner's bed, so I helped change the sheets and put in a fresh load in the never-ending laundry cycle. I stayed downstairs so as not to wake Lulu by trying to slide back into bed.

I sit up from the couch, my back practically reconfigured thanks to the evil springs of the pull-out. Despite being tired and sore, I can't stop thinking about a different fresh load. The one I was supposed to put inside Tanner last night.

Tiredness is no match for horniness.

My ball hurts as much as my back. It felt incredible confessing my love to Tanner last night. I am so happy he is my husband—legally, technically, and now romantically. I am so grateful to be part of this family. But I also want to consummate this marriage. I want to feel Tanner vibrate and moan under me, feel my cock stretching him in real time.

Maybe tonight? If I can hold out.

I blink and find Dean and Davy in front of me.

"What are you doing down here?" Dean asks.

"Did you and Dad have a fight?" Davy wonders.

"No. Lulu was sick. Too much cotton candy." I rub not-quite-sleep from my eyes.

"Can you make us cheese omelets?" Dean asks.

I rub my head, currently weighed down by tiredness. I should not be operating machinery or things that emit flames. "Uh, why don't I show you guys how to make your own omelets? You're old enough."

They look at each other, then shrug. "Sure," says Davy.

They scamper into the kitchen. I can supervise from the kitchen table drinking coffee. Did I just figure out a solution to a parenting problem? Maybe I am cut out for this dad shit.

A little bit later, I am in dad heaven: the boys are making omelets while I supervise. They're following my directions and not fighting. Lena enters the kitchen and grabs a Pop Tart from above the fridge.

"Hey," she says. "Thanks again for..."

I nod at her, neither of us needing to get into it again. I put my hand over hers. *I got you*, I tell her with my eyes.

"Guys," I yell. "Can you make a third omelet for your sister please?"

"Coming right up!" Dean concurs, like they're line cooks at a diner.

"Sit. Chill." I point to an empty chair beside me. "So what are you going to do about Matthias? He is a puppy dog in love with you."

"I'll let him down easily. And I'm going to start taking the bus."

A little bit later, Lena downs half her omelet before heading out to school. Then Lulu skips into the kitchen full of energy as if she was never sick. Tanner has the circles under his eyes to prove she was.

I pour him a coffee in the largest mug he owns. He tucks into the kitchen chair beside me.

"I'm sorry about last night," he says.

"It's all good. Life happens."

"I had an idea." He scoots closer to me. "Do you get a lunch break at work?"

"I can take lunch whenever. Why? What were you thinking?"

"We could meet...at your condo."

Tanner in my California king bed? Taking him on my eight hundred thread count sheets? A view of the river as I fuck him senseless? Yes to all this.

"Works for me."

The thought of having Tanner begins to get me hard.

"Can I have Cheerios?" Lulu asks standing right in front of me.

I cross my legs again, snuffing out my erection.

Tanner bolts up. "I'll get it, sweetheart." He shoots me a knowing smile.

————

MY MORNING CRAWLS. It's a rule of physics that the clock slows to a virtual halt whenever one is expecting to get laid. Time is a cockblocker.

We are one week out from the Silq Cosmetics pitch. My team and I have been working like crazy to finalize the pitch, scrutinizing every word of copy, every image, every bullet point on our PowerPoint. This has to be perfect.

I summon all my cognitive powers to focus on work, even though all I can think about is getting to make love to Tanner in a few hours. Fortunately, we realize that one of our commercial pitches is weak, so we spend a good hour brainstorming new ideas. It allows me to forget about sex for a little bit. Miracles can happen when you believe.

When the clock strikes noon, I turn into the Road Runner, ready to *meep meep* the fuck out of here.

"You're going out for lunch?" Craig asks, laying down on the couch in my office.

"I have to run an errand and help Tanner with something. I'll be quick." I stop at my office door and reconsider. "Not that quick. But I'll be back soon. Keep working on honing that new commercial premise we cracked, but also get some lunch. Let your brains relax. They'll come back stronger."

That's what I'm doing. I'm not shirking job responsibility. I'm going to clear my mind and my ball and come back to the office sharp as hell.

I walk so fast to the elevator, I hear wind whoosh past my ears. My dick is like a dog pulling at the owner's leash.

The elevator doors open, and Stan steps out.

"Des, how's the Silq pitch coming?"

"Great. We're ready to go for next week."

"Excellent. I'd like to swing by your office and hear the pitch, offer some feedback where I can."

"Now?"

Stan raises his eyebrows.

"I actually have to help Tanner with something. For the kids. This afternoon?"

Stan's face doesn't move, and I wonder if I just fucked myself over for the promotion in one fell horny swoop. Then he breaks into a laugh, the wrinkles on his face creasing with joy.

"Kids will keep you busy!" He laughs to himself. "How's three?"

"Perfect!" I give him a thumbs up and slide into the elevator. I heave out a breath as the doors close.

Twelve long, agonizing minutes later, I pull into my apartment building's parking structure. I have to drive down one long, agonizing level to my spot. At this point, I could crash my car into a wall and just buy a new one. Anything to cut down this commute and be inside Tanner sooner.

I trudge up the stairwell to the lobby, heart pounding in my ears. My dick throbs at the sight of Tanner leaning against the mailboxes scrolling on his phone.

"Hey!" He looks down, those bright blue eyes sparkling, inviting me in. "Did you have trouble leaving the—"

I push him against the wall of mailboxes and plant a steamy, epic kiss on his lips. Fuck, are we doing this right here right now? I could. I've had sex in public places before.

Tanner pulls back, his face flush, eyes heavy-lidded. "Good afternoon."

"Sorry, babe. Been a long morning." I don't have more witty

banter in me right now. I take his hand and lead us to the elevator. I push the up button a few times, waiting waiting waiting. If Tanner so much as breathes into my ear, I may come in my pants.

"Lulu still felt a little nauseous when I dropped her off this morning, but fortunately, I haven't heard from the school, so she should be fine," Tanner says.

"That's great."

The ding of the elevator makes my dick jump in my pants. I hustle us inside and press the door close button a few dozen times. I could ravage Tanner, but then I remember the security camera in the corner. It's a miracle with all the sex I've had that a sex tape hasn't leaked. Let's not start today.

"You look so hot," I whisper in Tanner's ear. My dick is poking his leg, and I don't have the good manners to stop.

"I'm wearing a T-shirt and old pair of jeans."

"I know. Like I said. Hot." I kiss his neck. I'm teetering on the edge of sex tape elevator. Only Tanner's good manners can stop me.

He leans in close. "I can't wait to get fucked by you."

A sexy, sinister smile slashes on his lips. Good boy gone bad. Cursing sounds hot coming from him.

The elevator dings. The doors fly open. We walk like gentlemen to my apartment, but halfway there, I lose all social graces.

I run to my door. Grab my keys. Fiddle with the lock that can be stubborn. I'm two seconds away from breaking the door down before imagining the bill I'd get from maintenance. The lock clicks into place. I throw the door open.

"Come over here." I sound like a fucking caveman, but how dare Tanner take his sweet time. I pick him up, throw him over my shoulder, and rumble into my apartment. After kicking the door shut, I march us directly to my bedroom where I throw him down onto my bed. The comforter and sheets billow out from under him.

He stares at me, pupils blown wide, cock outlined in his old pair of jeans. I stare back transfixed. There's this unspoken thought that simmers between us.

This is happening.

I'm about to have sex with my best friend. For the first time, I'm about to have sex with someone I truly love.

My horny devil brain calms down. I don't want to ravage Tanner as quickly as possible. I want to savor this. Every moment. Every inch of him.

I lower myself on top of him. I breathe in his manly scent through his shirt, drift up his neck where his stubble tickles my nose, until our mouths meet in a union of sweetness and heat. I'm still ravenous for him, but steadier, taking in the taste of hot tongue, the roughness of his lips. I comb a hand through his hair, letting each strand dance through my fingers.

Tanner is mine. And I am his.

I rut against him as we make out, feeling his thickness press into my leg.

"You feel so good," I moan against his lips.

"Am I getting the standard Des treatment?"

"Premium package, baby. Reserved for our most valuable customers." I take his hand and hold it against my premium package.

"I could lay here kissing you all day."

The sound of our lips smacking together fills the space.

"I could spend all day in this bed with you, Tan." Too bad there's work and school pickups and kids who insist on receiving dinner. "But time is of the essence."

I push my hands under his shirt, flick my thumbs over his nipples, savoring this glorious chest. He groans against my mouth desperate for relief.

I lower my mouth and slick my tongue over his left nipple. He tenses and shudders as he whispers, "Yes."

"You don't have to whisper," I tell him. We aren't at home with kids sleeping down the hall. "Be loud. Be proud."

Tanner abides, unleashing a bellowing moan as I go from one nipple to the other, teasing and playfully biting.

"Need you, Des."

I pin his arms over his head and meet him for a hot kiss, our tongues lapping over each other like two dogs roughhousing.

He breaks free from my grip and yanks my dress shirt from my pants.

"All these freaking buttons," Tanner says as he begins undoing them.

"I did not dress for a quickie," I laugh.

Eventually, Tanner gets through all of them, but instead of taking my shirt off, he reaches around and grabs my ass with both hands, squeezing each cheek like they're therapy stress balls. His finger drifts down my crack, sending shudders of heat rippling through me.

"I love watching this ass on the ice." Tanner smiles against my lips.

"You're supposed to be focused on the game."

"I'm a single dad with four kids. I'm a master at multitasking."

"Fair point." I rut against him, the friction of our cocks sending heat to my core.

I sit up and pull him flush against me for more making out. I yank his shirt over his head while he pushes my shirt off my arms. Our hands travel across our chests and arms, like new visitors to a foreign land wanting to experience everything.

I've long admired Tanner's body. We've stolen illicit glimpses in the locker room over the years and had quick grabs in the dark during our bedroom sexy times. Now I get to have fun. I get to explore. I get to feel the way his biceps and triceps weave together to form his lean, muscular arms. I get to tumble my fingers over the ridges of his sorta-there abs.

"You are one hot dad," I growl.

"And you are one hot stepdad."

There's fire in his eyes, but I also sense a hint of hesitation. And that's when I remember that this is all new for Tanner. Not only has he not had sex in two years (I'm still not over that revelation), but as far as I know, he's never been with a guy.

Is he scared? Is he being a good sport and not wanting to speak up? I tangle a thumb in his hair. "Hey, how are you doing?"

He glances down at his rock hard cock. "Pretty good."

"No, I mean...this is new for you. How are you feeling about it? I want this to be a good experience. If there's anything you don't like, or if you want to slow down, please say something."

"I will." He nods, yet the hesitation remains on his face.

I lift his chin to face me. "Tanner, I know when you're bull-shitting."

"I'm not really sure what to expect. I…" He laughs, his cheeks reddening. "I can't believe I'm admitting this, but I'm worried I'm not going to be…good. Like, if you had a Top Ten, would I make it in?"

I hold myself back from guffawing. I can't imagine not giving him a ten out of ten, no notes. The idea of this being lousy sex is as plausible as Martians taking over the planet.

"Tan, you're my number one guy. The only thing you're not good at is being a shithead. And bowling."

"That was one game years ago."

"And you were so bad it's stuck out vividly in my mind ever since." I plant a soft kiss on his lips, letting him know he's safe here. "I can't wait to have amazing sex with you. And it's going to be amazing because it's you. One of the benefits of having sex with your best friend is we can be honest with each other. We can laugh. We can call each other out. I don't care if we both come in ten seconds. I'm just so grateful I get to be here with you."

He pulls me into a hug, kisses my shoulder. "Des, how did I get so lucky to wind up with you in my life?"

Same, buddy. Same.

He pulls back, fixes his heavy-lidded eyes on me. Sweetness is slowly being subsumed by lust. "Des, since I'm a newbie at this, I want you to take lead. Tell me what to do. I'm yours."

My dick pulses with renewed vigor. I'm going to show this man a great time.

27

TANNER

There are times in my friendship with Des when he can be a bit bossy. A know-it-all. A guy who has to be in the driver's seat because he knows best. We're all human, and he means well.

Well, today, I really, really want that Des to come out and play.

While this is my first time with a man, and my first time in a long while that I've had sex, I'm not scared about what to do. Gay sex isn't rocket science. I know I can figure it out. But I want to be led today. As a parent, I'm always the one in charge, the one planning and executing. Today, I want to be the one taken care of. I want to put my trust completely in Des's hands.

He pushes me back on the bed and undoes my pants. He pulls them and my underwear off until my cock unabashedly sticks up like a national monument. I'm completely naked and exposed for him, a fact that makes precome leak from my tip in anticipation.

"Get on all fours," he commands in his low voice. He is looking ferociously hot. His smooth face accentuates his sharp jaw. A few stray strands of hair fall in his face. There's a sense of play twinkling behind his eyes.

I do as he says. Cold air hits my ass. He has me scoot forward, then unbuttons his pants. I've seen his cock in the dark during our nighttime fooling around, but now I can see it in the light of day. It's nice and thick, heavy in my hand.

When I take it in my mouth, it fills the whole space, hitting the back of my throat. I savor the feeling of being filled, eager for what comes later.

"That's it. Nice and slow," he says. "How are you doing?"

Since my mouth is full, I give him a thumbs up. He laughs, and the vibration rumbles down my throat.

"Only you can make a thumbs up during sex super hot." He strokes a hand through my hair, gently pushing me down to his base, then pulling back up. It's controlled, steady, thoughtful. My body tingles with excitement of being controlled by my friend, trusting him absolutely.

"I can see you in the mirror. Your ass is so sexy. Look at that pink hole," Des says. Until today, it was a body part I'd never thought of, let alone thought was sexy. Des makes all of me feel special.

He massages my shoulders, then my back, then keeps going until his hand slinks down my crack. He uses two hands to spread my cheeks and rubs a finger over my opening, causing my whole body to convulse with a type of need I'd never experienced before.

"You okay?"

I groan hungrily into his dick. I give it some hardy strokes and circle my tongue over the head, licking up his precome. Des grunts his approval, and I'm instantly addicted to that sound.

He licks his finger and puts it back on my hole, circling my tight opening, making me shiver with heat. And then he dips. The finger. Inside. Me.

Fireworks. No, not fireworks. Explosions. A skyscraper blown to smithereens in a ball of fire. I pump his cock harder. Lust consumes every fiber of me, a dire want to chase that glorious new feeling.

"I take it you and Katie didn't do any butt stuff." He chuckles.

"Only you can make the phrase 'butt stuff' super hot," I shoot back at him.

He winks at me, and I go back to work. More grunts of acclaim for my dicksucking work. I steady my hands on his massive thighs, feeling them flex and tense.

He pulls back, circles his thumb around my slicked-up lips, letting the saliva coat the pads of his fingers. Goosebumps prickle up and down my skin merely in anticipation of what he'll do. He presses a slick finger back inside me, pushing through my clenched ring of muscle.

"Oh God," I cry out.

"You are so fucking tight. I can't wait to stretch you."

I hunger to feel him inside me, hitting new sensations I've never experienced. I take his thick cock to the base as he plunges his finger deeper into my ass. He adds another finger, opening me wider, making me crave his dick in there. I shiver with need, my arms shaking to keep my upper body upright. How did I not know I was so sensitive down there? He's unlocking a whole new world.

"I love watching you take me. Your ass is so damn hot."

Sure enough, Des is watching himself finger me through the mirror. The thought of being watched sends a tidal wave of lust crashing through me. My late wife and I had very nice, very gentlemanly sex, and it was wonderful. But being with Des can help me explore new things in the bedroom, perhaps a kinkier side I didn't know existed.

I slap his cock on my tongue, lick up drops of bitter precome. I'm both excited and concerned about how he's going to fit inside me.

He fingerfucks my hole in short, manic thrusts. I moan and gasp, holding onto his thighs to catch myself, overcome with heat. My cock is so heavy between my legs I could blow right here. But something tells me to wait until Des is fucking me. That's where the real fireworks will happen.

"Okay. That's good." Des pulls his fingers out and gives my ass a pat, not unlike a coach commending his player's hustle.

I fall back on the bed, my knees and shoulders tight from being on all fours. Hockey and turning forty have done a number on my joints. Des sits beside me and runs his fingers up and down my back.

"Uh, so we never discussed who would top and bottom," Des says.

"One of the things you need to get used to as a gay couple. Unless you and Katie were into pegging."

We weren't and we should've been. Good Lord. Having my ass played with was life changing, like I can sense a Tanner pre-AP and post-AP, and they are not the same man.

"I want to bottom. I want to feel you inside stretching me."

My dick twitches at the statement. Des bites his lips in anticipation too.

"I will warn you, it's not going to be all kittens and rainbows. Since it's your first time, it may hurt a little. But I'm nothing if not a thoughtful, attentive lover. Like my dentist says to me, I'll do everything I can to make it as painless as possible. Ironically, I was getting a cavity filled."

"That reminds me. Davy is due for his six-month checkup. I need to check the calendar and see when that is. You book those appointments so far in advance."

"Tan, I just had my cock in your mouth and my fingers in your ass. Now is not the time to contemplate pediatric dentist appointments."

"You're right." Juggling four schedules on my own has broken my brain. "Sorry."

"It's all good. I'm still hard. And let me check you..." Des pushes me onto my back and lowers himself to my dick. He takes me in his mouth, licking up my shaft and taking me into his mouth. His slippery tongue polishes my crown. I hiss out in pleasure, so much pleasure I don't know what to do with it all.

My dick pops out of his mouth.

"Yep. You're still hard, too." He delivers his sexily smug smile. "Do you want to get back on all fours?"

"Actually, I think my knees and back need a rest."

"No worries." He throws my legs up and onto his shoulders. Cool air hits my slicked-up hole. Under the suaveness, there's an innocent giddiness in his expression, like we're teenagers in my bedroom again, except this time instead of sneaking up beers, we're experimenting with sex.

With an ease that reminds me he's done this many times before, he leans to his bedside table and pulls out lube. "Did you want to use condoms? I was tested recently and came back STI-free, and I haven't been with anyone since we got married."

"And I haven't been with anyone in...a while." Saying two years aloud will deflate my erection. "Let's go condom free."

Des uncaps the lube and preps his cock, then my hole. The cold lubricant sends a non-sexual shiver up my spine.

"Before you...do it. I just want to remind you that I'm not as experienced as you. As we've established, it's been...a while since I've had sex. So, you know, keep your expectations in check."

"Too late." He winks at me.

"I'm serious." How does one ruin a dream relationship? Be a lousy lay.

"Tanner, I love you. There's nobody else in the world I'd want to have awkward sex with." He drifts a clean thumb on my cheek, immediately settling me. "This is new for me, too. I've never had sex with someone I love. I'm just as much of a newb as you. This is going to be epic lovemaking or it's going to be an awkward debacle. Either way, I'm pumped that I get to experience it with you."

I've never been more excited to have sex. I love this man more than words can describe.

Des gives me and him one more coat of lube. He tosses the bottle on the nightstand. "So to quote that kid in *Love Actually*, let's get the shit kicked out of us by love."

And then Des takes my last remaining virginity.

When he enters me, there isn't pain. It's discomfort. A new sensation. A sharp stretch. A realization that something can go in, not just come out. Whenever the odd feeling hits, I look up at Des, and his gaze soothes me. We're in this together.

He pushes past my tightness. Hair falls in his face and his lips pout as he gets focused on bringing me pleasure.

I moan, but Des moans louder, his breath shaking, eyes rolling back in his head. "Fuck. You feel so good."

I take it all in, literally and figuratively. Des slides out of me, then back in. The weight of his body pushes against my sensitive opening. Quickly, like a sand castle melting against a wave, the discomfort fades leaving only ecstasy and connection.

"How are you doing?" His chest and abs flex with each thrust inside my ass.

"So good. This is incredible. I love you so much," I say through stilted breaths, keeping my eyes locked on him. The pleasure grows inside me, taking over me, consuming every cell.

He interlocks our fingers and pushes them over my head. He leans down and kisses me, over and over and over again. We pant against each other as he speeds up.

The sound of his thighs slapping against my ass with each hump echoes in the bedroom. It's then that I remember we aren't in my house. There are no children sleeping down the hall. This is a nice condo. The walls must be thick.

"Don't stop! Feels so good. Yes!" I yell, unleashed, the sound of my pleading voice only serving to make me hornier.

"I fucking love you, Tan. And I love fucking you." He swirls his tongue in my ear without slowing down his thrusting. Impressive. That's where the experience comes in handy.

My body is all his to play with. He's stretching me like Play-Doh, having a grand ole time. I am both powerless and powerful in his arms. Nothing has ever felt more right.

He gets back up and grips my legs before jackhammering my hole. "I'm going to make you come hands-free."

His confidence gets my dick harder. He hits my hole with repeated jabs. Sweat trickles down his chest. My dick and balls are tingling with the urge to blow. If I could wrap my fist around myself and pump, I'd blow. I want to so badly. But Des watches me, forces me to keep my hands away.

My dick becomes indescribably sensitive, desperate for touch and desperate for release. A simple gust of wind could turn me into a geyser at this point.

"Don't stop. Please don't stop."

"You are clamped around my cock. It's so hot. Remember, no

touching." He is getting a twisted glee from my desperation. And it only nudges me closer to release.

Every part of me clenches as my balls draw up, the avalanche of lust burying me. I am completely out of control, like I'm on the verge of fainting and unable to catch myself. My heart pounds in my ears, my vision blurs. I can only make out Des and the sparkle in his eyes. All my muscles tighten and flex as the orgasm rips through me.

"FUUUUUUUCK," I scream, part moan and part cry. The load shoots out of me, hitting my chest and stomach. Even Des is taken aback by the intensity.

One could say I needed this.

"Whoa," Des says without stopping. "Jesus, that was hot."

He speeds up again, wanting to join me on the other side. His face tenses and twists, and I take in every detail of this beautiful man I get to call my husband and my best friend.

He empties himself inside me. After a moment to catch his breath, he pulls out, leaving me a changed man. He collapses next to me. Before I can say anything, he kisses me with the fragments of intensity he has left.

"Whoa," he says again.

"You sound like Keanu Reeves."

"If your ass was the Matrix, I'd never leave."

I crack up at the corniness. Des joins in. Laughter fills the room.

"Come here." Des uses his shirt to wipe my torso off. Then he pulls me against him for a sweet kiss that makes me fall further in love with him. "Well..."

"Yeah."

"Now I know how to get you to curse."

28

DES

One week later, I'm pacing and sweating in my office. Today is the day of the Silq Cosmetics pitch. The marketing team should be arriving any minute to a conference room filled with pastries and a fruit platter. Outside, it's a gloomy early November day. The colors of fall are giving way to bare trees and the impending winter bleakness.

My team and I go through the pitch, analyzing every detail, leaving no stone unturned. Craig sits on the couch, his leg bouncing with nerves. Lisa analyzes every slide like she's a scientist looking for atoms.

This week was stressful, but at least I was able to blow off steam by fucking my husband. If I thought Tanner was hot before, he was the human equator in the bedroom. I can barely keep my hands off him. We brush against each other in the kitchen when pushing the kids out to school, and next thing I know, I'm pulling him onto the couch for a quickie. We had two more lunch breaks in my apartment, too, making me reconsider selling the place.

And then there are times when I watch him read Lulu a bedtime story or cheer on Davy at his hockey game, and my heart gets so full it may explode. I am filled with gratitude at the crazy twists and turns of life that brought us together.

Craig snaps a finger in front of my face.

"Focus!" he says.

I glare back, and all seven feet of him turn white. I stand up from my desk.

"Sorry." He looks at his shoes.

"Unless there's a martini in your hand, your fingers aren't allowed to get that close to my face again."

Lisa laughs. "Des is still in the honeymoon phase."

She may be right. I hold back a sloppy grin. Maybe it's because I refused romantic relationships for my whole life, but being with Tanner has turned me into a fucking puppy dog.

"We all need to focus. How is the ad copy?" I ask, pacing in front of my wall, covered in ideas and notes. "Let's go over it one more time."

Don't Hide Who You Are. Enhance It. says the sign we had made up with our proposed tagline. Our conversations about using makeup to conceal eventually turned to the more positive flip side. Use Silq Cosmetics to enhance your best assets, to show off the contours of your face that make you uniquely you. Bring out the fullness of your lips, the color in your eyes, the angles or roundness of your cheek-bones. You are one of one; let Silq be your megaphone.

"I love it," says Craig when Lisa reaches the final slide.

"Never fall in love with your own work. Never lose that objectivity," I tell him.

"It's good. I'm really proud of this. I'd buy Silq for my daughter," Lisa says. "How about you?"

Right. I have daughters. My daughters will be wearing makeup. Lena already is. "Me, too. I never want them to feel like they have to wear makeup to look like someone else."

I can't protect them from all the horrors of the world; I just have to hope that Tanner and I can give them the necessary armor so they can protect themselves.

"You know, Des. I don't think you would've come up with this campaign before you had kids." Lisa knocks her elbow against mine. "Isn't it funny how those little critters can change you?"

"Yeah." I chuckle to myself, letting my eyes drift to the family photo debacle.

I have kids! And they're wonderful! I mean, they're pains in the asses, but also wonderful!

"Let's huddle." I signal for them to come close. "Look, we've worked our asses off for weeks on this. I am impressed at everything we've done. Know that whatever happens, we left it all on the field. We have a great pitch, a great insight that their company will jump at if they're smart. That's all we can do."

One of the unexpected highlights of my job is getting to mentor my junior staff. I love watching them grow and develop. Craig could barely string a cogent sentence together when he first interned here, but over the past year, he's become a great copywriter.

"Knock, knock." Stan enters the office, twisting my stomach into a tighter knot of nerves. "How are we feeling?"

"Good," I tell him. "Silq would be fucking idiots not to hire us. They're not going to find a pitch like this from other agencies."

"I love the confidence, Des." Stan fixes his bowtie. "I'm going to be there with you."

Stan supports his teams, and I know he'll only interject if he really has something to add. He's not the kind of boss that loves hearing himself talk. But I also know he'll be judging me. This pitch is make or break for my career. He wants to see if I'm creative director material. If I bomb in front of a huge potential client, that's it for me.

But no pressure, right?

"You got this," he says to me, and it almost sounds like a warning.

Speaking of people who love to hear themselves talk, Kyle struts into my office. He's never good news, but the way he's smiling puts me on high alert.

"I wanted to wish you good luck, Des," he says.

"Thanks."

"It'd be a shame for you to bomb this presentation because you're a liar."

Sweat pricks at the back of my neck. My heart pounds in my ears. "What the fuck are you talking about?"

"Kyle, they have a big pitch today. They need to focus," Stan says.

"I'm sorry, Stan. I know this isn't the best time, but I'm very concerned that we have a con artist working here. Wouldn't you want to know if someone you worked with, someone you were thinking of handing the company to, was conning you?"

My mouth goes dry, my limbs stiff. There's a certainty in Kyle's glare that makes me want to throw up.

"What do you mean?" Stan asks, sounding a teensy bit receptive. "Des is a con artist?"

"Yes. His 'marriage'...is a SHAM. It's all a lie he's using to project this family man image in the hope you'll promote him."

"Kyle, get the hell out of my office," I say with a low voice to intimidate him, but my words sound hollow, and he knows it. "Tanner is my husband."

"Legally yes. You went to the courthouse and got a quickie wedding. How funny that right around when Stan announces his retirement, you became a husband and stepdad."

"You checked on my marriage license?"

"It's public record." He shrugs.

"Why are you digging into Des's marriage?" Craig asks. "That's creepy AF."

"What's creepy AF is that Des enlisted his friend Tanner Chance to be his husband, and forced his kids to lie for him. Tanner and Des played hockey together in high school. They play on a hockey league today. They've been friends for a while. And we're supposed to believe that they are suddenly in love?" Kyle scoffs. He prowls around my office, strengthening his grip on the upper hand. "And there's more! Because this isn't just a lie to get a promotion. This is insurance fraud."

Oh shit. Shit, shit, shit.

The team looks at me, as does Stan. His forehead creases with concern. Kyle's never been this convincing in a pitch, but I guess there's a first for everything.

"I checked with Tanner's old employer. He was recently laid off. And a week later, he and Des are getting married. One week later," Kyle stresses, his head shading into a strawberry. "Hmmm...a single dad with four kids who's about to lose his employee insurance plan out of nowhere marries his friend, whose company has great benefits? I don't know about you, Stan, but that smells like insurance fraud to me."

Kyle sits on my desk. I want to punch the smirk off his face. I still can't move. I thought Tanner and I were being smart, but we were the dumbest fucking guys thinking this scheme would work.

"We have two friends who hatched a plan. You give me insurance, and I'll give you an instant family to impress your boss." Kyle shakes his head in disgust. "Am I getting all this correct, Des?"

"Fuck you," I spit out. How long has he had this figured out? He naturally waited until today to make sure I bombed the pitch.

Kyle softens his stance and walks up to Stan. He puts a hand on Stan's shoulder. "Stan, I am so sorry I had to bring this bad news. I know my timing isn't great, but as soon as I discovered this web of lies and deceit, I had to tell you. You are a man of honor. If Des will go to these lengths to secure a promotion for himself, what else is he capable of?"

Nobody speaks. My office goes dead silent. People have gathered from the hall to rubberneck.

Stan looks to me, but I can barely keep eye contact. I stare at the rug like a fucking chump.

"Thank you for making me aware of this," Stan tells Kyle. He claps him on the shoulder.

"Anything for you, Stan." Kyle puts his hand over his heart.

"I had been struggling with who to promote to creative director. But after hearing this, you've made it remarkably easy to choose Des."

I whip my head up. Craig and Lisa's eyes go wide. Huh?

"What?" Kyle asks, all the wind leaving his body.

"The fact that you would concoct this gross, hateful story just to knock Des out of the running for creative director shows me that you are not a team player. Maybe if you'd spent less time searching for Des's marriage license, you would've had more time to land a big fish like Silq."

"S–Stan, you can't be serious. I'm not the one who's lying!" Kyle's voice short circuits into a high-pitched yelp. "Des and Tanner are in a fake marriage. They've pulled the wool over your eyes, over all of our eyes!"

"Let me tell you something, Kyle," Stan says, adding some old school spice. "I went to their house. I spent time with them, before your kids decided to act like demon spawn. I saw two men who are madly in love with each other, and a stepdad who is crazy about his kids. You can't fake the love that was in that house. I've been on this earth for over seventy years. It takes a lot to fool me." He steps closer to Kyle. "And you know who hasn't fooled me? You. I've had your number since the day you started here. An entitled, smarmy individual. A nepo baby asswipe."

Craig guffaws a nervous laugh. My sentiments exactly. Like Tanner, Stan's use of profanity is scant. When he drops an expletive, he's either ecstatic or you're fucked.

"Kyle, as one of my last duties as the boss...you're fired."

Kyle stands there like a chump, mouth agape. For once, no comeback.

I put a comforting hand on his shoulder. "And as one of my first duties as boss, it gives me great pleasure to tell you to get the fuck out of my office."

My comforting hand turns into a forceful one, shoving him into the hall.

"Fine! I'm going to start my own agency then. You better be scared," he says.

"Oh, Kyle. To quote my youngest: you are so delusional."

I slam the door shut.

29

DES

Celebrations for me used to mean steakhouses and lounges with sleek pianos and gorgeous views.

But now I prefer Caroline's, the greasy spoon diner in downtown Sourwood.

The six of us are seated around a table erupting in chaos. Lena is watching something annoying on her phone. Lulu keeps wanting to show me what she's colored on the kids menu. Dean and Davy are flicking paper footballs across the table.

It's madness, but it's my madness. And in truth, it's not so bad. I used to look at families like these and pity the parents. The loud noises, the stress. But I've learned that you get used to it. You can start to predict their needs and their tantrums. I know that Davy and Dean will calm down once their food comes, and Lulu just wants to show off her artwork.

Maybe there is a method to this parenting madness.

Tanner and I lock eyes across the table. He has that tired but proud look. He is so hot in dad mode.

I nudge Davy with my elbow. "Hey bud, how about we get back on the ice and practice this weekend?"

After not making the team, Davy said he was quitting hockey. I didn't believe it for a second. The game is in his blood.

He doesn't offer an answer.

"I'll make a deal with you. We do one practice this weekend, and if you absolutely hate it—like, hate it more than going to the dentist—then you can quit for good. But I really need to see with my own eyes how much you hate hockey first. Deal?" I hold out my hand to shake.

It takes him a few seconds, but he eventually shakes. That competitive spirit in him can't be held down.

Tanner shoots me a wink from across the table. He wraps his glass with a knife. "Everyone, raise your glass. We're here to toast Uncle Des."

We haven't decided yet what the kids should call me now that I'm their permanent stepdad. Lena and Davy are probably too old to switch to calling me dad. I think dad is a label that will be earned in time. I'm happy to be Uncle Des for the time being; I'm just glad that I'm a part of this family.

"Daddy, I ordered strawberry lemonade. This is lemonade!" Lulu cries out.

"Can I get chocolate milk?" Dean asks.

"Negatory!" I shoot back. "You'll get full on chocolate milk and won't eat your dinner."

"We'll get you a strawberry lemonade, sweetheart. But let's cheers to Uncle Des first," Tanner says in a gentler tone than I could muster.

"Okay," she says plainly.

We all raise our glasses.

"To Uncle Des, the new Creative Director of the Petty/Marsh Agency!" Tanner says. "Congratulations on Silq Cosmetics and the promotion. We're so proud of our stepdad."

"Woot woot!" Davy yells through his fist.

"Des for president!" Dean says. "I knew you could do it. I never stopped believing in you."

"You're still not getting that chocolate milk," I say.

We clink glasses in the center of the table. I get some combination of water and Diet Coke on my sleeve. All in a day's work.

"We love you," Tanner says, raising his glass to me one more time.

I never realized being in a family meant having your own built-in cheer squad. I'll take it. I keep my glass hoisted.

"We have some other good news to celebrate," I say, pointing my glass at my husband. "Daddy got a great new job. He's going to be a senior project manager!"

"What does a senior project manager do?" Lena asks.

"That's a good question." Tanner laughs, but he has the appearance of a deflated balloon sagging on the floor.

"We're proud of you." I wink at him. He pulls on a smile that has fake news written all over it and clinks glasses with each of his kids.

"It's nice to be employed again. It's a great company." He raises his hand to get the waiter's attention and immediately sets about putting this moment behind him to order Lulu a strawberry lemonade.

A little bit later, while we're chowing down on our dinners, a familiar face strolls up to our table.

"Maya." I look up from cutting up Lulu's hamburger, stunned to see her here. She is equally stunned at the scene in front of her.

"Des?" She holds a to-go bag in one hand. "Funny running into you here. Are these your nieces and nephews?"

"No. Uh, they're my kids."

Her eyes fall to my wedding ring. Tanner waves at her from his seat. She takes it all in. The last time I saw Maya, she was on all fours on my bed. A few months ago, but also a lifetime ago.

An amused smile lights up her face. "Been a while, apparently."

"A lot's changed." I nod my head at the table and the chaos of a family meal.

"Congratulations on Silq," she says.

"Thank you for getting my name in there. Did you get my thank-you gift?"

A few days before the pitch, I sent Maya a basket of fancy jams. It's something I saw Stan do whenever he was referred new business. My wet-behind-the-ears self thought it was super classy. He sent it before he found out if he won a pitch or not because he never wanted someone to think their help was only appreciated if he succeeded.

"Yes. That was too generous."

"My pleasure."

"Daddy Des, who is this?" Lulu asks, still remembering to call me daddy in front of strangers.

"This is my friend Maya."

Maya gives a polite wave to the family. She and I trade a friendly, weighted look, one that acknowledges the past but doesn't dwell on it. Life is just kinda funny in the way that it keeps moving forward.

"Being a daddy suits you, Des. Lord knows you have the stamina to handle four kids." She shoots me a wink and exits the restaurant, taking with her my former playboy self.

———

AFTER DINNER, when the kids go to sleep, we sit on the couch folding laundry and half-watching a bloated limited series that should've just been a movie. We fold in comfortable silence.

"Hey, since we're married, we can talk to each other about anything, right?" I ask.

"Of course." Tanner makes quick work of pairing socks.

"How do you feel about this new job?"

He shrugs, doesn't stop folding. "It's a good job. I'm happy to be employed. Seems like a nice company."

Tanner and I have discussed a myriad of topics throughout our friendship. No subject was off limits. But I'm realizing that he rarely talked about his job or general career ambitions. I could go on and on about my agency work. I love it. Tanner never came close to showing the same fire for any of his jobs.

"Are you excited about it?"

"It's a job, you know? It's keeping a roof over our heads and putting food on the table."

I take his hand, making him drop the fresh laundry. "Tan, have you ever had a job you loved?"

He squints his eyes, really thinks it over for a moment. "I loved being a counselor at this hockey clinic I worked at the summer between sophomore and junior year."

"Of high school?"

He nods yes.

"That was like almost thirty years ago." I rub his leg, a pang of pity shooting through my chest for my friend and husband.

"Look, some people have careers, and some people have jobs. I've never had a passion for the corporate business world. I love being a husband and father, which I know makes me sound like a Stepford wife. As long as the hours aren't too crazy, and I work with nice people, then I'm happy."

Something sparks within me, the pure joy that comes from looking out for someone you love.

"What if you didn't have to work?" I arch an eyebrow, awaiting his reaction.

He laughs, takes out an assortment of shirts to fold. "That'd be nice."

"I mean it." I stop his folding hands. "I mean it, Tan."

Beneath his dismissive eye-roll, a glimmer of hope twinkles in his sparkling blue orbs.

"This creative director promotion comes with a sizable pay bump. I can sell my condo and move in here permanently. We can make it work."

"What do you want me to do?"

"What you love most: be a dad. Take care of the kids. Coach all the little league you can handle. Not spend forty hours a week sitting at a soul sucking job because you feel you have to."

"You're being serious right now?"

"I am. You have given me so much love and support throughout our friendship. You helped me get through cancer, for crying out loud! Let me do this for you. You deserve to be present for your kids. Fuck, Tan. I don't know how the hell you managed to keep going these past two years. Working full time and raising a gaggle of kids. Constantly worrying about money. You deserve a break."

He throws a hand over his mouth as the reality of my offer sets in. Something cracks within him, a shackle being unlocked.

"Des…"

"I love you, Tan. I want to take care of you. If that's what you want."

He nods, his eyes watery.

I pull him into a hug. He wraps his arms around me so tight I may crack a rib.

"I promise I'll keep this house spotless, and there will be a home-cooked dinner ready every night."

"You don't need to go full trad wife. Although, the idea of you wearing nothing but an apron is tempting."

"Thank you." Tanner wipes away tears welling in his eyes.

"Now be honest with me: how were you feeling about this new job?"

"Dreading it. I could tell my boss was going to be a micromanager. And I don't even know what a senior project manager does!" His face splits into a wide, brimming smile full of relief.

"Who knows? Maybe you'll discover a passion for something while you're hanging at home." I reach for a pair of black shorts that I instantly identify as Dean's. Tanner rips them out of my hands and throws them back in the basket.

He grabs the laundry basket and puts it on his side of the couch. "You are not folding laundry ever again."

"I'll remember you said that." I remove the shirts from his lap and lean him back on the sofa. "Speaking of taking care of you…" I palm his crotch. "My husbandly duties should start now."

Tanner looks to the staircase as I massage his hardening cock through his sweatpants.

"Don't worry, Tan. They're all asleep," I say.

"To be safe, we should be quick."

"Luckily, I'm so good at what I do that we will be." I wink at him. I know it's wrong to be boastful, but I'm merely stating a fact proven out over the course of several sexual partners.

Though none of them can hold a candle to Tanner.

He arches his hips up, one eye still watching the staircase. "The second I hear a stair creak, this is done."

"You got it," I say. Although, the tent in his pants believes otherwise. I pull down his sweats, releasing his mallet of a cock.

I swirl my tongue around the crown, licking up his bitter precome. I decide to be antagonistic and slowly lower myself on his dick, taking my time down his shaft. He hisses with pleasure.

"Is this quick enough?"

"F off."

I laugh against his erection, eliciting another hiss out of him. He's warm and heavy in my mouth. His hips shift and buck under my touch.

I lick down his cock to his balls, taking them in my mouth.

"Yes," he says, barely above a whisper.

I fist his shaft and stroke him as I tongue his balls, lapping up their sweaty taste. He is rock hard, pulsing against my hand. He humps into my fist, unraveling with lust.

"Faster," he begs. If I tease anymore, he might scream.

And honestly, I'm kinda scared of one of the kids waking up.

I bob on his dick, taking him all the way down, letting him hit the back of my throat. Tanner presses a firm hand on my head, moves up and down with me like he's dribbling a basketball.

My cock is ragingly hard; this won't end at a blow job. I flip Tanner's legs up and flick my tongue over his hot hole. He bites against his arm, restraining a moan I know he wants to let out.

"We can't have sex, Des," he says in a strained whisper.

"I think it's already happening." I swirl my tongue around his most sensitive area, opening him up. His mouth is saying no, but his ass is saying yes, please, and thank you.

"We have to be quick. Really quick," he says.

"I'm going to be." It's difficult holding myself back with Tanner. He's so damn hot. It's a miracle I can last over a minute after sliding inside his warm opening.

I undo my pants and spit a few times into my hand. I coat my aching cock with nature's lubrication. I lick around his ass a bit more to slick him up, too.

"You ready? I know this isn't with lube...let me know if it hurts."

Tanner's pants bunch at his knees. His face is red with desire and want. And maybe a little discomfort. He's so beautiful, so eager.

"I love you," I whisper.

"Need you."

I plunge inside, sinking into his warmth, keeping eye contact with him. I slide in and out, the sensation of tightness and release making me dizzy with lust. I'm slow but deliberate, pumping his cock, too.

"You feel so good, Tan. How is it for you?"

"Don't stop." Tanner bites his lip, holding back moans I know he wants to erupt. His restraint is a big turn on.

I look down at the pretty sight of my thick cock disappearing into his hole, watching Tanner take all of me. I brush my lips against his muscular thighs.

He throws his head back, flush with need, when I begin jerking his stiff cock. Precome leaks down my fingers.

"I love stretching you out. Are you gonna come for me?" I ask in a low voice.

He nods ravenously, his cock bulbous and red and on the verge of exploding. My ball draws up as I barrel closer to release.

I could luxuriate in Tanner all night, but he's right: there could be a kid sighting at any moment.

The more Tanner twists under my touch, soft groans escape his lips, the harder I fuck him.

"Gonna come," he whispers.

He desperately reaches into the laundry basket and grabs one of his athletic socks. His fingers scramble as if trying to dismantle a bomb. As the piece of clothing falls from his grip, I snatch it and hold it over his cock just as he comes.

I manage to get all of it in the sock. Even off the ice, I can still catch Tanner's passes.

"Don't put it back in the laundry," Tanner says, heaving big breaths.

"Duh. I know." I pump my hard cock into his ass, wanting badly to jackhammer him, but also wanting to be quiet. We'll have lots more sex. It's okay for some of them to be quick.

"Fuck. I need a sock of my own," I huff out as the orgasm builds, making my whole body vibrate.

"No. Come inside me."

Damn. Hottest thing Tanner has ever said.

I pull back until only my cockhead is in him, then plow back inside. He hisses with desire. I go dizzy as the need takes over me.

"Tan..." I empty myself inside his hole, filling him up like a gas tank. I stroke a lock of hair back from his face, admire how beautiful he is, his cheeks bright with color.

"A guy can get used to this regular stuff," he says, pulling up his pants and catching his breath.

30

TANNER

I wake up absolutely refreshed the next morning. I tiptoe out of bed so I don't wake Des. The first thing I do is email my future employer to tell them things have changed and I won't be accepting their offer. My family needs me. Old me would've felt bad about leaving them in the lurch, but after getting unceremoniously let go, I now know loyalty is non-existent in corporate America.

I tiptoe into the kitchen and toast two Pop Tarts. You never realize how hard things have been until you're through them. It feels like I've been in crisis mode for the past two years, and finally, I can breathe.

I take the Pop Tarts upstairs and knock on Lena's door. When she was little, she'd lay in bed for a good thirty minutes. She wouldn't let us get her. She wanted to talk with her stuffed animals alone. I'd listen on the baby monitor, chuckling at her conversations, my heart full with gratitude that this little person was in my life.

Of course, parent life is always a dream when you have one kid. But as more kids got added to the mix, I had less time to enjoy those little moments.

She's sprawled across her bed, a tangle of spaghetti-like arms and legs. Lena picks her head up, flutters her eyes open.

"Morning," I say. I sit at the edge of her bed. "I brought you some breakfast. Do you remember how you and I would eat a Pop Tart together before you went to preschool?"

Lena rubs sleep from her eyes, her hair all asunder. "No. We did that?"

"Yeah. You were four. We'd toast them like champagne glasses and wish each other a good day."

"I don't remember that."

It's the blessing and curse of parenting: millions of little moments get lost to time. All the tantrums and yelling "no," but also all of those tiny golden morsels in between. They all get washed away.

"We need to talk, Lena."

"Is everything okay?" Her eyes bolt open. I can see that she, too, has been living in crisis mode.

I rub her hand, feel the bump of her knuckles. "When we lost your mom, I tried to step up. Everything your mom did, I could do. I told myself I could handle all the talks, all the lunches, remember all the school things. I didn't want you all to feel her absence more than you would. But along the way, I started to rely on you. I needed help, but I didn't want to admit it."

"It's okay, Dad."

"No, it's not." I fight back tears that insistently spill down my face. "I wasn't fair to you. Asking you to babysit your brothers and sister all the time. Making you become an adult way too soon. Yes, as the oldest, there is an expectation on you to help out more. That's just the price of birth order. But I overstepped. You're still a kid. I hate that you had to grow up fast, that I put that on you. We never talked enough about how you're doing. You always put on such a good front. I never questioned it."

There's no parenting manual. No coach who can watch me play and give me instant feedback. I never know if I'm doing things the right way. I wish parenting could be an exam with actual right answers, and if I did something wrong, it would get circled in red ink and I'd know for next time.

Parenting is easy. Good parenting is hard.

I push tears off my cheeks. More come.

"It's not your fault, Dad. You couldn't help what happened. Did Des tell you..."

"He told me that maybe you weren't doing as fine as you present. But I should've seen that. I'm so sorry that I didn't see that."

"I'm okay, Dad."

"You don't have to be okay, though. If you're scared or upset or angry or lost or confused, you can come to me. Please don't feel like you have to put on a brave face. I want to help you. I want to hear about what's going on in your life, even though I know as a teenager, you won't tell me. But know that you can."

"You just assume everything is fine with me. You never ask."

"I'm so sorry. I'll do better." The sad part is that even if I do better, I won't forget this moment. I won't forget how I let my little girl down, how I wasn't there for her like I should've been. And she'll tell me that it's fine, that I did the best I could, but still, I won't forget.

She nods, her lips slightly pouted. Sometimes, I miss when kids were younger. Small people, small problems. But having emotionally complex kids means we get to have these interesting, deep conversations.

"There are so many things I'd do differently. Number one: tell your mom to see a doctor ASAP. But we only go forward." I tuck a lock of hair behind her ear. "I want to go out to dinner with you this week. Just us two. Anywhere you want to go."

"Really? Okay, that's cool." Under her jaded response, it's not hard to spot her excitement.

"Cool, cool." I try to be chill, but that's not my strong suit. "And just because Uncle Des and I are married, it doesn't mean your mom is forgotten. I will love her forever. I see so much of her in you, Lena. You're kind like her. And thoughtful. And you do this thing where you itch your ear just like she did. It's uncanny."

She laughs, tears falling down her face.

"She would be so proud of you."

"No, she wouldn't. I met up with shady guys in abandoned parking lots."

I clench slightly. Grateful she's safe, but residual panic about how that could've wound up. Thank goodness Des waited to tell me all of this.

"Your mom told me about this boyfriend she had in high school who smoked clove cigarettes and brought a flask to class."

"Are you serious?"

"Your grandparents hated him. She said she was bored with him after a month, but she kept dating him just to piss off grandma and grandpa."

Lena erupts in laughter. It's been too long since I heard her laugh this hard.

"She would've loved Matthias," Lena says.

"Nah. She would've seen that he's too boring for you." I sigh, and silently pour one out for Matthias. He gave me some good gardening tips.

"You're a great dad." Lena wraps her arms around my neck. "I love you."

I breath in her scent. "I love you, too."

After I leave her bedroom, I stand in the hallway reliving our exchange. Was this a successful parenting moment? Was I wrong to apologize? Should I have reprimanded her for lying to me and hanging out with unsavory characters where she could've gotten herself in real trouble? Is it so terrible that as the oldest, she helps out more?

I'll never know. Again, no answer key in parenting.

You just love your kids and hope that's a strong enough guide.

31

TANNER

"I knew that Third Eye Blind CD was a lucky charm," Hank says in the locker room before our next game. "You guys...just beautiful."

Usually celebration happens after a game when we win, but my teammates are in a celebratory mood already. Des and I told them the good news. We're in love.

Have you ever seen big hockey players get schmoopy? It's a very weird sight.

"If you guys decide to have a proper wedding, the Stone's Throw Tavern is always open to you," Mitch says.

Griffin throws an arm around both me and Des. "I'm not one to get choked up like Hank, but I think this union is a wonderful thing. Tanner, we're so happy you found love after experiencing a devastating loss. And Des, seeing you become a father to those kids—seeing you actively wanting to be around kids—is beautiful."

"Des also experienced a devastating loss, too," Derek cracks in the corner as he pulls on his padded pants. He points down to his crotch.

Des flips him the bird. I put my hand over his chest, signaling that I have this.

"I assure you that there is no loss in that department," I say. That's about as close to trash talking as I get.

Des gets dressed in his hockey pads. He keeps looking up and smiling at me every few seconds, like he's checking that I'm still here.

"You look very sexy in your hockey gear," he says to me under his breath.

"Funny. I was going to say the same thing myself."

We share a look that makes the whole locker room melt away. Des really does look hot in his uniform. It makes him tougher, stronger. Yet his hair is perfectly coiffed. The debonair man and the hockey goon. Two sides to the man I love.

Bill claps his hands between us, breaking up this moment. "We're very happy for the both of you, but we need to establish some ground rules."

"Lighten up, Bill," Derek says. "It's cute."

"Yeah, I thought now that you have a boyfriend, you'd be more of a romantic." Griffin laces up his skates.

"What's more romantic than banging your assistant?" Hank jokes and puts his hands up as a shield, seeming to predict Bill's response.

"Hank, for the final, final, final time, I wasn't banging my assistant. Tate stopped working for me before we started dating." Bill stays calm, as if talking to his child, but the vein pulsing in his neck is a warning that he's always close to snapping.

"I think technically he was still working for you when you guys..." Hank wiggles his eyebrows.

Bill is not one to talk about his private life, but when he and Tate were snowed in during a work trip last winter, apparently things happened. In his new romance high, he divulged the whole thing to us. The night in a Chicago hotel room that sounded so hot my ears almost burned off listening to his retelling. It was one of the only times Bill gossiped about himself.

Yet Bill is not in a gossipy mood currently. He turns his attention back to Des and me.

"I said I'm happy for the both of you. As we all know, this wasn't exactly a surprise." Bill arches an eyebrow.

"I think I take offense to that," Des says.

"But we're laying down some ground rules so that this relationship doesn't interfere with what's most important: winning." Bill paces in a circle so we can all hear. He's naturally inclined to these types of speeches. His jaw remains tense. "Number one, in this locker room, you guys are teammates, not husbands. Any marital drama... you leave that in the parking lot."

I don't see us having big fights. In thirty years of friendships, we've never had a blowup. But I nod that I understand.

"Got it. Compartmentalize or die," Des says.

"What's rule number two?" I ask, trying to be peacemaker.

"I think all of these rules are number two," Des whispers to me. I fight the urge to crack up.

Bill shoots daggers at him. "Rule number two. No PDA."

"The fuck?" Des shouts back. "Is this a hockey team or a nunnery?"

"Again, once you enter this locker room, you are teammates, not husbands," Bill explains.

"Do you think we're going to have sex in front of everyone?" I ask.

Griffin seesaws his head. "I wouldn't put it past Des."

"Griffdog, don't make me gouge out your other eye," Des says.

"Look, I don't think it's going to happen, but I want to address any potential conflicts before they arise. This way, we're all on the same page. Rule number three, no calling each other romantic pet names when we're playing. We will use our hockey nicknames on the ice. We don't want to mess up our good juju," Bill says.

I open my mouth to object, but he has a point. I can't imagine calling Des sweetheart in the middle of a play.

Hank raises his hand. "Rule number four, Bill is banned from talking for the rest of the game."

"I second that," Griffin says.

"Third," says Derek.

"This is mutiny," Bill says.

Des gets up and throws his arm around Bill. "Billy boy, don't worry. We will abide by all of your rules. We're here to play hockey and win. But I promise that if Tanner and I accidentally have locker room sex in front of our teammates, we'll make sure to call out your name when we climax." Des pulls Bill to him and kisses his head. Bill looks like he wants to vomit, although I have this sneaking suspicion that he and Tate have probably gotten it on in this very locker room.

We put on our helmets and charge out of the locker room. Des tugs me back by the jersey. He whips off my helmet and pulls me into a kiss that sets off fireworks in my chest.

"See you on the ice, husband," he growls between us.

"Love you."

Bill clears his throat behind us. Yet even he has the tiniest bit of a smile on his lips.

"That wasn't what it looked like. I was giving him preventive CPR," Des explains.

EPILOGUE

EIGHT MONTHS LATER

Des

It's another chaotic morning in the Chance-Desmond household. In between getting the kids up, getting them dressed, and making sure they brush their teeth, I've gotten my cardio in for the day by eight.

And then there's also the matter of feeding Big Guy, the rabbit Tanner got Lulu and Dean. The kids may forget to do their homework or where they left the remote, but they clearly remembered the time Tanner promised them a pet rabbit for keeping our fake marriage ruse alive.

Big Guy hops around in his cage as I put pellets in a little bowl for him. Despite the kids really wanting him, I'm the one who does most of the rabbit maintenance, including trimming his nails, which is as difficult as it sounds.

On a sunny summer morning, Dean hovers near me while I perfect my omelet flip.

"I have an idea for the next omelet. We should put the leftover mac and cheese in there," Dean says, acting as if he just discovered alchemy.

"Maybe next time, pal." I flip the omelet. One half flops onto the other in a beautiful, fluid motion. If they handed out gold medals for omelets...this one probably wouldn't come close. But it'd score gold in the Chance-Desmond household.

"Look at it." I slide it onto a plate and hand it to Dean. "That is a work of art."

"Eh." Dean takes the plate and heads to the table without acknowledging my hard work. Luckily, I'm used to this treatment from my clients.

He plops into his seat and lets out a loud pfffft. "Hey!" he yells, pulling a whoopee cushion from under the kitchen seat cushion.

Lulu laughs so hard milk threatens to spew from her nose.

"That's payback for the can of snakes in the pantry last week," I say.

"Tushy." Dean slaps the whoopee cushion on the kitchen table.

"I told you, it's pronounced *touché*," says Lena, who eats a bowl of cereal next to him.

"I want a cwoissant," Lulu says, emphasizing its Frenchness. "Those eggs smell magnifique. Bonjour." Lulu bows to me. "Beaucoup."

Lena used Lulu to help her practice French this past year. Lulu has become quite the Francophile in response. I chuckle to myself. "Cheese omelet?"

"Mercy," she says as Americans pronounce it. "Did you know there's a street in Paris called Chomps Ulysses?"

"You don't say." I have fond memories of dropping six grand on an Omega watch there, then sitting in a café, people watching with the most delicious coffee I've ever had. Another life. Perhaps one day, I could take Tanner and the kids there. Vacationing with four kids: what could go wrong?

Over the past eight months, we've gotten into routines with the kids, while I've been learning to balance new work responsibilities with new domestic duties. I may take work calls while cleaning up the kitchen, or hop back online for a little bit after everyone's asleep. I'm making it work. As much as I love the work I do, I'm grateful to have a family to come home to every night. It reminds me that contrary to what I used to believe, work isn't everything. That no matter how stressful a day I have, I can unplug from my phone and get lost in their worlds. (And when living in a quaint house with four kids gets a little too stressful, I'm grateful to get lost in my work. Like me, it goes both ways.)

My future travel mate swoops into the kitchen and grabs a banana.

"Omelet?" I ask my husband. I lean back from the stove to give him a morning kiss.

"No thanks. I gotta run." Tanner pulls his gardening gloves from his back pocket. The extra time at home has allowed him to reconnect with his love of planting and hoeing. He meets up with a gardening club on Friday mornings to work on elaborate flower beds at Renegade Park. I man the fort. Luckily, Lena has work, the boys have day camp, and Lulu loves coming to the office with me. My coworkers can't get enough of her, and she gives the bluntest feedback on all of our advertisements.

Matthias knocks at the back door. Lena turns red and puts on her best smile.

"Matthias!" I give him a rousing high-five. He still acts nervous and scared around me after our carnival skirmish, despite the fact that I'm always friendly to him. He kind of reminds me of a cat perpetually seconds away from dashing under the bed.

"Hey everyone!" he says when he comes in. "Mr. Chance, are you ready to go?"

"Yes! Let's do this." Tanner claps Matthias on the shoulder. "Are you ready to plant some hydrangeas?"

"I've never been more ready for anything in my whole life."

Even though Lena and Matthias broke up, Tanner was able to retain custody of him. They're now garden club buddies. Lena and I share many an eye-roll at the development. Fortunately, Matthias started dating a girl two months ago, effectively ending his crush on Lena. She has yet to shed a tear about the one who got away.

"Can I talk to you a second?" Tanner pulls me into the living room.

"Are you nervous?" He asks in a low voice moments later.

"About what?"

"Today is your annual checkup for...the C-word."

"Curmudgeon?" I smirk at him.

"Cancer." Tanner crosses his arms. "Your appointment is this afternoon."

"Will you be back in time from hoeing it up with the gardening club in time to hang with Lulu?" I've used the hoeing joke a bunch since he joined. Hasn't gotten old yet. I rub Tanner's shoulders, hoping to bring about that smile I love so much. "I've been cancer free for four years. Statistically speaking, I should be fine. Don't get yourself worked up over nothing." I kiss his forehead.

"There's always a chance...a chance I could lose you." Fear clouds his eyes, and I wipe the smirk of my face. I kiss him softly.

I pull him to me. "Tan, it's going to be fine."

"This is serious, Des. This is...curmudgeon."

I rub my hands up and down his arms, trying to bring him calm. His eyes are saucers of worry. My far-off fear is right in his face.

"It'll be okay," I tell him. "And if it's not, we'll get through it together." I rest my forehead against his. "I love you."

"Love you more."

"It's not a contest."

"But if it was, I'd win." Tanner pulls me into a kiss that sets me ablaze. I told him that when the kids start school in the fall, I'm taking a day off work and spending it in bed with him. No exceptions.

"Matthias is waiting for you," I whisper.

Tanner

It's amazing how much my life has changed since I married Des. Being able to be a full-time dad has allowed me to stop and breathe for the first time since Katie died. Heck, for the first time since my twenties. I'm able to make better meals (and less take-out), spend quality time with the kids without the incessant dinging of Slack notifications in my ear.

I keep meaning to do some job searching, but Des says there's no rush. I want to do something. We have four kids we'll need to put through college, after all. In the meantime, I'm gardening, cleaning our house, and getting sucked into more PTA volunteering alongside Russ.

But for now, I have bigger things to worry about. Des. His test. He said there's very little chance of a recurrence, but that's not zero. I never expected to go biking with my wife and have her die twenty-four hours later. Things happen.

He hasn't called or texted all afternoon. As the day wears on, my nerves get more heightened, until I find myself chowing down on two red velvet cupcakes at For Goodness Cakes. Lulu and I joined Cal there for his weekly 'You Made It Through Another Week' red velvet cupcake. But not even Cal's theatrics could distract me.

I check my phone at every red light on the way home.

"Dad, you can't text and drive," Lulu says.

"Sorry, sweetie. You're right."

Things will be okay. They will. If Des has a recurrence of cancer, we've likely caught it early. He can get treatment. He got treatment last time.

I keep thinking of him in that hospital bed, in the chemotherapy chair. We played cards and watched hockey games together, and I could tell he was in pain. But he kept it to himself.

At a red light, I close my eyes and say a silent prayer. There are so many people in the world who are hurting. I am low on the list of priorities for the big guy in the sky. But please let Des be okay. But let our family stay intact.

"Dad, why are your eyes closed?" Lulu asks.

"Can you think really good, really happy thoughts?" I ask through the rearview mirror.

"Like about ice cream?" Lulu asks.

"Exactly."

She squeezes their eyes shut. Lulu mumbles to the Lord her

request for ice cream. It's so cute how unself-aware little kids are. There's nothing so pure.

My heart pounds louder and louder in my ears when I pull onto our street. It becomes full-volume bass between my ears when I spot Des's car in the driveway.

Did he forget to text because he's fine? Or did he get bad news he's afraid to share?

We go in the house; nobody's there.

"Hello?" I call out.

The silence is eerie. My house is never this quiet. The opening of a door makes me jump. Dean exits the bathroom. A flash of parental approval distracts me when I notice his hands are wet and freshly washed.

"Hey, Dad," he says nonchalantly.

"Where is everyone? Where's Des?" I ask.

"We're all outside." Dean strolls through the living room and kitchen to the sliding patio door.

Des runs with a football through the backyard, my three oldest kids chasing after and tackling him in the end zone, as the sun shines above us. Their overlapping laughter echoes in the wind. It's an image reserved for catalogs.

"That's a touchdown! That counts! I'm still holding onto the ball," Des says, wiping grass off his old T-shirt.

"The ball touched the ground. It doesn't count," says Davy.

"Where's the instant replay?" Lena manages through laughter.

"According to official NFL rules, I was over the line with the ball in my hands. Counts. Now if you'll excuse me, I gotta do my touchdown dance."

Des struts a few steps back and spikes the football. He proceeds to do the most ridiculous dance I've ever seen from him. Something between a moonwalk and the funky chicken. "Stepdad Des for the win!"

"I wanna play!" Lulu wails.

"Lulu's on my team!" Des cheers. He squats down so she can give him a double low-five. "Alright!"

"You're going down!" Lulu taunts her siblings.

I could watch this scene all day, all year, until the end of time. In that moment, I feel this overwhelming gratitude that this gets to be my life. Married life has been magical. I get to kiss Des every day and share a bed with him.

Des jogs up and scoops me up in a kiss, all sweaty and warm and smelling just like home.

"Negative," he says between our lips. "All tests negative. I'm curmudgeon free."

I pull him into a life-affirming hug. I look at this man, study his beautiful features. Those thick eyebrows and full lips and eyes as transfixing as the ocean.

"I love you so much," I say.

"I love you more." Des grabs the football and spins it in his hands. "For dinner tonight, how would you feel about going out for ice cream?"

Dean and Lulu scream for pure joy.

"Daddy Des, you are acing this stepdad thing." Davy bumps fists with him. We're still working on the right name to call Des. Daddy Des started as a joke, but I think it's sticking around.

Des gives me an impish shrug. He's already said it aloud, and ice cream for dinner is one thing you can't take back. I respond with an approving nod.

"Can we play more football first?" Lulu asks.

"Of course! I need my quarterback." Des tosses her the ball and has her toss it back.

The two uneven teams get into starting positions. Des squats down, football between his legs. He pauses.

"Wait. Dad, you want in on this?" he asks.

"Dad is coming on our team," Lena says.

"I'd love to." I jog to my team and give them high-fives, then get into position. Des and I make moony eyes right before he hikes the ball to Lulu.

Lulu misses the catch, but we wait for her to pick up the ball. Hugging it to her chest, the football nearly as wide as she is, she scurries down the yard. Lena and Davy pretend to block her, but don't put up a resistance when she darts around them. Dean jumps in front and swipes at the ball.

"Over here!" Des calls to his teammate.

He moves behind back and takes the ball in a surprisingly agile play. Oh, he's really going for it. He's running to the end zone designated by our old sprinklers. I catch up to him, and we tumble to the grass, followed shortly by our kids. It's one big pile.

I'm laughing so hard, I can barely catch my breath.

Lulu jumps onto my chest. "Daddy, we're having ice cream tonight! My wish came true!"

"Mine, too."

Des extends a hand and helps me up. I lean against him, tip my head against his shoulder, and watch our kids set up the next play.

I can't wait to grow old with this man. I can't wait to attend high school graduations and hockey games and college graduations and weddings and recitals and school plays with this man. I can't wait to go wrinkly and gray with this man. I can't wait to argue about turning down the thermostat with this man. I can't wait to experience the highs and lows and mundane middle of life with this man.

The best is yet to come.

———

Thank you for reading!

>> What happens when Hank falls for a new teammate...who is secretly a crown prince? Red white and royal WTF?! Find out in book 3, *King of the Crease*, coming in 2026.

In the meantime...

>> Where to find other couples referenced: Griffin and Jack fell in love in *Gross Misconduct*. Russ and Cal went from enemies to lovers in

The Falcon and the Foe. Mitch and Charlie have quite a love story in *The Barkeep and the Bro*.

\>> Go deeper into the world of Sourwood by joining my Patreon. Patrons get spicy and SFW art, exclusive sexy stories, access to hardcover special editions, and the first look at what I'm working on next.

\>> How did Bill Crandell wind up banging (and falling for) his assistant? Read their love story in the free prequel novella *Cherry Picker* when you sign up for my newsletter: **www.ajtruman.com/ outsiders.**

\>> Please consider leaving a review on the book's Amazon page or on Goodreads. Reviews are crucial in helping other readers find new books.

\>> Join the party on Facebook, TikTok and Instagram. Follow me at Bookbub and Amazon to be alerted to new releases.

And then there's email. I love hearing from readers! Send me a note anytime at info@ajtruman.com. I always respond.

ALSO BY A.J. TRUMAN

The Comebacks

Gross Misconduct

Scoring Chance

South Rock High

Ancient History

Drama!

Romance Languages

Advanced Chemistry

Single Dads Club

The Falcon and the Foe

The Mayor and the Mystery Man

The Barkeep and the Bro

The Fireman and the Flirt

Browerton University Series

Out in the Open

Out on a Limb

Out of My Mind

Out for the Night

Out of This World

Outside Looking In

Out of Bounds

Seasonal Novellas

Fall for You

You Got Scrooged

Hot Mall Santa

Only One Coffin

<u>Big Boys Small Spaces</u>

(co-written with M.A. Wardell)

Marshmallow Mountain

Cut to the Feeling

ABOUT THE AUTHOR

A.J. Truman is a gay man living in Indiana with his husband, kids, and fur-babies. He writes books with **humor, heart, and hot guys.** What else does a story need? He loves spending time with his family and occasionally sneaking off for an afternoon movie.

www.ajtruman.com
info@ajtruman.com
The Outsiders - Facebook Group

www.ingramcontent.com/pod-product-compliance
Lightning Source LLC
Chambersburg PA
CBHW020129120726
47903CB00007B/2173